"You Dropped This."

The burned man came forward, his shoes slowly scraping on the dirty concrete as he walked into the light cast by the single hooded bulb. Danny saw his feet come into the light, his knees, his waist, his chest. He stopped there, his face masked in shadow, and extended a hand.

It was a skeleton's claw held together by tendrils of dead skin and baked muscle. Clamped between the chalky fingers was a rumpled one-dollar bill.

"See you sometime," he said in his dead, wheezy voice, and Danny discovered, after he snatched the dollar away, that he could run pretty fast in the dark.

D1601154

DARKMAN #1

THE HANGMAN

A NOVEL BY RANDALL BOYLL
BASED ON CHARACTERS CREATED BY CHUCK PFARRER AND SAM RAIMI & IVAN RAIMI AND DANIEL GOLDIN & JOSHUA GOLDIN

POCKET BOOKS
New York   London   Toronto   Sydney   Tokyo   Singapore

This book is a work of fiction. Names, characters, places and incidents are either products of the author's imagination or are used fictitiously. Any resemblance to actual events or locales or persons, living or dead, is entirely coincidental.

An *Original* Publication of POCKET BOOKS

POCKET BOOKS, a division of Simon & Schuster Inc.
1230 Avenue of the Americas, New York, NY 10020

ISBN: 0-671-78764-0

First Pocket Books printing February 1994

10 9 8 7 6 5 4 3 2 1

POCKET and colophon are registered trademarks of
Simon & Schuster Inc.

Cover art by John Alvin

Printed in the U.S.A.

THE HANGMAN

PROLOGUE

He was dying in his sleep, but that was not unusual. He had come close to death enough times to know the sight and smell of the Grim Reaper closing in on him, its skeletal face chalky and gleeful, its scythe madly swinging. Not long ago the man had had a name: Peyton Westlake. He'd had a career: university research scientist. And he'd had a fiancée: Julie Hastings. All that was gone now, bombed and burned out of existence. He was alone and friendless, scarred so badly that his face frightened everyone, even him. The old name had vanished along with the old face, and with the burial of Peyton Westlake he had acquired a new one.

Darkman.

He turned over fitfully, caught in a dream populated by grotesque memories. His bed was an old slab of plywood covered with dirty fiberglass wall insulation that might have been pink a few years ago, a few decades ago. His home was an abandoned soap factory in the heart of the city's most squalid slum. He had been living on pizza and beer for months; the factory he called home looked like the inside of a Dumpster that had been parked between a very busy pizzeria and a tavern. But

1

this, too, was acceptable, because the more wretched the place became, the more likely it was that people would stay away. Darkman did not need visitors.

He turned again. A groan slipped between the charred remains of his teeth. His head was wrapped in gauze to prevent a heart attack on the part of anyone who might be fool enough to blunder in and find him here. His hands were also wrapped, for they were skinless and skeletal. Even for Darkman it was frightening to wake up and find his head resting on his own bony fingers. The sight of them tended to make the breakfast pizza harder to gag down.

And now, enmeshed in a ghastly nightmare while the moon floated cold and high outside and sent its beams through the gaping windows and cracked walls of this former factory that reeked of age, he relived some of the nightmare that had been his past.

The horror had started, it seemed, with the toy bird.

The toy had been a gift from Julie, a bobbing plastic bird that rocked up and down, dipped lower and lower until it dunked its beak into a small cup of water. It wasn't a new car or a trip to Tahiti, but Peyton Westlake had consoled himself with the knowledge that Julie's legal career was in its early stages and that, contrary to popular opinion, not all lawyers made millions. Especially not recent graduates.

He had been working in his ramshackle lab as usual, trying to work the bugs out of his newest project, the creation of artificial skin for burn patients. For reasons he could not understand, the skin would be perfectly fine for ninety-nine minutes, but then it would disintegrate into popping blisters and yellow smoke. The smell of it was "pretty goddamn rotten," as he would tell his prospective lab assistants, most of whom would quit within a few weeks, bored absolutely to death watching phony skin do nothing for ninety-nine minutes, then get greasy and puffy and yellow in the space of two seconds. There had been a rumor at the university, Michigan's own Wayne State, that staring at the clock for so long had driven Dr. Westlake insane and given him a phobic hatred of clocks. The latter was true—he had smashed a few with a hammer and tossed some others into the river that bordered his lab—but he was no more insane than the average professor.

Strack Industries—that was the beginning of the end, no doubt about it.

Julie had discovered some unsavory treachery going on in that huge conglomerate. Shady deals and kickbacks and payoffs—classic corporate greed. She'd left a memo filled with damaging evidence in Peyton's lab one sunny day during the previous October, and a squad of Louis Strack's goons had come to search for it. Find it they did; angry they were. They shot Peyton Westlake's lab assistant in the face. They hooked Peyton up to his own high-voltage equipment, which quick-fried his hands. They dunked his head in a boiling acid solution, cackling like hyenas. As a final gesture of dissatisfaction, they opened tanks containing flammable gas and then set his electronic lighter directly under that toy bird's beak and, *tap,* set the bird in motion.

By that time Peyton was on the floor, stunned by excruciating pain. He tried to get to his feet, but his balance was gone. Gagging on chemical fumes, aware of what would happen if that lighter ignited the gas, he began to crawl to the lab table where the colorful bird was doing its dance.

With the last of his strength he grappled his way up the table with his ruined hands, reached for the bird— missed it.

The explosion blasted him all the way to the river, a remarkable distance. His clothes were ripped from his body by the impact. While debris from the lab and the body of his assistant rained down around him, he tried to swim, desperate to stay alive. But his memory ended there, a blank until he awoke in a hospital and found himself being studied like a bug on a pin.

A man with no face and no name.

Darkman jerked upright. The echoes of a scream were chasing each other throughout the factory, skidding off the grimy walls, telling him what he already knew.

Another memory, another nightmare, another late-night awakening to the sound track of his own misery. He heard rats scampering through the debris in the lab; rats were his only companions now. His head ached brutally, and the taste of old beer was sour in his mouth. He was a tall and lean sort of fellow, and since his transformation he had taken to wearing a black felt hat that concealed the naked bone where his scalp had been, and a ragged old raincoat, also black. His outfit seemed fitting; a black shroud to mourn the loss of himself. It also made him hard to see in the dark, a definite advantage when a platoon of cutthroats was after him. But that was old history now. He had fought the corporate thugs to the last man, and he had beaten them.

Sweet revenge? In retrospect it seemed closer to mindless revenge, even mindless savagery. There was still one enemy to be faced, and that enemy was time. The months were dragging by, and he was edging past thirty-five, well on the road to the big four-o. Since the night he had faced Louis Strack in the skeleton of an unfinished skyscraper and fought him to the death, he had been doing only three things day in, day out: eating, sleeping, and working with his computers to solve the maddening mystery of the artificial skin.

He had been able to repair or replace much of his ruined machinery and was free to work on the endless project, but he had learned nothing new, except that the skin would not self-destruct in darkness. This was dangerous business, he knew, this constant solitude, this moribund self-analysis, this tendency to consume a six-pack of beer every evening while brooding and reliving the past. And oddly—*very* oddly—whenever he thought back to that afternoon when Strack's helicopter had towed him, hanging on to a rope ladder, over the entire city, his heart would speed up, and if he'd had a face, he would have smiled.

Danger. He liked danger. He *loved* it! Death and murder were terrible things, but danger was a refreshing drug. Peyton Westlake had been a gentle man; Darkman was not. Darkman had been created by hate and a experimental medical procedure called the Rangeveritz technique. The pain of his burns would have been excruciating, so the surgeons had dug inside his brain and flipped the pain switch off, just like that. Now you feel it, now you don't. Darkman had read not too long ago in a day-old newspaper that there had been an investigation into the Rangeveritz procedure. It seemed the patients on whom it had been performed often experienced unbearable rage, even went insane. A congressional committee had put a halt to the use of it. Fat lot of good it did Darkman. He was only thankful that his nervous system had simply been tampered with, rather than shut down entirely by those medical fools. With no feeling in his feet, he supposed, it would have been hard to walk, just as it was hard to whistle after having a dentist dull your facial nerves with Novocain.

He took a long, heavy breath, turning his head to look dully at the walls and heaps of debris and the ghostly discarded pizza boxes that graced his home. When he wasn't working, he was vegetating. He had sunk so low that his greatest interest now, aside from perfecting the skin, was seeing how many pizza delivery persons he could scare the living daylights out of when they dropped off their wares here. The great scientific genius had been reduced to the role of prankster.

An inner voice taunted him: *Sounds a lot like self-pity, Darkman, my old friend.*

He nodded slightly to himself in the dark. Self-pity could become an art. But dammit, he had a lot of good reasons to feel bad.

Is a hangover topping the list?

"Ah, shut up," he grunted. One of these days he was going to drill a hole through his head to get at that damned voice. With an exhausted groan he flopped back down on his pallet and let his eyes fall shut.

In his memory he saw the toy bird bobbing. It was painted red and blue.

His eyes sprang open again. He had found nothing to do all day, and now he couldn't sleep. It was as if all of the demons that could plague a man with misfortune were doing a rush job on him. He didn't want to be awake, and they wouldn't let him go to sleep.

It occurred to him that he could see a psychiatrist.

He laughed, a cold and bitter sound that the echoing factory repeated for him. Hey, Doc, I got this problem, see. I look like a reject from a horror movie. Oh, you want to see what's under these bandages? Hold on a sec while I unwind this gauze. . . .

Eyes full of horror. A lifeless gasp. And then . . .

"Yaaaaaaahhhhhhhhhhhhhhh!"

And of course the crashing plunge through the window of his ten-story office building.

Darkman, old pal, you are losing your mind.

"No thanks to you," Darkman said aloud and turned on his side. For most humans sleeping on fiberglass would have been unbearable, because the fibers would inflame their skin, which would itch enormously. No problem after the Rangeveritz operation. The calendar had recently flipped over to October, and the air was dank and cold here in the Peyton Soap Factory where once Fresh Splash soap had been manufactured, but Darkman didn't mind sleeping without a blanket. With his pain reflexes muted, he supposed he could step into a bear trap and hardly notice it. More than once, while padding around the factory barefoot, he had felt a tiny tickle and only later realized that he had stepped on a tack or a rusty nail. For reasons he was not sure of, this usually made him angry. Dangerously angry.

He shut his eyes again, determined to find a nice dream floating around somewhere inside his head, wanting to avoid the door in his mind labeled Nightmare Department, Enter at Your Own Risk. He visualized instead a door marked Dream Department, Happy Darkmen Only, and to his own surprise he chuckled aloud, then laughed, then roared, wallowing around on the pallet holding his sides, the brim of his hat getting crushed, made helpless by his own keen wit. It came to him that the rats were probably looking on in horror as he laughed himself to death, but that only brought more laughter.

The spasm lasted five full minutes, and would not completely leave him for another half hour. Just as sleep beckoned he would see that door, see those rats packing their bags to get the hell out of this loony bin, and suffer a bout of the chuckles again, very sure that he was losing his marbles.

In the end he visualized Julie's face, her blond hair, her wonderful eyes. As he did slip into a sleep, someone switched the labels on the dream doors.

An unpleasant image—too real, too recent—drifted into his mind through a mist of purple and black. He saw the construction elevator that had carried the three of them almost to the top of the unfinished skyscraper: Darkman hidden behind a mask of artificial skin, Julie bound and gagged, and Louis Strack holding a pistol. Julie had tried to expose Strack, and for this she was to walk the plank to a twenty-two-story fall, here on a cool and windy night while the moon glared at them and the stars shimmered like diamond dust in the sky.

Strack knew his secret. "Time for the unmasking, Westlake," he had said with a grin. "Show us just who you really are."

Darkman walked toward him on a long girder made of dreams and steel, where hundreds of feet below the dirty river reflected colorful dreamy lights. Vertigo swept over him like a wave of terror, and he edged back, panting.

"So glad my father made me work high steel," Strack said. "At the time I hated him. Now I love him for it. Watch what I can do."

He jumped up from the girder and clicked his heels together, then landed solidly on both feet again, arms outstretched for balance. "It took me sixteen months when I was young to get the courage together to try that. Do you know what it feels like? Death ready to grab you at any moment? Sure you do. So come on and get me."

Darkman ground his teeth. He jumped for Strack, launching himself skyward, parts of his face disintegrating in the cold wind. He smashed down onto the girder where Strack had been, but Strack was gone and Julie was alone on this bleak beam, wavering and bobbing to stay in place, her eyes twin lamps of terror. Darkman swung around, hands ready to stab and claw, but Strack was in the moon shadows of building's interior.

"Bravo, Mr. Westlake. I applaud your clumsiness. I would love to shoot you right now, but for all the trouble you've caused me, I will wait to hear your screams when you fall."

Darkman jumped toward the voice, a ragged scream of hate wheezing past his lips. He landed hard on a stack of plywood and searched the dark, his eyes narrowed to slits.

"What do you really look like?" Strack asked him.

Darkman swiveled his head, noting that Julie was sidestepping off the plank, retching on the red gag in her mouth, moving slowly. For now, at least, she was okay.

"You want to know what I look like?" he shouted into the darkness. "I look like you, Strack. You hide behind money and lies, but all I've got is a false face."

There was a pause. Then Strack said, "I guess we both belong to the same club, Westlake. Let's call it the pretenders' society. I pretend to be nice and admirable and generous. You pretend to be human. I live a lie, you live a lie. Who's worse?"

Damn, Darkman thought, damn, damn, damn. The bastard had brains, unlike his lackeys, and he knew how to use the shadows. Julie came to a vertical beam and leaned against it, a white ghost against the sky and the stars. Strack was silent, possibly moving, possibly not.

"Strack!" Darkman shouted.

The reply sounded weary. "You are a killer, Westlake. I live only to build—skyscrapers, malls, office buildings, whole towns. I create. All you can do is destroy."

Darkman kept his mouth shut, looking without seeing. Seconds passed. A minute. Two minutes. Something winked in the darkness just to the right—gold metal catching a moonbeam. A cuff link? A belt buckle? A ring? The gun? He gathered himself and pounced toward the light.

His fingers brushed against soft fabric, and then there was nothing but air. He snatched out wildly and caught the edge of a girder. Strack leaned over and began pounding his hands with the butt of his revolver. Darkman looked down, looked for something to land on, but there was only cold air and steel and one hell of a drop.

He tried to pull himself up. Strack kept pounding his fingers. It was a minor irritation, not painful at all, but when Darkman brought his head into range, Strack started pounding it, too. The blows didn't hurt much, but they were growing very tiresome.

Tiresome . . .

Tired . . . too tired . . .

Finally he realized that this could not be happening, that this scene had taken place a long time ago, that he was trapped inside a dream. But he could feel things, could feel the butt of the gun whacking his bare head, could feel the cold wind blowing through his clothes. A dream? Yes or no?

He considered letting go, letting himself fall these twenty-two stories, waking up just before impact. But what if this was real?

His hatred for Strack ended the idea. Even in a dream Strack should die. He swung out and captured one of Strack's ankles. Strack cried out and grabbed a vertical beam while Darkman clambered onto the girder, breathing hard, balanced between fear and rage.

Strack jerked, trying to free his foot. Darkman pulled, managing to tear Strack's shoe off. It tumbled out of sight. Nice going, Darkman thought sourly, chiding himself. The poor bastard would certainly miss that wing tip.

He tore Strack's sock off, just for the hell of it. Strack grunted, stretched taut between the vertical girder and Darkman's hands. The artificial skin of those hands ripped free with a squelch. Strack looked at Darkman's scorched claws, his eyes growing wide in the moonlight.

"If your face looks as bad as your hands," he said, noisily straining to stay in place, "I'd sure hate to see it. You're a damn carnival freak."

Darkman growled. It wasn't nice to call a freak a freak. He pulled one hand free of Strack's bare foot, feeling

9

a surge of extra strength, the partner to his anger. He considered twisting Strack's foot until something snapped, but a better idea surfaced, a more fitting punishment for this creature made of money and lies.

He tore his mask and wig off, glad that the moon was shining directly in his face. Strack let out a loud gasp.

"Go ahead," Darkman sneered. "Pass out. Go blind. You did this to me, Strack. You stole my future and my wife. I hope you're happy with the results."

Strack put on a false smile. "They have a carnival going in town, part of the Octoberfest. You could get a job, a free cage, straw to sleep on."

"Never lose your nerve, do you? Mr. Smart Guy to the end."

Strack nodded, his own face strained as his grip on the girder weakened. "Get yourself a bag, cut an eyehole in it, and you can be the Elephant Man."

Darkman twisted his foot. Strack groaned, his hold getting weaker. Anklebones crunched as Darkman rearranged them. Strack gritted his perfect white teeth, the pistol still in his fist but quite useless unless he let go of the girder.

Walking on tiptoe, Julie edged toward them, the wind blowing her hair, making it shift and billow. Darkman turned and saw her. He turned his head quickly away, not wanting her to see him unmasked. "Stay away," he said, unconsciously easing his hold on Strack's foot.

With a huge jerk, Strack pulled his ankle free. He aimed the gun, hopping on one leg. "Say good-bye, Dr. Westlake," he crowed triumphantly. "This bullet's for you!"

Darkman ducked in time. The bullet thunked against steel and ricocheted away, whistling crazily. Julie wobbled and started to fall. Darkman crawled across the girder and caught her elbow, steadying her. The moon showed her eyes as they shifted down to his hands. She emitted a terrified scream.

"Do you see him now?" Strack shouted at her. The wind picked up, whooping past the unyielding steel, moaning with a hundred cold voices. "He isn't a man anymore, Julie. He isn't even human. Look at him!"

Darkman snatched his hand away from Julie and covered his head and face with his arms.

"A freak, Julie. A nightmare, a spook. Is that what you want? Come back to me and we'll forget that this Peyton creature ever existed. Forget, too, that damn memo that caused all this trouble." He extended a hand. "Together, Julie, you and I. Just the two of us. All grudges set aside."

She stared at Strack, gagging on the rag jammed so deep in her mouth, her hair billowing in the wind. Darkman peeked through his arms and saw her nod. She edged toward Strack, stopping where Darkman blocked her path on the beam. Strack reached out and steadied her as she stepped past him. He was smiling gently. He pulled her close and jerked the soggy cloth out of her mouth.

"Dr. Westlake," he said, "I believe our business is almost ended. Just one thing remains to be done and we will all be released from bondage."

Darkman turned his back. He did not want Julie to remember him as Darkman but as the Peyton she had loved.

"Only one thing left to do, Mr. Circus Freak," Strack said. "Julie will live, but only if you can prove your love for her."

Darkman shuffled around, uneasy, shielding his face from the light.

"You will take an extended hike off this building, Mr. Nobody. I want you to jump."

Strack spun Julie around and hooked an arm around her neck. "Either you jump or she does. Who will it be?"

Darkman stared at him.

Strack smirked. "Once you are in your coffin, I will make Julie my bride." He stroked her breasts with his free hand. She stiffened but said nothing. "All of her, just for me."

Darkman jumped at Strack, sick with rage, no longer afraid of the height, no longer afraid that Julie might see him, no longer afraid at all. Strack swung the gun up, too late. Darkman smashed it aside and tore Julie from his grasp. She wobbled, arms pinwheeling, a high-pitched scream of terror slipping out, but Darkman steadied her until she regained her balance, then stood face-to-face with Strack at last, boiling with hatred for this human devil.

"Now who jumps?" He snarled in Strack's face and grabbed him by the hair. With one move he threw him into the air. For a moment Strack was outlined against the moon, a windblown scarecrow, legs and arms wildly flailing, a thin scream of fright bursting out, and then he was falling . . . falling.

Darkman reached out as he plunged past. He snagged him by one ankle, the bare one, gloating inside that as Darkman he was stronger than Charles Atlas, stronger even than Schwarzenegger, the victim of a surgical procedure that had made him powerful and deadly. He laughed at Strack.

"If you can't fly, now's the time to learn, Strack," he said. "Better learn pretty fast, too."

"Wait!" Strack screeched, hanging upside down, coins and keys clattering out of his pockets. "Listen to me! If you kill me, you'll be as bad as I am. Maybe worse. If you drop me, you'll be the monster you look like. I know you. Julie told me a lot about your values. If you kill me, you'll never be able to live with yourself. Right?"

Darkman dropped him. *"Wrong."*

Julie gasped.

Strack screamed for a remarkably long time before punching through the reinforcement bars and splatting on the concrete that his own workers had poured just two days before.

"I'm learning to live with a lot of things," Darkman whispered, and covered his face. He let himself lean forward, past the point of balance, and began to fall.

He jerked upright, his body sticky with sweat. His own screams echoed, echoed.

If you do not find something to do besides work and dwell on the past, his hated inner voice said gravely, *you will go insane.*

He drew up his knees and propped his forehead against them, nodding at that voice.

He was going insane.

CHAPTER

1

A Little Discipline
Never Hurt Anybody

Danny's father always turned mean when he was drinking. His father slapped him around when he was drunk. Today Danny's father was not just drinking and not just drunk; today he was fried to the gills and reeking of the blackberry vodka he favored.

"You little shit!" he screeched in a tone usually reserved for the criminally insane. "You stop that! You stop that!"

In the ruins of the living room his son Danny was doing a fairly good duck-and-dodge routine, ducking a fist here, dodging a foot there. His father was a big man in green janitor's clothes with the shirttails flapping, his heavy boots thundering on the floor, his out-of-style Afro hair protruding from his head in twirls like curly black wires. He ran his fingers through his hair when he was troubled, and getting laid off from his job on the night maintenance crew at the former Springdale Metalworks was trouble enough.

That had happened two, almost three months ago. Danny had watched his father slowly disintegrate under the pressure of filling out job applications when he could barely read and write, watched him grow lazy and mean as he stared at the boob tube all day, watched him skip meals to stay loaded on that blood-red concoction called Acer's Blackberry Vodka.

"I'll kill you!" he screamed.

Danny Frakes had turned ten years old a few months before, in June. He was a shrimpy kid for his age, a little too short and a little too skinny—just little enough, in fact, to make his life at Garfield Elementary a living hell. He looked soft and scrawny and had a baby face that would make any mother smile. Unfortunately there were no mothers in his fourth grade class at Garfield . . . except for the kind whose names were spray-painted all over the rest room walls and in the hallways, mother-blank this and mother-blank that.

Danny's unhappy standing at Garfield was also due, in part, to his mom's insistence that he never swear. Never swear! Imagine that, in a school like Garfield. But he was bound to his promise by the fact that his mom was dead, had been for seventeen months, and was very likely keeping watch over him from heaven. And even if she wasn't, he *had* made the promise.

Quite a kid, that Danny, his teachers thought.

The midget's gonna die, the big kids at school thought.

"Shit for brains!" his father shouted. "Shit for brains! You ain't nothing but a shit for brains!"

His dad had been drinking since morning, sitting morosely in his useless uniform at the table, his gaze frozen on the blank gray wall beside the broken refrigerator, the bottle in one hand, the other clenched into a taut fist, his jaw muscles soundlessly working as he ground his teeth. What's going on inside that head? Danny wanted to ask, but the mood in the kitchen was so cold that Danny imagined he could see his own breath.

He went off to school without breakfast. Food had become scarce lately anyway, though the sagging metal cabinets in the kitchen held plenty of vodka and a dozen cartons of generic cigarettes. The free school lunch had tasted pretty good, a dry hamburger on a bun, some floppy fries, a carton of milk, and some carrot sticks. Word had it that Garfield would be closed this year and the students bussed out to the "white" schools on the perimeter of town. There would be new friends to make and new dangers to face.

Danny had not had much contact with white people in his ten years, save for the ones he saw on television and that old coot Charlie Troy who worked with his dad and had visited a few times to get drunk and raspberry-red in the face before staggering off. He seemed all right.

What a world, and he was only ten.

"You killed her!" his father yelled. "It was you!"

Danny scuttled down the short hallway and stiff-armed the bathroom door open. It hit the wall with a bang, the knob punching a hole through the plaster that was already cracked there. He spun around and smashed it shut, leaned his weight against it. And down the hallway came heavy, thudding steps, slobbers, and growls.

He was afraid he couldn't hold the door. He was sure he couldn't hold the door. He braced his feet against the base of the toilet, hoping the porcelain couldn't be shoved from its moorings when his dad crashed into the door. One hand went out and clutched the towel bar; the other held the knob to keep it from turning.

"Yeah, and you had to have a brother!" his father howled. Danny felt his breathing hitch, felt his eyes becoming hot. His mom had come down with something they called a tubal pregnancy that had burst and they didn't even find it out until the autopsy. Sure, he had wanted a brother. Sometimes even the kids on TV wanted a brother.

"I'm coming for you, you little shit!"

Danny swallowed, waiting. His throat was dry as ash. A trickle of blood was sliding down his chin from the one hard blow his father had landed on his mouth. It dripped steadily onto the floor and the legs of his pants, bright splashes that were as crimson as the candy-apple bicycle paint he had once seen at a Schwinn shop on the rich side of town. He tilted his head back, thunked it against the door, squeezing his eyes shut. Dripping tears joined the blood on his chin.

A force like a locomotive slammed into the door, cracking it in a dozen places. Chips of old paint blew out around Danny's head and spattered on the floor. He heard his dad grunt with surprise. The weight on the door went away.

"Daddy, please," Danny sobbed. He knew well enough what was coming next: another good run at the door.

Footsteps, receding. A pause, a harsh intake of air. A locomotive hit the door again. Danny locked his knees, begging the toilet to hold fast, begging his legs not to break.

Crunch!

Danny howled. The pain in his back from the blow was enormous. He opened his eyes and saw that the toilet had scooted a few inches toward the wall. The water inside lapped at the porcelain. Something behind it was hissing, and water was dripping onto the floor. The water pipe had been damaged.

"Daddy, no! Please! It wasn't my fault that Mom died!"

Footsteps, receding. A pause, a harsh intake of air. A locomotive rushing toward him again.

Danny realized the hopelessness of it and jumped to one side at the last possible second. His father smashed through the door in an explosion of wood chips and noise. Momentum carried him into the wall as his knees slammed against the seat of the toilet, knocking it completely off its position. Plaster cracked as he dead-ended on the wall. Water geysered up from the pipe that fed the toilet, squirting crazily, and he began to scream, holding his shins, his face twisted in agony, while water jetted under the shelf of his chin.

Danny did some quick thinking. His father had always been rough with him, especially when he was loaded, but ever since Mom died his drinking had increased and he had gone steadily haywire. Even old Charlie Troy no longer came by for an occasional evening of boozing and complaining about the world and how it had betrayed him. Danny had not lived in this city all these years with his eyes closed. Most of the kids he knew had part-time fathers; a lot of them had no father at all. Danny knew it was hard for a proud man to grovel and scrape at some joke of a job. Harder yet to support a family on a minimum wage that was an even worse joke. Mom's death had ripped his father's heart out; losing his job had taken everything else.

Danny had to leave. Now and forever. He looked at his dad and saw a man sinking slowly to the floor in a loud torrent of water. His face was twisted up into horrible lines and angles as his work boots slid across the floor to push against the wall that had kayoed him. The guttural sounds he was making were cries of pain and defeat, worse than defeat. They were the cries of a man on the road to early ruin and early death.

His dad was still in his twenties, but he was already ruined, hopeless. As he clambered out of the bathroom and ran toward the door of the apartment, Danny swore that life would be different for him. He would make it, make it big.

He gave his father one last glance. He had passed out, splayed on the floor with his crazy hair gathering glistening drops of water as the bathroom slowly started to resemble a swimming pool. Danny would make it. Oh, yes, he would. But he needed to answer one question before he tried.

Where, exactly, was he trying to make it to?

Danny wandered the city for three days, hands rammed deep inside the pockets of his jeans, his white high-top shoes fashionably untied, his white T-shirt slowly turning gray from exposure to the dirty air. He discovered, after not eating for a day or so, that the burger joints and the chicken restaurants dumped incredible amounts of unsold food into the trash each night and that he could usually find a dozen slices of cold pizza in one of the Dumpsters.

To his own surprise he was left pretty much alone, too young to be of interest to the gangs, obviously too poor to be of interest to the pickpockets and muggers. It was the winos who scared him the most, faceless men dressed in rags, warming themselves over a fiery trash can at night, sleeping on the sidewalk or on a warm grate. They eyed him with their mysterious gazes, mumbling things, sometimes reaching for him in delirium. He saw men passed out with a bottle nestled protectively in their arms, and the bottles were strangely monotonous: Thunderbird, Boone's, Wild Irish Rose. What those men lived for he did not know. Where they vanished to when they died was equally hard to figure out. They were gray specters with gray faces, aliens on planet Earth.

But just eating and walking and staying out of trouble was not what Danny had in mind. Something waited for him out there in the world, something that was better than anything he had ever known before, better than most people ever dreamed. He saw men driving fabulous cars that seemed to skim above the surface of the road, people dressed in wild finery, women burdened with jewelry, kids with their noses in the air. Money, tons of it, but money was not the issue here. What he really wanted was . . . was . . .

He didn't know. He wouldn't know until he found it. And there he saw grounds for despair.

His fourth day on his own dawned damp and ugly, streaks of dull purple crisscrossing the horizon above the dark bulk of the high-rises, the air cool and damp and smelling heavily of bus exhaust. Danny had spent the night in an alley on a slab of cardboard with newspapers for blankets and—eureka!—a discarded old pillow. Barricaded behind trash cans, camouflaged as a pile of paper, he lay groggily awake wondering how his dad was, wondering if the broken pipe had filled the whole tenement up with water, wondering if his mother was looking down on him, dismayed at his having deserted his father. At her funeral he had prayed for her to come back to them, had sat there while the minister droned on, inwardly imploring her dead body to sit up and end this nonsense. That would have provided a good scare, and shown that religious guy that no mother of Daniel Zack Frakes was going to be planted in the ground forever, no, sir.

But she did not sit up. Nobody was surprised, nobody was scared. Danny was dismayed by her insistence on staying dead and by the realization that he would never, ever see her again in this life.

He sat up wearily now, sending the newspapers cascading off of him. His back ached and his bones felt heavy. He looked around, smacking his lips, idly wondering if today it would be burgers or chicken or pizza. He stood up and tucked his pillow under his arm, not willing to part with something so grand. It was probably worth its weight in cash in this crummy neighborhood so near the river. He sauntered out of the alley, glad that the sun was not high enough in the sky to spear his eyes with its unbearable light, and turned left for no reason at all. Maybe today, he thought, he would figure out exactly what he was looking for and where to find it.

The first building he passed was gutted, its doors gaping open, nothing but blackness inside. The next one was a red brick structure, its windows smashed and boarded up. This had to be the worst neighborhood in the city, or close to it. The atmosphere here was heavy and dead, the bustling sounds of city life absolutely missing. Danny thought of ghost towns in the wild West; he could even picture vultures perched high in the rubble, waiting.

He crossed one nameless street, then another. Once this had been a busy area. Many of the buildings were abandoned factories sitting dumpily in shambles, victims of the malls and businesses that were now clustered on the south side of the city. Danny could imagine people living here, going to work next door, stopping at the tavern down the way. Laundry flapping on lines, kids playing.

Something caught his eye and he stopped. Etched onto a rusty steel plate set in the wall of one huge building was an odd word: Reyton.

A large hasp and padlock held the big double doors closed, but the lock hung open, chipped as if recently fought and defeated. Out of pure curiosity, and in the hope that the new streetwise Danny could make use of it or peddle it, he took the lock out of the hasp and stuck it in his pocket.

The doors drifted open, revealing the black maw of an empty factory that had once probably employed thirty or forty people. A dismal wooden sign hung from small chains in the ceiling: Reyton Soap Company, Home of Fresh Splash Soap and Other Household Products.

Peachy. Danny patted the lock in his pocket and was about to head away again on the journey to his future when something very odd, even for this part of town, happened.

A howl unlike anything he had heard before came billowing out of the dark interior.

"Nooooooo!"

His heart switched gears from neutral to drive in the space of a second. He had heard a lot of hollering from his dad, but those were the screams of rage. This one was a mixture of terror and agony. He listened, frowning, hearing the echoes of the cry being swallowed away— going, going, gone.

And then nothing at all.

Danny took a cautious step inside, then another. He was old enough to know that the only way to stay in one piece around this area was to mind your own business. What lurked in the old soap factory was none of his concern. But curiosity got the better of him, and he walked deeper into the guts of the building down a long and confusing hallway that angled to the left and then to the right until it opened on a huge dark bay where he could hear someone, or something, shuffling around in the dark.

It began to mumble and curse to itself. A man, then, a man in a bad mood. Danny knew he should leave, that this was none of his business. Nothing here but trouble.

Instead, he went farther inside, on tiptoe, his breath locked tight in his lungs, a small sprinkling of sweat beginning to form at his hairline.

Ahead, something clunked. Something wooden rasped across cement. A small thing whickered through the dark and shattered against a wall, something made of glass. Shards of it rained down on the cement floor.

This dude must be *crazy,* Danny thought. Crazy or drunk.

Muttermuttermutter.

It sounded very much like a wino mumbling to himself, mumbling to the hallucinations his dying brain produced for his enjoyment. The best thing for a ten-year-old boy to do in this case, Danny decided, was to get the hell out and stay the hell out.

He went in deeper. A dark misshapen thing loomed on the floor—some kind of machinery—and Danny sidestepped it. There was a smell in here that was growing stronger as he sneaked into the depths of the factory, a smell very much like that of an electric appliance overheating and, below that, a hint of stale food. Stale pizza, come to think of it. Danny was becoming an expert on stale pizza.

Muttermuttermutter.

Enough of this. Time for a silent retreat and back to the business at hand.

He took two more steps and stopped. The sun had risen higher in the sky and was streaming in through a hundred tiny cracks and holes. Dimly he could see a junkyard of debris, chunks of machinery, huge spools and coils of wire, slabs of wood suspended from chains to form tables. All kinds of dark shapes were perched on them—small televisions, radios, stereos, computers. In a movie the scene might serve well as the laboratory of a mad scientist, the maddest of them all.

A black figure stalked toward him as suddenly as a bat flapping through a cave. Danny ducked, nearly letting out a squawk, and held his hands in front of his mouth to silence his breathing; his eyes were round and huge. The dark man stopped at one of the hanging tables, leaned forward, and turned something on with a click. A small green light began to flash in the dark. More clicks. A computer screen glowed alive, bathing the man in gentle green light.

He was a mummy.

Danny mashed both hands hard against his lips to keep from gasping out loud. The man wore a rumpled old hat and a long coat like any wino, but his face was wrapped in cloth and his hands were tightly bandaged with the same fabric. For eyes he had slits; for a mouth he had a hole. Danny could hear him breathing now as he tapped out something on the computer.

21

He stepped back and turned the computer off. His voice was harsh, ragged. Semidarkness took over again, and the specter stalked away.

Danny waited, listening to the man move around muttering to himself, hearing the scrape of his footsteps as he wandered away. He waited longer, counting out the seconds. After perhaps five minutes with no sign of the mummy-man, Danny collected his courage, assured himself that he was in no danger, and found the hallway again that led outside.

That was when his troubles really started.

CHAPTER

2

I Should Have Known
He Was a Jerk

The day before Danny left home, Penny Larsen returned to her snug little apartment on the fashionable south side at about six in the evening. She flipped the television on, not caring what channel might be found there, and went into her bedroom to toss her jacket on the bed and slip out of her shoes. She worked as a secretary to one of the many assistant district attorneys in the city, those young go-getters whose profession was merely a stepping stone on the path to their real goal: the mayoral chair, a Senate seat, the Oval Office of the president himself, where they would sit surprisingly wondering just what was going on in the world.

At twenty-three, Penny Larsen had found out fast just what the law business was really about. Her boss, John McCoy, was not much older than she, but while Penny was the blushing daughter of a Kansas wheat farmer, McCoy was the shameless son of a minor politician in New Jersey who had been indicted three times for malfeasance. Penny was not sure just what malfeasance was, but in her ears it rang like the words "corruption" and "graft." She was not exactly sure what graft was, either, but she knew it was a crime.

23

Her phone rang as she was in the bedroom peeling her panty hose off. She had good legs, a handy match for the rest of her, which of course was a problem for any woman brave enough to work for John McCoy. At times, in despair, Penny had considered never wearing makeup, getting her hair cut into something awful, wearing baggy clothes. She had not yet been able to bring herself to do it, fairly sure that as long as she was still female, John McCoy would want to bed her down, no matter how ugly she made herself.

She walked to the phone, almost groaning with the relief of being barefoot on the cool gray carpet, and picked up the handset. "Hello?"

It was McCoy. She covered the phone with a hand and groaned for real; whatever the man wanted, if it involved his long-suffering secretary Penny Larsen, it couldn't be good. She took her hand off the phone. "What's up?" she asked, trying to sound sprightly, and looked at her watch. Just past six. If he needed another memo typed up in a hurry, he could damn well type it himself. On a muggy, dreary day like this one, driving through rush-hour traffic would be awful. No matter how much he cajoled or threatened, she was prepared to say no—something she had never been very good at but had been forced to learn fast.

"I need to see you," he said. His voice was low and secretive, almost a whisper. "I'll be at the Blue Flame on your side of town. Bring your steno stuff."

She sighed. "I don't know where any Blue Flame is, Mr. McCoy."

"Corner of Port and Washington. By the boulevard. It's practically in your back yard. Be there in twenty minutes."

She felt her ability to say no shrinking inside her. McCoy was her boss, and bosses were always coming up with projects and paperwork at odd hours. Other secretaries did it. But then, other secretaries didn't work for a D.A. whose knowledge of the law was shaky at best. McCoy had failed the bar exam three times before getting it right. Penny knew that much. Along with his incompetency came an ego the size of the moon, trailed by a dedication to the judiciary the size of a grain of sand. Of course he hoped to enter political office soon, but God save the country if he ever made it.

She sighed into the phone again. "Can I wear something casual? I don't feel like getting dressed."

"Oh?" he drawled, sounding intrigued. "You're not dressed? Right now, on the phone? You're talking to me naked?"

"Twenty minutes," she snapped, then slammed the phone back into its cradle. A wisp of her light brown hair had fallen over her face and she blew at it, muttering unhappily to herself. The Blue Flame? Probably a sleazy bar with peanut shells and chewing gum all over the floor. But at least it wasn't all that far away, as McCoy had said. If he tried to molest her and her car wouldn't start she could at least run home. Some consolation.

And so on the day before Danny's father got drunk and tried to kill him, Penny Larsen found herself negotiating the heavy traffic with the bloated evening sun streaming in her eyes, with drivers honking for unfathomable reasons and pedestrians hurrying across the crosswalks like frightened deer. Her car was a very clean and shiny Delta-88 that had slid off the assembly line at about the same time she was born. Belching blue smoke, rattling what threatened to be its last gasp at every stoplight, held together by paint and not much else, the car made its way in the lazy heat to the Blue Flame. The parking lot was jammed almost full. The building itself was indeed blue and apparently very popular. As she guided her oversize beast into a parking slot a group of people wandered out of the lounge, dressed to the hilt—suits, nice dresses, jewelry. She looked down at herself in alarm. Old blue jeans and a blouse. Cheap slip-on shoes. The idea had been to look unappealing to McCoy and to discourage his amorous advances, not make him sick. She got out, wilting inside at what awaited her when she strolled into this elegant lounge dressed like this. Conversation would stop. Heads would turn. The piano player would pause in mid-song.

Penny would turn red enough to burst into flame. Probably actually do it, even.

She slunk inside like a criminal and got absolutely ignored. The right half of the place was a dining room, the left half a lounge. Plates and glasses clinked, voices droned. It all smelled very nice and restauranty, no mink coats sending out the aroma of expensive fur, no diamonds slashing her eyes with light. She saw a hand wave at the bar, saw McCoy nod to her and smile, saw him pat the empty stool beside him. Clutching her purse and its freight of secretarial gear, she made her way to him and sat down.

"Right on time," he said, tapping his watch. He was, of course, still in the suit he had worn all day, now with the tie loosened and his shirt unbuttoned to show a sprig of reddish hair. She had to admit that he was not bad looking. But if looks had to match the personality inside, he would have been a large and loathsome toad.

"I try to be punctual," she said, and put her purse on the slick wooden bar.

"What's your pleasure?"

She recoiled. Pleasure could only mean one thing with this guy. She squinted at him and said, "Hmm?"

"What would you like to drink?"

She looked at his glass. Traces of tomato juice, a celery stalk reclining there. "Oh. Beer."

"Beer? Women don't drink beer." He raised a hand and snapped his fingers. "Barman! Yo!"

The bartender strolled over, wiping his hands on a towel, a plump and pleasant-looking fellow. "Help you?"

"Yeah." McCoy snatched the celery out of his glass and bit into it, talking with his mouth full and jabbing the stalk at the air. "I'm an assistant D.A., and this is my secretary. Do you think the secretary of an assistant D.A. should drink beer in public?"

The bartender frowned. "Depends on what she wants, I guess."

"Bring her one of these. Me too."

The bartender eyed her. "Okay?"

She rolled her eyes. "Okay."

He went away. McCoy pointed his celery at her.

"Better. Much more dignified than beer. I have an image to create and uphold, and you've got to play along."

"Oh?" She looked across the bar at the mirrored wall. Duplicate Penny stared back, obviously unhappy. "Does that mean I have to chew with my mouth open and jab the air with a stalk of celery?"

He flinched, looked at his celery, dropped it in the glass, slammed his mouth shut. He dusted his hands off, his eyes flicking back and forth as if searching for spies. "Okay, then," he said after a minute. The drinks came and Penny dived into hers, needing something to knock the sharp edges off this meeting. "A new case got dumped in my lap right after you left the office. You really ought to have a cellular phone in that death trap of yours."

She scowled. "I can't afford one on my wages."

He brushed right past the remark. "It's called the Ice file. Kozinski dropped it off in person, if you can believe that, the frigid bitch. Hey, don't you want to take notes?"

"Okay," she said noncommittally, and got her steno pad and a pen out of her bag. She flipped it open, scribbled something. "Let's see," she said. "Kozinski is a frigid bitch."

"Ah, Christ," he grumbled. "One of these days you're gonna smart-mouth yourself out of a job."

She wrote, muttering, ". . . yourself out of a job."

He went for his drink. Penny watched his profile. Maybe she would indeed smart-mouth herself out of a job, but without this verbal jousting he would have his way with her. She had been warned by other secretaries and even by Jane Kozinski, who was an assistant D.A. herself, that McCoy cared deeply about only one thing in life—sex. And he'd almost gotten it from Penny less than two weeks after he hired her, back when she was starry-eyed about doing good work in the judiciary, helping the downtrodden and oppressed while ridding society of its evil elements, etc., etc., etc. She'd found herself nearly frozen with terror when he bent over her as she typed and announced his admiration of her cleavage. She'd let the incident pass, too scared to give it any real contemplation, but when no more than a day later he slid a hand along her thigh while admiring her dress, the fear gave way to anger, and that anger eventually became the repertory of put-downs and sarcastic remarks that had kept him at bay to this day.

He set his drink down. "Ice is the only name we have so far for a man whose crime career is flourishing like weeds in a rose garden. He—"

"Very poetic, that weed simile."

He glared at her. "Thank you. Ice is a black man in his early twenties. He has some kind of operation going, where he recruits other kids to steal for him. How original, I know. But this Ice character isn't content to have teenage punks doing his dirty work. He's recruiting kids ten years old, even younger, like seven or eight. They're little and inconspicuous and fast-running little bastards, too."

Penny looked at her steno book. A few useless scribbles, the name Ice, not much else. So why did she have to meet McCoy here, instead of tomorrow at the office? She wondered if he was involving her in a heavy case. Maybe it involved police corruption. God, but that would be scary and dangerous—real detective work. Scary and . . . fun.

"Kozinsky said she was ordered to hand the case and the file over to me. *Me!* I know she hates my guts, or at least she's going to keep hating me until I jump her snooty bones in bed and show her what a real man can do. Hah!"

Penny wrote down studiously: *Hah!*

"It's gotta be a trick," he went on. His eyes became slitted and wary. "I wouldn't put it past her to pawn this thing off on me because it's too petty for her to waste her time with, not exciting enough for her inflated ego. She probably thinks I'll work my ass off, and then when I lay it out get laughed out of the division. They'll say: 'Hey, McCoy really jumped for this one. He's already bagged a five-year-old pickpocket and a newborn with a flair for mugging.' Get it? Kozinski finally gets down off her high horse to toss a case at me, and she expects me to jump all over it and wind up looking like a weenie."

Weenie, Penny wrote.

"Well, this is what I'm going to do. I'm going to bury

that frigging file. I'm not wasting one minute of my time on it. I stuck it in your desk drawer and I want it to stay there. If Kozinski happens to ask about it, play innocent. Say it'll take some time to locate it.. That way the laugh is on her stupid ass, not mine. Got it?"

She nodded. "Got it."

"Fine, then. Drink up."

She slumped a little. "That was it? I drove here for that?"

His red eyebrows hiked up a bit in surprise. "You didn't expect me to spill this stuff over the phone, did you? Phones can be tapped, you know. Kozinski's tricky. And besides, you got a free drink out of the deal."

"I didn't even want the damn drink!"

"You'd learn to like it if you tried it more often. Better than beer, by a long shot, especially for a woman."

She frowned at him. "I like beer, Mr. McCoy. I like Chinese food and I like Tootsie Pops and I like day-old coffee. I like a lot of things some people don't." She snatched her bag off the bar and jammed her things into it, mashing them deep.

He cocked his head, looking at her strangely with his bright green eyes wide and surprised. "Gee, I didn't mean to piss you off," he said, and raised his hands in defense. "Honest, Penny, I wouldn't have dragged you out here if it wasn't urgent. I'm sorry, very much so."

She stopped. After a second she plopped her bag back down and picked up her drink. "Guess I've had a tough day," she said, smiling wanly at him. "Sorry."

"No problema," he said, and smiled. He raised his glass. "To us."

"To us," she agreed, and started to drink, but stopped when she saw that he wasn't quite finished.

"To us," he said again, this time very gravely. "Us, and the quickie you're just dying to give me."

She should have known.

29

CHAPTER

3

Some Mornings
Just Plain Suck

The sun was still low in the sky, the dirty streets and alleys that bordered the Reyton soap factory were cut with sharp black shadows when Danny Frakes finally found his way out and stood squinting in the morning light. It was better to be outside than in there with the mummy-man, whoever he might be.

Danny took a deep breath, shivering a little in the brisk October breeze. He did not know what he would do when winter came, but for now, he had to concentrate on surviving each new day and let the rest take care of itself. Hunger was gnawing at him in earnest now that his fright was leaving him, and he knew there was a Wendy's some twenty blocks away where he might find a stale burger with two slabs of rock for a bun in the Dumpster. His stomach rolled slightly at the thought of it. Fast food was slipping off his list of favorite things pretty fast.

He stayed long enough to swing the big double doors of the factory shut. When they swung open again of their own accord he relented and threaded the padlock back through the hasp, doubting that a busted padlock could be worth much anyway. How the mummy-man got in and out of the place was anybody's guess; Danny's guess was that the factory had a few other doors and maybe some big docking bays.

Down the street to the right he could see a couple of winos warming themselves over a fire in a trash can, rubbing their hands together and pausing often to pull a bottle out of their clothes and slug down some cheap wine. How they could do that so early in the morning seemed miraculous. Danny's own father spent a lot of his time in the bathroom when he drank too much noisily throwing up. And even a drinker as accomplished as he had to relent and eat something once in a while. Danny had yet to see a wino eat.

Thinking of his dad made him feel lonesome and hollow inside. All of his thoughts about making it big in the world were starting to dim a little, a wave of childish hope battering itself to pieces against the shores of reality. He was ten, he was little, and he did not have a pot to piss in, much less a window to throw it out of, as Charlie Troy liked to say about himself after the metalworks closed down and he walked away jobless. Danny's clothes were showing neglect, his hair was probably a mess, his face was greasy, and he was smelling more and more like a Dumpster himself. It was probably time to go home, make apologies, and let time pass until his dad forgot the fracas. Danny could patch things up, cook his father a nice breakfast, shine his shoes, whatever. Anything to leave these hostile streets.

Danny turned to the right and stepped headlong into a wall of clothing. He jerked back, apologies already forming in his brain to be routed to his mouth, but two bony hands dropped down on his shoulders, clamped themselves there hard enough to make him cry out. He looked up and saw the cold, leering face of a stranger.

"Hey-hey," the stranger said. His eyes were dark and shiny. His breath on Danny's face was all sour wine and doom. "Better watch where you're going."

"Sorry," Danny squeaked. Those hands were digging deep into his flesh, nearly lifting him off the ground. Terror wrapped cold fingers around Danny's heart and tried to freeze it in place.

"C'mere," the wino growled, and manhandled him around the corner of the factory, back into the dead-end alley where he had spent the night. Danny squirmed and struggled, his face twisted up, fear scrambling his thoughts and making him clumsy. He tried kicking, tried biting, but the wino was thickly padded with layers of clothes and coats. He forced Danny to the end of the alley and pressed him hard against the cold brick wall of the factory. Danny noticed that his guess had been right: there was a metal door set in the wall just beyond his reach, a big folding panel that could be raised like a garage door—for all the good it did him.

"Pretty boy," the wino grunted, his gaze traveling over Danny's face as he held him against the wall. His skin was red and mottled above his scruffy beard, his teeth brown and broken. His eyes were crazily gleeful as he took in the sight of a young boy fresh out of luck.

"Pretty boy," he said again, leering insanely. One of his hands left Danny's shoulder. Cold fingers wormed under his belt. Danny squirmed and twisted. When he shouted, the alley simply spit the sound back at him as an echo. Terror was raking through his veins, shrieking inside his head, making it impossible to fight back.

He felt his belt being undone, felt his jeans being unsnapped. *"Noooooo!"* he shrieked. The wino clamped one hand over his mouth, crushing his face, splaying his lips apart. The wino pressed closer, grinning.

Danny screamed again, this time through his nose, a huge cry of horror and helplessness. He knew that there was probably no one close enough to hear except the other wino at the flaming trash barrel, and that he would either mind his own business or come and join the festivities. But he screamed anyway, screamed, because it was impossible to stop.

Darkman jerked his head up at the sound, realizing at once that he had been asleep again and that this time the screams had not come from him.

He sat up, his tattered face under the bandages trying to pull into a frown. He remembered having paced about trying to calm himself not long ago, remembered turning one of the computers. Then he had flicked it off in disgust and dropped back down on his pallet to chase after sleep again. Couldn't have been more than two, three minutes ago.

He sat up to the tune of an inner groan, got wearily onto his feet, and set out to locate the noise. He could hear a tussle going on just outside one of the docking bay doors as he neared it, a tussle punctuated by muffled screams. He nodded to himself unconcernedly. Just a couple of street bums going at it, probably fighting over a bottle of that ghastly toxic waste called muscatel, nothing but another nuisance to keep him from sleeping. He considered going out to scare them away, the inconsiderate bastards, only now it sounded very much as if one of the bums was a woman. A woman street bum? A female wino? Pretty rare. Most likely a bag lady, and in this part of town the bag ladies had to be tough. So to hell with her, and may she shut up soon.

He was halfway back to his bed when it struck him. That was no woman screaming her lungs out; that was a kid, whether boy or girl he could not tell. He turned and ran back to the docking bay, dodging by memory the junk on the floor, heading toward the rectangular outline of light where the sun was poking in through the gaps between the wall and the huge door. A battered length of pipe served now as its lock; Darkman lifted it out of its hasp and let it drop with a clang onto the floor. With one huge jerk he flung the door up. Its elderly springs and rollers screamed in unison as it clanked into position overhead, and then he leaned out into the cold morning air and saw what the commotion was.

A dirty old wino was pressing a little black kid against the building, his hand crushed against the boy's mouth. Darkman gaped in horror when he saw the wino plant a kiss on the boy's forehead. His insides went cold and hollow. The shock gave way instantly to revulsion, to anger. The wino looked over at him. Alarm washed in a fast wave over his features. He jumped back, his clunky shoes gritting on the ruined asphalt as he moved.

Darkman stalked toward him. "You filthy bastard," he heard himself growl. The rage was there suddenly, it was growing, the rage that was another terrible side effect of the Rangeveritz procedure, the same rage that had driven others to mental asylums, prisons, suicide. He saw his own bandaged hands reach out, felt his own legs propel him into a fantastic flying leap. He dropped down in front of the wino, his vision clouded with the red mist of Rangeveritz-driven hate. One hand clamped down around the gray and sagging chicken skin of the old wino's neck. Darkman lifted him overhead like a barbell and hurled him into the trash and junk at the end of the alley. Garbage cans spun and rolled like bowling pins, spewing garbage and muck. The wino howled, rolling in the trash, then staggered drunkenly to his feet while the crashing echoes of the cans chased each other off to nowhere.

Darkman went for him again, feeling bloated and sick with rage, wanting to see blood and see it fast. He stalked past the boy and closed the distance between himself and the wino, who was desperately trying to untangle himself from the garbage and run away. Darkman had a vision of himself and the perverted old wino, and in that vision Darkman was ripping the man's heart from his body and stuffing it in his filthy mouth.

Darkman stopped. The vision remained. He was going to do it, *had* to do it or go mad with this stunning, overpowering rage.

He was able to force himself to turn away from the wino, but it was like trying to swim against a high tide. He shambled robotically toward the wall of the factory and leaned against it, gasping, his bandaged fingers clawing at the bricks, a line of drool staining the gauze around his mouth.

"Run," he was able to croak.

He heard the wino crashing around among the cans. Something made of glass shattered noisily, and soon the disgusting tang of fortified perry wine was wafting through the air. Darkman pressed his eyes shut and willed his heart to quit hammering.

"I didn't mean no harm," he heard the wino blubber. "That kid started it, not me."

Darkman turned again and sagged against the wall, watching him through that mist of red, of blood. The wino was zipping his pants up, looking, of all things, somewhat angry just past his fright. He patted his clothes and put his nose in the air.

"You will be hearing from my attorney," he snapped.

Darkman eyed him.

"Run!" His voice was a screech this time.

The wino eyed him. Something sparked in his eyes, a twinge of new fear. He edged sideways. "Fucking mummy," he grunted. He sidled past Darkman with his back against the wall of the adjacent building, got some distance between them, and took off at a dead run, his shoes slapping hard and fast on the street.

Darkman pressed an arm to his forehead. The beginnings of a headache were forming inside his skull, thudding to the beat of his heart. He looked to the left and saw that the boy was unharmed and was staring at him, his eyes dull and shocked. "You okay?" Darkman asked. His voice was thready and weak, his knees trembling, now that the rage was funneling itself off to wherever it stayed until its next curtain call.

The kid nodded. He sniffed and wiped a hand over his nose. To Darkman he looked as frail and helpless as a baby bird. He was surprised to feel a twinge of affection for the kid, an emotion he thought had been erased from his mental tapes.

"Want to come in, maybe have something to eat?" he asked him gently.

The boy shook his head. "I don't need nothing," he said sullenly. "I just gotta get home."

Darkman went to him and pressed one bandaged hand on his arm. To his surprise the boy didn't flinch, didn't charge away screaming. "You're shaking like a leaf," Darkman said. "I could make you some hot tea. There's probably a teabag lying around in there someplace."

He found himself being ignored.

"Want me to walk you home?"

The kid turned wordlessly and ambled away. Darkman watched him go, full now of the urge to escort him to wherever that home might be. The city was a rough and mean place; the world in general was unsafe. No kid should have to face its dangers alone.

He watched the boy turn to the right, watched him walk around the building and out of sight. For a while Darkman stood there rubbing his chin with his fingers, thinking, wondering, aware of something new happening inside his mind, but not sure what it might be. He was looking for a purpose in life, looking for a place in society where a man with no face and no future would be welcome.

A thought struck him. He nearly jerked from the force of it. Once again he leaned against the wall, puzzling this time. The rage was gone.

"Ah, don't be silly," he said aloud, and shook his head. Some ideas were so harebrained they were almost funny.

He went inside and lowered the door, locked it, and wandered away to do some thinking.

CHAPTER

4

Jonny's Got the Blues

The morning before Danny left home the phone was already ringing when Jane Kozinski opened the door to her cubbyhole office and dumped an armful of folders and files on her desk. One of the many assistant district attorneys who occupied offices in the courthouse, she was a few pegs higher on the judicial ladder than John McCoy, a few pegs lower than her boss, who occupied the more spacious adjoining office. The time would come, Jane Kozinski knew, when her boss would be promoted and she would take over his position. It was like a game of musical chairs. Just as the system ground out new criminals to replace the old, the criminal justice system ground out new A.D.A.'s as the others got promoted or went into private practice. At this rate by the time she reached, say, forty years of age, she expected to have an office the size of Rhode Island.

She grabbed the phone up. "Kozinski."

It was her boss, calling from next door. Not exactly a prime physical specimen, he found it easier to let his fingers do the walking than to leave his own office and enter hers. "Got some bad news for you," he said. "Can you handle it this early?"

She rolled her eyes. No, she could not. "Go ahead, Frank," she said anyway. "Make my day."

"We've got a very dead corpse at the morgue waiting for identification," he told her. "They want you to do it."

She frowned as her heart began to tick faster. "Me? What, it's one of my relatives?"

"No, of course not. It's a kid, about twelve years old. He's got a long scar on his forehead."

"Jesus." She found her chair and dropped into it. "Jonny Bates."

"Yeah. Sorry to drop a bomb like this so early."

"Bomb is right," she said tonelessly. "Back to square one." Jonny Bates was her star witness in the ongoing and seemingly endless investigation into juvenile crime. The kid had finally opened up and promised to tell it all, and now he was dead just a few days away from facing a grand jury. Coincidence? Don't be funny.

Frank was silent for a moment. Then: "I think it's time to call it quits on the Ice case, Jane. We're wasting the taxpayers' money on small fry. We need to refocus on the issues we can effectively deal with."

Frank's political-sounding oratory slid right past her. All she could think of was Jonny Bates lying on a slab in the morgue with her entire case forever locked inside his head. She had worked on the Ice case since April, and here it was October. Jesus.

"Jane?"

She blinked. "What?"

"I'll need a complete workup on that new murder case—the Hobson case. Could I have it by lunchtime?"

She blinked again. "How did he die?"

"Who? The guy Hobson shot? He got, uh, shot."

She waved a hand. "No, no, I mean Jonny. What killed him?"

"Oh." She heard papers rustle. "Prelim reports suggest that drowning was the probable cause, since they found Jonny's body in the river. The final report has to come from the coroner's office, and you know how swamped they are."

"Yeah." She nodded absently. Jonny on a slab, dead at age twelve. Unbelievable.

"So then, I'll see you when you've got the Hobson case packaged," her boss said, sounding a little uneasy. "Hey, are you okay?"

She came to herself, jerking upright in her chair, making it squeak. "We can't drop the Ice case," she blurted. "Ice is out there recruiting babies! We've got six-year-old boys committing grand larceny!"

"All we have is conjecture," Frank said immediately. "Without Jonny, our case won't hold water."

"But you heard Jonny's statement. You and I were both there when he made it."

She heard him pause, heard him sigh. "I'm surprised at you, Jane," he said. "You've only been out of law school for a few years. Breeze through some of your old textbooks if your memory's short, see what they say about secondhand testimony and how reliable—and admissible—it is."

She felt heat rise in her face. "I'm aware of that. I just need some more time to find another kid like Jonny, one kid who's willing to talk, and I can split this Ice business open like a—"

"Rotten tomato?"

She suddenly felt a wave of cold dislike for her boss. "Go ahead, Frank, tell me I watch too many old detective movies, tell me I'm being a fool. But I've worked long and hard on the Ice case, and the death of my star witness—"

"Your *only* witness."

"Okay, the death of my only witness simply means I have to keep plugging until either I or the police round up another one."

She could hear Frank tapping his fingernails on his desk—his desk was never cluttered like hers—obviously impatient with this conversation. "I don't intend to argue with you all day," he snapped. "I want the Hobson report by lunchtime."

"Fine," she snapped back. "Hobson by lunchtime. But don't ask me to drop the Ice case."

"What if I demand that you drop it?" he said.

She paused, thinking. "Please don't."

"You've become obsessed," he told her bluntly.

"You've put your heart and soul into this case, and you should know as well as I do that hearts and emotions and all that other sentimental crap don't belong in the judiciary. I want Ice out and Hobson in, no two ways about it."

She suddenly felt like weeping—for Jonny, who had been an okay kid, and for the case, which had been ripe and ready to pluck. Jane Kozinski did not like to be beaten. Maybe that was why some of her colleagues considered her a bitch. She knew how they felt about her, and she knew she should ignore them, but their attitude hurt her just the same. She was the Iron Lady who was soft inside. Right now a dive out of the nearest window sounded attractive, but that was silly. Why should she kill herself just because a major criminal case had fallen apart? Maybe it was time for a vacation.

"I can't drop the Ice case," she said anyway, utterly without hope. "I want to work it on the side."

"Hold on." On Frank's end of the line she heard muffled conversation and knew he'd slid his hand over the mouthpiece. Then, after a bit, he came back to say, "Jane, I'll keep the Ice file open on one condition. If you can't abide by it, say so right now."

"Let me hear it," she said dully.

"Okay. The Ice case stays open, but you hand it off to someone else. You're too emotionally involved to handle the case objectively. If you don't mind my saying so, I think you've lost your perspective."

She opened her mouth to speak, then shut it. She was being offered an easy alternative, and very lucky to be getting it. "I'll hand it off," she agreed.

"Good. See you with the Hobson file later, then."

"Wait," she said. "Who gets the Ice case?"

"Oh." He breathed into the phone for several seconds. "Give it to John McCoy. He's never very busy."

She jumped to her feet. Her chair scooted away and banged against the old ornate steam radiator along the wall; some of her folders—most of them containing Ice material—slipped off the desk to the floor. "McCoy?" she said incredulously. "He's a walking advertisement for lobotomy! He keeps his brain between his legs! He failed the bar exam so many times they put a revolving door in just for him!"

"Nevertheless," Frank said, his voice stern, commanding, "I want you to give it to him. And I'll brief him myself as to what approach to take with it, now that your boy is dead."

"But he's—"

"But he's a licensed and accredited lawyer. That, in my book, is sufficient qualification."

"But, Frank—"

"Hobson by lunch, and get that morgue identification business settled," he said, and Jane's phone went silent in her hand. She pulled it away from her ear and looked at it as if it were something newly invented. When she left work yesterday, the path of her career had looked bright and long. Now it lay in ruins, waiting to be repaved with mundane cases like the Hobson affair and maybe a dull little hit-and-run case, maybe an assault and battery. If there was a second thing in this world that Jane Kozinski could not stand besides defeat, it was boredom. To fit in with the happy crowd was not her goal in life.

She put the handset back in its cradle and remained posed that way, lost in her thoughts. Anyone strolling past her door would have seen a tall, pretty woman in a pitifully tiny office wearing a conservative black skirt, a sensible jacket and blouse, a chrome clip in her dark hair. "You can rely on *this* lady lawyer," her clothes seemed to say, but a little boy named Jonny Bates had relied on her and was now lying stiff and blue in a morgue cooler, waiting for her to stop by and report his name so that his toe-tag ID could be filled out, his body shuffled off to whatever relatives he might have.

Her shoulders slumped as she thought of Jonny. Relatives? She knew of none. He had been adopted by a street gang run by a man known only as Ice. This was not a gang that fought for turf or "honor" or just out of plain meanness; this gang was as smooth and dangerous as hot oil. This seemed to be their philosophy: let the other gangs hack each other to bits while we get rich. Jane's best estimate of the amount of money that fell into the hands of Ice and his crowd of thieving kids and the invisible manipulators hiding in the wings came to thirty grand a week, at least. And Frank, in his wisdom, was handing all of her work over to the one man in this building who would do an absolutely incompetent job of it. John McCoy. John McCasanova, she had heard him called once. He was a disgrace to the law profession, the male sex, and the human race in general.

Bending over, she picked up the disarrayed stack of folders, deciding that if she handed McCasanova the entire weighty bundle it would frighten him half to death. She located the very first file she had assembled, the one labeled, simply, "Ice." She had started it a long time ago, in April.

"You're the one for him, I guess," she said unhappily to it, looking as upset as she felt. She retrieved her chair from the wall near the ancient steam radiator, dropped into its creaking seat, and began the task of distilling these hundreds of pages into a few important dozen that even an idiot like McCoy could understand and—if she knew him—utterly ignore in favor of chasing his pretty secretary, Penny, around the office.

The job took until noon, past noon. Lunchtime came and went. A man named Hobson was sitting in a jail waiting for his court date to come up, waiting to see what kind of evidence the D.A. had besides motive and blood on his clothes and the gun with his fingerprints all over it.

She worked, consciously putting off the task of identifying Jonny Bates's corpse until she could stomach it. Jane Kozinski did not give the slightest damn about Hobson or Frank or anybody else currently alive and breathing on the planet, except one.

It was the elusive demon named Ice she wanted so very, very much.

CHAPTER

5

As If the Morning Wasn't Bad Enough Already

Danny Frakes stood at the foot of the stairs that led up to his father's second-floor tenement apartment. He stood there and examined the steps one by one, imagined his feet clomping on them as he climbed up, imagined opening the door and having to deal with his father, who was probably sleeping off another night of drunkenness on the couch or on the floor, or maybe on the toilet, where he had dozed off a few times before.

Danny imagined this and more.

He saw himself later in the morning, scurrying to school with no excuse for having missed three days, dodging the hangouts where the bad guys loitered, perhaps suffering the indignity—not for the first time—of being crammed screaming into his own locker and hearing the door click shut, that narrow gray door that could not be opened from the inside. Once the boys had stripped his pants off and left him on the playground shivering in the January cold while the girls looked on and laughed and the principal, old and useless Mr. Pargessy, staggered around telling them to shush.

The memories were sickening. Why had he come back here? He was like a burned man jumping back into the

43

fire because the frying pan was too hot. The image was weird, but Danny could recall his mother having said something similar about a man who was wanted by the Mafia and who chose to live in prison just to stay alive. Did he, Danny, have any more choice than that unfortunate man?

He swallowed hard, staring at those steps. He could almost see the ghost of himself, his former self, tromping up and down on the creaking wooden staircase through summer and winter and fall and spring. His whole small life had been cast and produced and played out here to the small audience of himself. Did he want to go back to it?

He stepped forward and put a hand on the shaky post that supported one of the handrails. It was naked and greasy wood, eroded out of shape. Whatever varnish had graced the rails remained only on the bottom sides now. Kids used to slide down these rails. Even Danny had slid down one of them, ripping his new jeans on a splinter and getting a little physical education from his mother. But now the children were gone, the people gone, and this home for half a hundred tenants stood deserted and empty. Where had everybody gone?

He climbed the first step. It groaned under his foot. He supposed a musician could have identified the sound as an A-flat or the like. He stepped on number two. G-sharp? It would be fun and utterly useless to know.

He kept climbing to the crazy music of the stairs, reached the first landing, and climbed again up to his own hallway, where he stopped, unnerved.

His father's door was down this hall, number twenty-two. It was still warm here on the second floor, the remains of yesterday's heat. The smell was, as usual, old dusty carpets and sour baby diapers left to rot. But where had the babies gone? The place was like a tomb.

Danny made himself walk. The incident with the wino was tucked far and deep inside his brain, awaiting later analysis. Perhaps the memory would cause him to wake screaming in the night, or perhaps it would be completely and mercifully forgotten. A kid on these mean streets should not be surprised at anything, he knew; by the age of sixteen most of them had seen it all. But he was barely ten. Chalk another one up to experience. He just hoped it was the worst of the worst.

It wasn't.

He came to the apartment where the number twenty-two had been gouged into the door by previous tenants, and stopped. He stood there as if waiting for a bus or a train or a chariot to drop down from heaven and whisk him away to his mother's new home. Nothing of the sort happened, of course, but that did not matter much. He was beyond the age of believing in miracles and was now quickly moving toward the age of believing in nothing at all.

It occurred to him to knock. Perhaps, though, better to just walk on in. But the door would still be locked this early in the morning, the chain in place, the dead bolt thrown. And what worse way to announce his return than by waking his father out of a drunken stupor into a killer hangover? Maybe it would make better sense to come back later.

His fist swung out with no help from his brain and pounded on the door a few times; the doorbell hadn't worked since, roughly, the Stone Age. The door itself was splintered and scarred, layers of graffiti sandwiched between layers of paint. This year it was painted green; last year it had been brown. Danny stared at its battered surface, entranced by the color and the memories of past years that it evoked, unwilling to think of what lay beyond. It could be anything from his father stone drunk on the floor with no memory of what had happened, to his father just plain vanished, unable to face the memories in these walls, this paint.

Nobody answered. He knocked again. Distantly, from downstairs, the wailing of a baby drifted crisp and sharp up the stairwell, a sign of life in this desolate slum after all. Danny knocked, then pounded on the door with the side of his fist.

Nothing.

He tried the knob. It was unlocked. Dismal morning sunlight was trying to seep through the grimy window at the end of the hall, but it was still too early for any effective daylight, and certainly too early for the door to be unlocked. Danny pushed it slowly open, frowning, peering into the dimness inside, aware of the smells of home and booze and food left out to spoil. No problem here, apparently. Dad had just been too drunk to even bolt the door before he passed out.

Danny slipped inside and eased the door shut behind him. He knew that almost all of the windows were draped with comforters and sheets to keep the light out: since becoming a full-time drunk his father could not sleep with the sun pouring through the windows. This way he could doze far past noon without any light in his eyes. He had adopted the timetable of a vampire.

From memory Danny wended his way through the little living room into the kitchen, then into the bathroom. Something sucked mushily under his shoes. When he snapped the light on he found himself standing on a field of colorful wet towels. The geyser had been turned off and the toilet repositioned, probably by the landlord's flunky and fix-it man, that big fat guy Danny hardly ever saw. Other than that, everything was just the same as it had been when Danny left. He turned the light off in case his dad was passed out nearby, and used the toilet in the dark, wondering, hoping, feeling safe enough again here in the confines of his apartment to maybe go to his bedroom and shut his eyes, to sleep and sleep and sleep, the world and every rotten thing on it be damned. Dad wouldn't wake up for hours; that left little for Danny to do except sleep. The thought of having a real mattress underneath him made Danny feel almost woozy with fatigue and anticipated pleasure. He believed that after some sleep and some time to think, he could somehow patch up the rift between his dad and himself. Maybe they could strike a deal, come to an agreement, draw boundary lines on the floors, never speak to each other. Anything would be better than the streets.

He zipped up and went to his bedroom, passing by the dim bulk of the couch where no father slept, treading cautiously to avoid stepping on him if he happened to be on the floor. The trip was short and uneventful, enough to convince him that his dad had probably made it to his bed before giving up the struggle this time. Perhaps things were looking up a bit.

He wafted his door open, already able to smell his bed, which seemed to carry a pleasant scent of its own, the aroma of long, sleepy nights. That spoiled-food odor seemed stronger here, though it couldn't be, unless his dad, in a fog, had eaten one of his rare meals in here and left the scraps for the flies.

He moved a hand out and found the light switch. He flipped it up.

It was the shadow on the floor that he noticed first. It had a head and arms and legs. Danny's eyes jerked up to the edge of the bed, which was an unmade mess, then farther up. Long legs and big bare feet were frozen in a ballerina's pirouette there, an inch or two above the twisted blankets and sheets.

His eyes snapped fully up.

His father hung there, a length of white clothesline reaching from his neck to the light fixture. His eyes bulged crazily, and his purple tongue stuck out of the side of his mouth in a grotesque and mindless leer. Flies crawled on his open eyes. The rotten smell came from Dad hanging there like a horse thief caught in the act. The smell came from the decomposing ruin of his body in the permanent heat wave of this tenement, and from nowhere else.

Danny thought he should scream. That was what people always did on TV. Instead, he stared at the corpse hanging over his bed and wondered why his dad had killed himself in here. Had he chosen this room because he missed his only son? Did he feel guilty for having driven Danny away? Was this one last attempt to show his love? Or was this just the sturdiest light fixture in the apartment, the only one capable of holding his weight?

Danny walked calmly out of the room and went into his father's room. He turned the light on.

It was a miracle that the light still worked. The whole fixture had been pulled from its moorings and now dangled by its wires, one dusty white, one dusty black. There was a puff of plaster dust on the bed with footprints in it.

He went wordlessly back to his own bedroom and the ghastly body hanging there. He looked briefly for a suicide note, a farewell, a good-bye to the cruel world, any last word at all.

Nothing. *Nada,* as the Puerto Rican kid across the hall liked to say. Danny's father had had nothing whatsoever to say to his only son.

He turned again and went into the kitchen. He opened the refrigerator. There was almost nothing inside it—a jar of mayonnaise, a jar of pickles, a greasy black banana that looked old enough to light up and smoke, a jug of cold water for the dehydration that accompanied his dad's hangovers, a block of government cheese that had turned mostly green.

He pushed the door shut. There was nothing left here, nothing at all. No food, no mom, no dad. For quite a while Danny stood there looking blankly at the wall, his thoughts drifting without haste like a lazy stream, detached from reality, drifting on senseless memories and the need to sleep.

Around noon he dozed off on the couch. Just before darkness came, he woke up. He went straight from the couch to the door, opened it, and trudged down the steps of his home for the last time.

CHAPTER

6

Childhood's End

The day Jonny Bates died he had been doing business as usual for the man known only as Ice. In the hierarchy of professional gangs, Jonny was ranked about as low as he could get, a peon doing the hard work so that the fat cats higher up could attend to other, less dangerous things. It was Jonny's job on the streets to rob and mug and pick the pockets of as many people as he could during the course of a day. He often brought in thirteen or fourteen hundred dollars at a time. Not bad for a twelve-year-old fat kid whose only real talent seemed to be eating.

Beside gorging on food, Jonny Bates was also good at being pushed around. It seemed to be the lot of all fat boys to be badgered and bullied by the thin kids, not to mention being called every humiliating name connected with obesity—fatso, porky, lard-ass, blubber-puss. Jonny had heard them all. The only respite he had found from the ugly realities of life was being in Ice's nameless gang. There, safe in that world, he was respected not for what he looked like but for what he could do. And he was such an innocent-looking kid that the adults he stole from would probably forgive him if he ever got caught. He was truant from school most of the time, but the

49

teachers forgave him. He spent most nights away from home, but his mother forgave him. He felt pretty sure that if he hosed down a crowded street with a machine gun, the cops would probably forgive him. Though he did not know it, there was one adult in the city who would never forgive him.

Ice.

Jonny had spent this Wednesday in one of the ritzier parts of town, the area surrounding the Diamond Square shopping mall where doughnut shops and department stores and convenience stores competed with the thirty businesses inside the mall proper. Jonny had seen the prices of the merchandise in these stores and the shops in the mall, and he didn't understand how anyone could earn enough money the legal way to buy stuff there. He knew that a pair of winter gloves would run about thirty dollars in the mall. At the army-navy surplus store on Grant Street he could get a better pair, the military kind, for six bucks. Ditto for the price of clothes and shoes, camping equipment, what-have-you. Cameras in the mall that sold for seven hundred dollars could be bought used at a pawnshop for about fifty bucks. Since beginning his criminal career last year he had become keenly aware of the dividing line between the rich and the poor of the city, an awareness that had become, with time, a general feeling of contempt for the people who blew their easy money as if it were nothing but green paper.

Their attitude was convenient for Jonny, though. In the beginning he had felt uncomfortable picking the pockets of strangers. He had felt guilty hiding behind cars in the parking lot, waiting for some rich broad to hurry by with her arms full of packages. When one appeared, he would just walk right into her and, boom, she'd drop her stuff. Then, boom boom boom, he'd grab as much as he could and run away while she shrieked her indignation. After a few weeks of this, Jonny had lost that sense of discomfort and guilt. What he never lost, though, was the feeling that Ice and his lieutenants were taking advantage of him. Using him. Out of a thousand-dollar haul, he averaged fifty bucks. Pretty good wages

for a poor kid from the wrong side of town; a pretty slim
little cut, though, considering that he did all the work.

He had been in one of his grouchier moods ten days
ago when two plainclothes cops jumped out of nowhere
and caught him racing down the sidewalk outside the
mall, his arms full of Bloomingdale's plastic bags. The
cops had handcuffed Jonny and read him his rights as a
crowd of gawkers assembled to watch his degradation.
He was taken on an extended visit to jail and assigned a
lawyer who looked about as old and wise as Opie Taylor
and could never stop yawning. Jonny sneered at his
suggestion of pleading guilty. He felt sure that when Ice
found out that one of his best street men was in the poke,
F. Lee Bailey himself would show up to defend him.

That didn't happen, though. Jonny was arraigned the
next morning. Bail was set at two thousand dollars. Four
days trudged past; no bail. His mother came to visit him
and spent the entire fifteen minutes crying. Finally a guy
named Sting, Ice's second-in-command, showed up and
stayed just long enough to inform Jonny that if he opened
his mouth, they would kill his mother. Jonny hadn't slept
much that night.

When a slick-looking lady breezed in the next morning
carrying a briefcase and tape recorder and introduced
herself as Jane Kozinski, Jonny was at least willing to
listen, if not talk. The deal she offered sounded fair
enough: immunity from prosecution if he told all. He
had precious little to tell, but they did not know that, and
he had sense enough to string them along. He gave them
one tantalizing bit of information: the head of the gang
went by the name of Ice. This tidbit sent Jane Kozinski
into a fever of happiness. She suggested wiring Jonny up
with a micro-recorder. He agreed. He fully intended to
tear the thing off and talk with Ice on his own, simply to
tell him what a son of a bitch he was.

That was old history now, though. He had no chance at
all of finding Ice; nobody could find Ice, except maybe
Sting. So Ice found Jonny.

It was broad daylight. Jonny was walking the streets
two hours after leaving jail as if sheer persistence would

locate the Ice Man. The big silver limousine hummed past him at the corner of Charles and Elderberry streets, its windows black, the little flying-wing ornament on the trunk glinting under the sun. The limo stopped, and a door popped open.

"Get in," someone said.

Jonny did not need a high school diploma to figure out who it was. He climbed into the limo, which was so new that it still smelled wonderfully of carpeting and leather, the smell competing successfully with that of the smoke from Ice's cigarette, and pulled the door shut. Ice was a large man in a shimmering blue suit with black accents. He had on enough gold and diamonds to finance ten limos, to Jonny's way of thinking. Behind his wrap-around sunglasses two eyeballs stared hard at Jonny in the dimness of the car. Jonny tried to organize his thoughts but found them whirling uselessly inside his head. This guy stank of money and power.

"Sit still, kid," someone said behind Jonny's head, and he jerked around. Man, but this was one big car. Sting and another guy were seated behind him in another pair of seats that faced each other. The driver pulled away from the curb so carefully that the martini barely sloshed in the glass in Ice's hand. "What are you doing out?" Sting demanded.

Jonny put on a wobbly smile. Sweat was beading up on his forehead despite the air conditioning. "They let me go," he said. That sounded damned lame, even to his own ears.

"They don't just *let* anybody go," Sting rumbled. Though Jonny had worked for him all year, he seemed now very menacing despite his age. Jonny knew that Sting was sixteen, maybe seventeen. All of the members of Ice's gang were under twenty. Why, he did not know, but had tried to guess once or twice. What grown man would have worked for such low percentages?

"They knew I couldn't pay the bail," Jonny said. "My mom talked to them, and she's real good at bugging people to death."

"Do tell," Ice grunted. His voice was a combination of smoke-ruined vocal cords and intense dislike. For the first time Jonny saw that he had a silver tooth in front. It reminded him strangely of an ax. An ax growing in Ice's mouth. With a word he could have Jonny killed. "Check our fat boy for security breaches," Ice said to Sting, and Sting leaned over the seat and began patting Jonny's clothes.

"I'm wired," Jonny offered, and lifted his shirt. The micro-recorder was taped under his right arm, the tiny microphone on his breastbone. "But I was gonna tear it off."

"Do tell," Ice murmured. He took a long drag off his cigarette and blew the smoke in Jonny's face. Then he leaned forward and parted the short curtains that separated the chauffeur from the passengers. "Warehouse after all," he said, and slid the curtains back together. He settled back on his seat and sipped at his drink. "What did you tell them?"

"Hmm?"

"The police. What did you tell them?"

Jonny could only shrug. His heart under its protective layers of bone and blubber began to speed up.

"Did you give them my name?"

Jonny tried smiling, then frowning. Nothing worked right, as if his face had come unglued from the rest of him. "W-well," he stammered, "not—not really. I mean, it's not like I even know your name, except for Ice. Just Ice, that's all I know."

Sting leaned forward again. "You mean you told them you work for Ice?"

"Well, yeah. But I mean, it's not his *real* name. Anybody could be named Ice in this town. I'll bet there's a dozen Ices."

"You lose the bet," Ice said.

They drove him wordlessly to a collapsing old building on the waterfront where the smell of the river was dirty and damp. They got out, Jonny squinting in the sunlight, his hands deep in his pockets, the mud sucking at his shoes. He wondered why he was here at an abandoned warehouse that had the number A-22 stenciled on its tin wall for no discernible reason. He was not about to believe that Ice would do any more than slap him around. He was, after all, one of the gang, and gangs had rules. Besides, he was just a kid. And he was willing to forget the whole matter of telling Ice what a son of a bitch he was.

Ice and the nameless boy escorted him up a sagging wooden walkway that led into the building while Sting trailed behind with the chauffeur. Jonny was reminded absurdly of old pirate movies where people were forced to walk the plank. He glanced back and saw that Sting had a length of rope wound around one shoulder. What a strange item to have in a limo. And what could they do with it? Keelhaul him?

He began to cry as the walk led him out of the sun and into the dark belly of the warehouse. As his eyes adjusted to the gloom he could see piles of old crates and junked machinery. The smell was a mixture of old vegetables and rotten wood, motor oil, and bird shit. A general-purpose warehouse and chicken coop, maybe. He felt a crazy urge to either laugh like a hyena or throw himself at Ice's feet and beg for mercy. He had never been whipped in his life, and that rope was new and stiff; it could shred all the skin off his back.

"Please," he heard himself bleat when they had stopped. Something was clanking behind him. He glanced back and saw Sting climbing a ladder hooked to the wall. "I swear I didn't mean no harm, Mr. Ice. The cops had me scared real bad, you see, and so I thought I could trick them with the tape recorder. It would've been funny! We could have said funny things into it!"

Ice turned and peeled his sunglasses off. His eyes were large and white. "Laugh this off," he said darkly.

Something slithered down from the ceiling and dropped on Jonny's left shoulder like a snake. He jumped back with a cry.

It was the rope. It had become a noose. A hangman's noose.

"Put it on," Ice said.

Jonny's mouth began to slobber out nonsensical pleas without any direction from his brain. He had been afraid before, but this was the Godzilla of fear, the King Kong of terror. He backed away and thudded into the kid whose name he would never know. The kid jerked his arms behind his back and forced him forward.

"Put it on," Ice said. In the semidarkness his blue suit appeared to shine. It occurred to Jonny that Jerry Lewis had worn a suit just like it in some movie, that *Nutty Professor* show where the scientific potion had turned him from a nerd to a cool dude. Buddy Love, that was the guy's name. Buddy Love.

"Ice, please," he mewled. *"Please."*

The kid let his arms go and settled the noose around his neck. He snugged it tight and stepped back. Jonny looked up and saw that the rope rose up to some sort of scaffold in the shadows above. Sting was up there with the other end in his hands. The rope was looped once around a metal bar, ready to be pulled taut.

Ice raised a finger and pointed it at Jonny's face. "Just look at how bad you fucked up," he said reprovingly. "And now I have to go and do *this.*"

He snapped his fingers.

The rope jerked around Jonny's neck. The noose tightened, pinching his skin in a dozen places. An involuntary groan bubbled past his lips. A wildly panicked voice inside his head said that his eyes were going to pop out of their sockets under this kind of pressure.

Sting lifted him an inch off the floor, two inches. Jonny jerked and flopped like a fish on a hook. The pain was huge and unbearable—no quick snap of a broken neck, not even total asphyxiation to end things. He tried to scream, but all that came out was a gout of hot blood that splashed down his chin. His breathing was a strangled wheeze through a throat that had been crushed to the size of a pinhole.

It took him five full minutes to quit twitching. While they waited, they chauffeur walked around Jonny taking pictures with an expensive camera, one that had been stolen by Jonny Bates himself.

They dumped Jonny's body in the river and went back to business as usual.

CHAPTER

7

Hail, Hail, the Gang's
Not All Here

Nightfall.

Danny did not know how long he had been walking. Since leaving home and his father's corpse, he had simply walked from here to there to nowhere, his mind still connected to the rest of him by only a few lines and relays, his brain on idle. As the sun dropped, the broken skyline at the western edge of the city was bathed in ugly shades of pink, then purple, then black. The streetlights in the better sections of town flickered on around nine or so; the ones in the slums, long ago shattered by children's rocks and gang members' bullets, had been left unrepaired.

It was in this darkness, lit only by a slice of moon, that Danny walked, the stench of uncollected garbage and oily streets hanging heavy in the dead air, and when something—someone—grabbed him from behind and pressed a straight razor to his throat, he felt only a peculiar sense of relief.

"Empty your pockets," he was told. It was the voice of a teenage punk, half boy and half man. Danny obediently turned his pockets inside out and raised his arms. A hand slapped at his buttocks—sorry, no wallet.

"Shit." The razor left his neck. Danny stood still, as limp as a marionette with broken strings. "Take a hike," he was told.

Instead, Danny sat down on the curb. He put his face in his hands and began to rock, his legs crossed like an Indian guru, the amazing rocking boy, sitting with his pockets inside out and heaving great, wrenching sobs into the palms of his hands even though he no longer remembered quite why he was crying. He knew only that he missed his mother so badly that the huge hole in his heart, which he'd thought was mending, had been ripped open again. The frightening word "orphan" lingered at the back of his thoughts like a leering ghost, a terrible secret no one should know.

"Hey, I didn't take nothing from you." It was the man-boy, still hanging around. Danny could hear his feet shuffle on the cement as he debated whether to go or stay. As far as Danny was concerned, it didn't make any difference at all.

"You on some bad dope?" he was asked, and was civil enough to shake his head in reply.

"Old man kicking ass? Mine does, when he's home."

Danny looked up. The world was dark and swimmy. He blinked and saw the other kid, a generic product of the ghetto like himself, an inner-city Joe Average. The only thing significant about his looks was the small golden ring in one of his nostrils. To Danny he looked like a scrawny little bull. Sometimes Danny would have a gut feeling about someone he'd just met, an instant affection or dislike. With this kid he got neither, despite the rude introduction. It was as if this boy were made of air. "My old man's dead," he said without emotion, and wiped his eyes with the heels of his hands. He scrubbed them on his pants. "And I don't even care."

"That's why you're crying?"

"I ain't crying."

"Pretty bad hay fever, then."

Danny looked at him again. "Who the heck are you, anyway?"

"Who the heck?" He looked as if he might grin. "I am the heck named Big Mac."

Danny went back to studying the sidewalk between his knees. "You ain't so big."

"It's a code name. Everybody uses one."

"Well, I don't."

"You ain't in a gang? Nobody in a gang uses their right name, not even those assholes who run the east side, those Marauders who think they're such hot shit."

"No gang," Danny said.

"I might could get you in mine, depending on where you live. A little kid like you keeps walking around by yourself you're gonna get stung, and I mean *stung*. Like I almost did to you, but worse."

Danny shrugged. "I don't give a darn."

"Darn?" The kid who thought he was a hamburger sat down on the curb beside him. "Man, where the fuck do you come from? Santy Claus Land?"

Danny shook his head. "I promised my mama I wouldn't ever cuss. She died, so she might be watching."

"Heavy shit," Big Mac said after a moment. "So who's got you now?"

"Got me?" Danny almost laughed, but it would have turned into crying. "Nobody. Nobody got me, and I ain't got nobody."

"Sounds like a song I don't like. Want me to get you in my gang? You ain't gonna make it long like this, as young as you are in this crummy town. Come on." He got to his feet. "You with me on this?"

Danny considered it. "I'm not much good at fighting or anything."

"Shit, we never fight," Big Mac said. He stuck a hand in one pocket of his jeans and pulled out a wad of money. "All we do is get rich."

Danny hemmed and hawed, not really interested in joining the boy's gang, not really interested in doing anything at all.

But in the end, at a loss for alternatives, he went with him.

He spent the night at Big Mac's house, where the name Big Mac didn't seem to exist. His mother called him

Loyell, another of those names mothers enjoyed tacking on their kids. Loyell's mother was a fat lady struggling to take care of eleven kids, all of them younger than he was, so all that Danny got from her was a nice-to-meetcha while she glared at Loyell. Danny could almost read her thoughts: Too many mouths to feed already, damn you. The apartment was small and smelled just plain rank from all the diapers festering in a pile in the bathroom, some cabbage cooking on the hot plate in the kitchen, and probably a plugged-up toilet no landlord concerned himself about. For Danny, this was nothing new—just the long version of the smells of home. His former home.

Loyell became Big Mac again and left to talk with his buddies in the gang. Danny helped one of the little kids with a coloring book and a handful of stubby jumbo crayons, finding that as long as he concentrated on working with his hands, he could ignore the bad feelings for a while. At times he would close his eyes—fatigue seemed to be his constant partner now—and see in a brief flash, an instant vision, the corpse of his father hanging above that bed. When that happened, a cold chill would spread from the center of his guts to the rest of him. Alone and abandoned at the age of ten. And just who gave a darn, anyway? He was rapidly becoming a tough kid, at least tough enough to hold the tears at bay.

Most of the kids were in bed by eleven, at which time Loyell's mother collapsed onto her ratty old couch and stared dully at the television. A rerun of "Family Ties" was on, that silly white family whose problems in life were no more severe than a stubbed toe but took a half hour to overcome. Booooor-ing. Danny dozed off lying on the floor with his chin in his hands, and it wasn't until Loyell nudged his shoulder that he came awake again.

Disorientation did a fast number on him. Who? Where? What? He staggered to his feet and recognized Big Mac, and then all the memories poured back into his head. Mom. Dad. His empty little life.

"I got you cleared to start," Big Mac whispered. Only one lamp was on now, and his features were nothing but shadows and stripes in its glum light. "Let's go."

Danny followed him out, needing to piss but able to hang on for a while, needing to eat but able to ignore his rumbling stomach. There was a surprisingly stiff breeze tooling down the streets outside, scattering the litter and the smells of the slum as it swept past, hinting at rain, maybe within the hour. Danny shoved his hands deep into his pockets and hunched his shoulders, hanging on tight to the only thing he had left in this world: Danny Frakes.

It seemed inevitable that he would wind up in Big Mac's organization of money-makers, but this entire gang business did not sit well with him. Several times his mother had mentioned how horrible the gangs were, with the shootings and all that, but his dad still wore the emblem of his former gang tattooed on the web of skin between the thumb and forefinger of both his dead hands. In dark purple letters against the brown of his skin the tattoos declared to the world that he had been a member of the Slayers.

The streets wound on, the blocks sliding past while Danny and Big Mac walked. He saw undamaged street signs he could remember having seen before through the fog that hovered over him as he wandered—Acton Street, Newport Avenue, O'Connor. It occurred to him that he had put in a lot of miles in the last few days, and gotten nowhere.

"You ain't scared, are you?" Big Mac slowed down long enough to ask him. He had been holding to a fast trot, his long legs hard to keep up with. "We really ain't a street gang, just a business organization. That's what they told me when I joined, and that's exactly what it is. I work for a cut."

"A cut of what?" Danny asked him. "The money you make from mugging little kids?" He realized that the question sounded sarcastic, even dangerous, but the fog he'd been in for the last few days had not totally left him, and if this Big Mac wanted to ditch him, fine; if he wanted to use that straight razor on him, fine again. Nothing mattered anymore. Nothing.

"That's just a sideline," Big Mac said amicably enough. "I can pop maybe twenty dollars in two hours, hitting up kids like you after work. That way the whole haul is mine."

Danny matched his smile, feeling nothing behind it but dead thoughts. He searched his mind for something to say as he speed-walked, and finally dredged up a suitable question: "So you mean you work for a living?"

"Damn right," Big Mac said, sounding proud. "Eight hours a day."

"You've got a time clock? Where my dad works he has to punch a time clock."

"No time clock for me," Big Mac replied. "But you just told me your old man was dead." He stopped suddenly and rounded on Danny. "You better not be feeding me bullshit," he said darkly. "One thing Ice won't put up with is bullshit. Or anything else."

Danny stepped back, vaguely surprised by his tone. "My dad's really dead. My mom, too. She had a tubal pregnancy."

Big Mac eyed him. "And the cops got your daddy?"

Danny nodded. "Yeah. He was in the Slayers."

"The who?"

"The Slayers. Big gang around where I live. At least it used to be."

Big Mac shrugged. "Never heard of 'em." He dug in a pocket and jerked out a huge old-fashioned silver watch on a chain that glinted under the moon. "Shit, man, we got to move."

They moved. Streets changed names as they ran past, some with signs, some without. At least there was life in the area; the windows in the tenements that bulked up on both sides of the street showed squares of yellowish light and shadowed figures inside—signs of occupancy. He was almost able to smell the residents on the breeze—people instead of empty rooms, tenants who paid rent and tried to get by on a couple dollars a day, and sometimes succeeded. But at the intersection of William and Nutmeg streets Big Mac turned left and stopped under a rusting streetlamp whose bulb was still lit.

Danny was struck with the feeling that he had been here before, or close to here at least, and with that idea came a twinge of dread. The area that still showed signs of life was behind him; up ahead lay desolation, untold acres of abandoned houses and factories that stood brooding and ugly in the thin moonlight.

"We wait here," Big Mac said. He seemed uneasy, maybe a little frightened. Danny picked up that emotion and made it his own.

"How come it's so far away from all the stores and houses?" he asked, looking around with large eyes. His shadow, cast by the streetlamp, lay stark and black on the sidewalk. "Are you sure this is the place? I don't see anybody."

"Oh, this is it, all right. They'll be coming pretty quick."

"Who's they? How many in the gang?"

"The business."

"Okay, the business, then. How many?"

Big Mac glanced at him sharply. "There's some things you don't need to know, kid, and that's one of them. All you need to do now is get through the test."

Danny frowned. "I don't know about any test."

"Didn't want to scare you," Big Mac replied. "To be in our business, you gotta pass a little test to see if you've got what it takes."

"Oh." Danny kept frowning. "Is there any arithmetic on it? I'm not much good at arithmetic. But I can count money okay."

Big Mac laughed, a bellow of raw humor that seemed strange and eerie in this quiet place. "You are so weird, man," he cackled. "We ought to call you the Santy Claus Man, or maybe the Kid from Mars. You really crack me up."

"Sorry," Danny said stiffly. It came to him that he had absolutely no idea why he was here. With everything gone, he was a vagrant, a homeless bum. "Maybe we ought to just forget the whole darn thing."

"No, wait!" Big Mac clamped his fingers around Danny's arm. "I ain't making fun of you, man, just laughing at myself. Hey, that could be them there." He released Danny's arm and pointed. Danny turned. A car with two very bright headlights was cruising toward him, lots of dark faces inside. He felt a new chill. The car was a limousine and had to be worth at least a hundred grand. As it swept around the corner its lights glinted off a metal plate in the wall of a falling-down building not far away, sending reflections into his eyes.

Danny looked up to the sky. The afterimage stayed with him, a purple rectangle floating in the center of his sight. He felt himself go weak. To hell with the chills; he was slipping fast into panic. He did not know what kind of test might be ahead of him, but if it involved darkness and winos, he wanted no part of it. He blinked to make the image go away, but it hung on, a taunting reflection that said, simply, "Reyton."

It was the soap factory where the mummy lived.

CHAPTER

8

Just Call Him Mouse

For lack of a better subject, Darkman was studying Dracula. Inside the dimly lit factory the vampire loomed against the eastern wall, a celluloid image cast there by a dime-store movie projector and a cheap 8mm novelty film, for the express purpose of keeping Darkman from going mad. The idea of creating a vampire disguise had formed fairly long ago, soon after his face was ruined in the fire, in fact, but until now he had let the matter lie. In seeking revenge on the thugs who destroyed his laboratory and his life, he had been able to imitate their voices when he masqueraded as them—at times masking his ineptitude with the feeble claim of having a cold—but he was not a skilled impressionist, and his limited ability had almost cost him his life.

Now he sat on the frame of a ruined old chair, studying the Dracula image on the wall and trying to match Bela Lugosi's memorable accent as it poured out of the projector's tinny little speaker. On the bank of computer screens to his right the wavelength of Lugosi's vocal pattern was printed in S-shaped lines. With one hand Darkman was pressing a miniature microphone to the base of his throat; with the other he was fine-tuning the pattern.

He stopped the film for a moment, and cleared his throat. "Good evening," he said. "I am the vampire."

He rolled his eyes and spooled the film backward for a bit. Once again Dracula was projected on the wall when he turned it on.

"Goot eefnink" the vampire said.

"Good evening," Darkman replied.

"I am dee vampiyah" the vampire said.

"I am the vampire," Darkman said.

He turned the projector off with a grunt of dissatisfaction, spooled it backward a little. He turned and tapped at the keys on one of the computers, sat back, and tried again.

"Goot eefnink. I am dee vampiyah."

Darkman repeated, "Goot eefnink. I am dee . . ."

He smelled smoke and snapped the projector off. Cheap piece of plastic anyway, he thought moodily, but when he reached overhead and jerked the string of his jerry-rigged electrical system for some light, he saw that the smoke was curling out of the side vents of his newest IBM. "Not again," he growled, and lunged forward to turn the computer off before any more circuitry could be fried. He was going to call IBM, he decided nastily. Sir, I demand a repairman. I don't care that he's deathly afraid of mummies.

He touched the bandages over his forehead, grinning without much humor. But it was better this way, he could easily acknowledge. At least he was doing something, inventing something. If he could get the voice synthesizer to match the vocal wavelengths of, say, the mayor of the city, he could cook up a batch of synthetic skin and look—and sound—just like the mayor himself. For ninety-nine minutes, of course. The thought of what he could do with that kind of trickery almost staggered him. Need some cash? Become the security guard at a bank. Need a new car? Become the manager of a Chevy dealership. Fool your friends, astound your neighbors. What, you're off to jail? Become the chief of police.

He stood up and began to pace. Something had

happened to him; something was still happening. He could not forget the sight of the wino and that little kid from yesterday morning. That had made his blood run cold. There were doubtless hundreds of people in this city being abused, attacked, and murdered every day. Nobody believed in Superman, and even Michael Keaton himself did not believe in Batman. The same was true of the Flash, the Silver Surfer, GI Joe, and Dick Tracy. When bad things happened to real people, the only help available was the cops. But there was only so much a cop could do, harnessed and held back by the rules and regulations of the criminal justice system, influential lawyers, and the constant danger of being accused of police brutality. He didn't see how the cops could stand it, the poor guys.

But Darkman had no need for cops or lawyers. He had been forced to become a creature of the night, living in secret, a man who was officially dead, officially buried. So he could, to make it short and sweet, do anything he damn well pleased. Anything.

Except get a spare computer part in the middle of the night. Having no face was, after all, a distinct disadvantage when it came to shopping, and whipping up a batch of new skin took time.

He inwardly said to hell with it and searched his tool kit—a greasy cardboard box full of weary old wrenches and odds and ends—locating some small screwdrivers. Getting the computer apart would be easy, and then he could cannibalize one of the older machines for parts.

He had disassembled most of an old NEC computer—seven years ago it had been the top of the line, but now it was a slow and bulky dinosaur—when he heard footsteps and voices outside. He quickly jerked the string to kill the lights and hurried over to pull the door shut on the generator room, where his fine Honda juice maker purred along a little too loudly for his taste as it cranked out voltage. That done, he crossed to the loading bay door at a trot and listened. On any other day he might have ignored the voices, but after the incident with that poor little kid . . . well, winos were now on his list of least favorite things, right there between monkey brains and yellow snow.

The voices were muffled, a little too far away to hear well. Darkman inched the loading bay door up one creak at a time, until the gap between it and the cement was big enough to stick his head through. Feeling sufficiently stupid, he lay down on his stomach and pushed himself out a bit.

The night was cool. He saw six, maybe seven kids, a hodgepodge of blacks and whites and Latinos, clustered under the streetlight at the start of the alley; a huge silver limousine was idling behind them. Voices and nervous-sounding laughter drifted down the alley. It struck him that these boys were about to do something sinister and that it probably involved him. Maybe the little kid had told the others about the mummy who had saved his life, and so here they were as a group, determined to see for themselves.

So explain the limo, he told himself.

He couldn't, so why worry about it? The only explanation that came to mind was silly: a rich man out there doling out cash to the needy and the downtrodden. Hadn't there been an ancient TV show like that once? But in real life the only people who got any easy money nowadays were congressmen voting their own pay raise.

He strained to hear, catching disconnected words— "dude . . . Big Mac," "Gotta do it . . . motherfucker," "One lousy dollar"—and laughter. At least one of the voices belonged to a little kid.

Darkman nodded to himself. A gang, obviously, looking about as dangerous as a collection of department-store dummies from the kiddie section. If they were up to mischief, he thought, they'd better think twice about it. Little kids could get hurt trying to fight the bigger boys.

He drew his head back in, mentally shrugging his shoulders, and got to his feet. He lowered the door to the ground again and wondered what to do. The computer voice synthesizer was out of action until he could find out what had gotten cooked inside it; the night was growing old; he'd seen the Dracula film so many times he had it memorized. So, then, what was left?

"Goot eefnink," he mumbled and trudged off to bed.

Danny could not believe what was happening. The chances of finding himself in this particular neighborhood again, after being held up by a kid named Big Mac a dozen streets away, of being drafted into his gang and agreeing to join it—the chances had to be one in a zillion, one in ten zillion. But here he stood with a knot of excited kids of various sizes and colors under the cold glow of a streetlight, the moon drifting high overhead behind a thin sheet of clouds, the threat of rain obvious and inevitable. And now he'd been told what he was supposed to do here. The initiation test to become one of these successful businessmen was—to roll a wino.

He could not believe it.

"If you're scared, just run away," one of the kids sneered at him.

"I ain't scared," Danny shot back. "I just need time to check the alley out."

Another kid pointed into the black maw of the dead-end alley. "There's about ten winos living in there. All you gotta do is steal a dollar from one of them, man. One lousy fucking buck."

"Hold it!" Sting, the tall kid who seemed to be running the show, had started pushing people aside. "Let the kid breathe, goddammit. Yo, Mouse!"

Danny frowned and looked behind him, then turned in a circle, pressing a finger to his chest. "Me?"

"Yeah, you. You look like a scared little mouse, so if you live past tonight, that's what we're going to call you."

"Okay," Danny squeaked.

"Everybody else, back in the car," Sting said. While the others climbed into the limo, Sting folded his arms across his chest and studied Danny. "You got two choices," he said as the doors slammed shut. "You walk away and forget the whole thing, or you don't. Myself, I don't give a rat's ass what you do. Nobody in the organization is gonna stay here and watch you, so if you decide to hike home and get a dollar to fake us out, fine. But we'll know. We definitely will know."

Danny felt himself trembling inside. Rain had started to fall. It stung like shaved ice against his skin. He had never felt quite so miserable in his life.

"Here, Mr. Mouse." Sting jabbed a scrap of paper into one of Danny's pockets. "You can find me at that address as soon as you're done. If you change your mind, have a nice life." He turned and went to the car, opened the door. "Remember," he said, "all you gotta do is steal one lousy dollar. Now that ain't hard, is it?"

Danny shook his head.

Sting dropped into the car behind the steering wheel. Before he could slam the door Danny raised a hand to get his attention. "Can I pick a different alley or does it have to be this one?"

Sting poked his head out. "This one or none."

"But—"

"You'll know why later."

The window slid smoothly up, muffling the laughter. Sting swung the limo into a tight U-turn, burning rubber. As the car slid out of sight Danny saw the wipers come on, and then it was gone.

His throat was as dry as sawdust, his knees about ready to wilt and drop him on the sidewalk. Of all the thousands—the millions—of alleys in the world, the gang had chosen to use this one to test the bravery of its recruits. There had to be a reason . . . and then it struck him that they knew perfectly well what awaited him in the darkness.

The wino. That particular wino. Or . . .

The mummy-man. They knew he hung out here.

Danny whimpered audibly. He had to steal one buck from a wino dead drunk to the world. It would be like taking candy from a baby, so simple that it was downright stupid. But what if the wino woke up? What if the mummy-man wasn't feeling all that friendly tonight?

The rain began to pour down in sheets, huge drops splattering on the streets and sidewalks, pummeling his shoulders and head. He heard the crackle of distant thunder, smelled that strange, oily aroma of wet streets that was so familiar. He stuck his hands in his pockets, stood there hunched over like a wet puppy, feeling extremely sorry for himself. If any other ten-year-old boy on the planet felt worse than he did, Danny could only wish him well.

Minutes passed, several of them. He was not debating whether or not to steal from a wino. He was not debating anything. His ears were full of the noise of the rain, his thoughts loose and tumbling inside his head. He believed he could fall asleep standing there in the rain, and wouldn't he look funny? But no one was around to laugh at him on this unfunny night.

The streetlight stuttered, off-on, off-on, trying to fail. How perfect that would be. Danny looked to his left and saw the shape of someone bumbling around in the alley. Light twinkled on an empty whiskey bottle, and the streetlight went off-on, off-on. Ah, a wino, Danny thought dreamily—or, better put, a whiskey-o—staggering about in the shadows of the alley. Danny watched as he collided with the walls. He could see that the man was black, and a bit of the burden lifted from his shoulders. The wino from yesterday morning had been white, though his face had been pocked and speckled with the little red flowers of alcoholism, but this man was black and absolutely plowed out of his mind. Danny took a hesitant step toward him. Lightning bracketed the sky for a moment; the streetlight went off-on, off-on. Somewhere in the distance a police siren wound itself up to a shrill scream.

The drunk keeled over. His bottle rolled away, clinking on the asphalt.

Now or never. Danny searched himself for signs of extraordinary bravery, signs of courage. All he found was a little kid who ached so bad inside that the outside things no longer mattered. With his hands still in his pockets and the streetlamp performing its dreary light show, he ambled forward and squatted beside the drunk. He was a man made of too many coats and a dozen pockets. Danny shoved a hand inside one and found lint.

The wino groaned. He twitched a little.

Danny went for another pocket—empty. Another—dirty and gritty with God knew what. Another—the fossilized remains of a sandwich. Danny tossed it aside and watched it head downtown in the flooding gutters. Even in the rain he could smell this guy, and he smelled strongly of . . . cologne. Figure *that* out. He shoved his hand into another pocket. This time he pulled out a wadded-up dollar bill.

Bingo.

He was starting to stand up when the wino grabbed his hand and twisted it hard. His eyes jumped open, sparkling and wet in the crazy light. Teeth shone as he grinned. "You thieving little shit," he growled, sounding very, very much like a wild bear. Several things happened inside Danny's head at that moment: a mental shriek of terror, a craving to wake up from this horrible nightmare, and the very real possibility of fainting dead away. Instead his overtaxed bladder let go for a second, sending warmth trickling down his thighs. He sucked in a breath and blew it out as a strangled scream.

"Bugga-bugga!" the wino howled, and let him go. "Bugga-bugga! Run, kid, run! Hah!"

Danny needed no second invitation from this cheerful fellow. He turned and sprinted away, in his fright somehow imagining that his feet were merely skidding on the wet pavement and taking him nowhere, like a character in a cartoon. Yet the stuttering streetlight was closer now, so he knew he was indeed moving. Then he looked back and saw that the wino was up and charging after him, roaring with laughter like a certified maniac. And Lordy, Lordy, look at that. The maniac was wielding a butcher knife.

Danny made it to the street, but he knew he couldn't outrun the wino, knew that he was about to be killed. Then he heard a strange noise to his left and turned his head to look.

A black raincoat was swooping toward him. A black raincoat topped with a black hat. It was the mummy, hanging on to a cable, swinging down toward him through the rain. They collided with each other, but instead of rebounding, Danny felt bony hands clutch at him, felt himself being lifted off the ground, being hugged so hard that it hurt, hurt bad. He tried to breathe or scream, but bright-colored pinpoints of light had begun to dance inside his eyes, pretty little dots. Then the world became dark and windy, nothing but a blur.

He passed out, listening to the wino's shoes slapping on wet asphalt as his footsteps faded away and away, to nothing.

CHAPTER

9

No Costume Necessary

When Danny came back to his senses, maybe ten seconds, maybe ten minutes later, something was digging into his back. A butcher knife? he wondered. He opened his eyes and found himself lying on a dirty cement floor, staring up at a network of cobwebs and pipes overhead. With a jerk he sat up.

He was in the abandoned soap factory again. He got unsteadily to his feet, feeling cold in his wet clothing, cold and miserable. He looked around him and saw doors hanging from chains to form tables for a host of computers. The huge room was littered with boxes, cans, and rat droppings. The only light came from a battered fixture hanging from the ceiling over the bank of PCs. He took a step, disoriented by the shadows, and jerked when a clap of thunder boomed outside. Oh, the rain. The wino. He had almost forgotten.

He made a short tour of the unearthly place, fascinated, feeling as if he had just stepped out of a starship into an alien landscape. Among the computers—one of which had been partially torn apart and lay in pieces—was other scientific apparatus. Vials and beakers, curly glass tubes, huge electrodes wrapped in copper wire. A

glass tank about the size of a large aquarium was filled
with what looked like pink Jell-O. On the floor was a box
of colorful wigs, makeup kits, lipstick, and fake fingernails. A glass container full of water held contact lenses
in many different colors. All very interesting, all very
baffling. So how had he gotten here?

He realized that his chest hurt when he breathed. More
memories came back. He had been running from the
wino, the air was full of rain, and the mummy-man had
swooped down out of nowhere and plucked him off the
street. Strong fellow, that guy. Danny knew now that he
had passed out in the man's arms, his breath crushed
from his lungs in a super bear hug. He tested his ribs now
with his hands. Nothing seemed to be broken, but did
they ever hurt.

He became aware of the sound of footsteps gritting on
cement, of someone breathing, hidden in the shadows.
Fear walked up his spine on cold feet, and he wanted
suddenly not to be here at all.

"Bad weather for rousting winos," a voice said. It was
harsh and a little wheezy, sounding somehow damaged
but familiar. "I thought you'd learned your lesson yesterday."

"Where are you?" Danny said, shuffling in a circle,
wanting to see him. The man's voice was raspy; Danny's
was quavering. Tonight was the night of weird voices, it
seemed. "Do you work here?"

He got the hint of a chuckle in reply. Then: "Yes, I
guess I do."

"This is the old soap factory, isn't it? Do you make
soap?"

Another chuckle. "Call it a hobby, kid. What's your
name?"

Danny squinted into the gloom, not seeing anyone.
"Da . . . Mouse. Mouse Frakes." Oops. He could have
slapped himself. What good was an alias if you gave away
your real last name? "Just Mouse."

"Okay, just Mouse. You're just a little young for that
line of work, aren't you?"

Danny shrugged. "Call it a hobby."

This time he got a genuine laugh in reply. But where

was it coming from? This old factory had more corners and passages than a battleship. "What's wrong with your head?" he asked the shadows. "And your hands? How come you wear all that mummy stuff?"

No reply for a few seconds, then a rather sad one. "I got burned."

Danny nodded to himself. It was starting to make sense now. In school there was a fifth grader whose mother had accidentally spilled hot grease on him when he was a baby. Half of his head was permanently bald. Half of his face was pretty much Freddy Krueger material. The big kids liked to torment him about his appearance. "I seen bad burns before," Danny said.

"I suppose we all have, Mouse, but mine are kind of special. I had to take the wet gauze off because it makes my skin kind of . . . decompose. Smell bad, if you understand that. I have to stay as dry as possible. So you wouldn't want to see me now."

Danny nodded. "Okay." He turned, looking for a way out. A boy-shaped puddle of water showed him about where he'd been hauled in; there had to be a door nearby. "I'd better go now," he said.

"Going to pick some more winos' pockets?"

"No." He meant it. Even a ten-year-old's mind can only take so much in the way of fright. The last thing he needed was a heart attack.

"Glad to hear it. And hey, Mouse?"

He turned back. "Yeah?"

"You dropped this."

The burned man came forward, his shoes slowly scraping on the dirty concrete as he walked into the light cast by the single hooded bulb. Danny saw his feet come into the light, his knees, his waist, his chest. He stopped there, his face masked in shadow, and extended a hand.

It was a skeleton's claw held together by tendrils of dead skin and baked muscle. Clamped between the chalky fingers was a rumpled one-dollar bill.

"See you sometime," he said in his dead wheezy voice, and Danny discovered, after he snatched the dollar away, that he could run pretty fast in the dark.

* * *

Darkman watched him go, the poor kid. Why had he so brazenly let him see one of his mutilated hands? Probably, he thought without much satisfaction, he had hoped Mouse would see it for what it had been, not for what it was now. But even Julie, his former fiancée, had been repulsed by the sight of someone so ugly.

He ambled through his worldly estate, these meager tools of the scientist, these salvaged computers that could help him achieve ninety-nine minutes of normalcy once in a while. Right now he could whip up a new face and a pair of hands and walk the rain-soaked streets as a man. In the dark the skin would last a long time, but he could not enter a lighted building, a lighted room, because the process of destruction would begin at once, and his face would literally go up in smoke. And at sunrise, like a vampire, Darkman would return to the darkness of his tomb.

He snorted, disgusted by his own self-pity. Everyone on earth had a cross to bear, everything from crippled limbs to horrible diseases, so why should he bemoan the fact that he had no face and no hands? Would he rather be confined to a wheelchair or dying of cancer?

He clapped his hands together. Enough of this damned wondering and thinking. It was time to do something useful, like perfect the voice synthesizer.

He turned to begin his work and then remembered the fried computer part. So much for that idea. What now? He knew he wouldn't be able to sleep after that gymnastic performance outside; he was still charged up with energy. It had felt good, though, to get some exercise and to save a little kid's life.

The idea, the one that had been taunting him for so long, resurfaced, the crazy one about . . .

No. It was too silly.

Not too silly for the Caped Crusader.

"Shut up," Darkman warned himself. He swept his gaze across his computers, his equipment, his home. There was a purpose for him, to perfect the damned artificial skin, help others just as tragically burned. And in the meantime he could help himself.

Captain America?

But he had tried and tried for years, had used everything from barn paint to staples to try to make the skin hold together. He could well spend the rest of his life in this haunted factory, eventually failing in the end, anyway.

Indiana Jones?

The most tempting dream of all occurred to him: he could manufacture a hundred faces and two hundred hands for himself, stick them in a lightproof bag, go find Julie, and live a normal life—except for the frequent trips to the bathroom to restructure himself. Okay, at ninety-nine minutes per batch, how long would a hundred faces and two hundred hands last?

The Hulk?

"That's going a little too far," he growled at himself. Okay, ninety-nine times one hundred, that's ninety-nine hundred minutes. Divide it by sixty, that's one hundred sixty-five hours. There are twenty-four hours in a day, but at night the skin would last longer, so I'd have to . . .

Chip 'n Dale's Rescue Rangers?

He stopped, frozen in place, afraid that his mind might split in two. Part of him wanted to work on the skin; another part of him—the stronger part now, it seemed —wanted him to . . . to . . .

Put on a Darkman suit and fight crime.

He waited for a reaction. He waited for the chuckles, the chortles, the guffaws, the merriment, the belly laugh, the howls. Instead he got a cold lump of certainty in the middle of himself, a feeling that was both awful and grand. He had fought Strack and his men, criminals of the worst sort, and he had beaten them. He had exacted revenge, pure and simple. But even with Strack dead and gone there was no lack of criminals in this city. Just by prowling the streets at night he could intervene in a dozen or more holdups, muggings, burglaries, rapes, murders—enough to keep a body busy, for sure.

He dropped onto his chair and made it squeak as he rolled it back and forth, his chin on the bones of his hand, deep in thought. The costume was of course a ludicrous idea—outlandish, even stupid—but the rest of it was sounding less outrageous with each passing moment. The Rangeveritz technique had given him unusual strength, there was no doubt of that. He had no finger-prints, for what that might be worth. He was legally dead, utterly faceless. He could fight crime like no one else. He could comb the city under the shroud of darkness. He could work for the benefit of all mankind. He could go where no man had gone before!

"You," he grumbled unhappily, "are deranged."

He rolled his chair over to the next computer and flipped it on. The monochrome screen, amber on black, glowed lazily to life, shining in the semidarkness to announce that it was ready for anything he could throw at it. At one time, in those hectic days during his effort to topple Strack, it had been connected via modem and phone line to the outside world. A good deal of time had elapsed since then, but he knew the phone still worked because he used it to order his meals. He plucked the receiver up—it had been pretty well melted in the fire and now looked like a toy Volkswagen, but it still worked—and held it to his ear.

Zzzzzzzzz.

Why the line remained in service in this desolate slum he did not know. He jammed the misshapen receiver into the modem and went to work on the keyboard, setting up the connection. When it was all there he dumped the memory into the modem and waited.

The screen locked up; the cursor quit flashing. If he'd had a face, by God, he'd have been frowning. This did not bode well. He reset the computer, got an okay, and tried again.

Everything on the screen froze. He pushed himself backward, absently tapping a finger bone on his charred front teeth. Either the modem did not work or technology had surged forward again. Hell, maybe they'd dumped the binary code altogether and he was trying to communicate in a language no computer now understood. He sighed. Naw, not likely.

He set the phone aside and began to pace. For almost a year he'd had nothing to do. And now that he had made this decision, his computer hardware was showing its age. In order to make this thing work—this *thing?* The

God-help-us-Darkman thing?—in order to achieve maximum resultage of the hemosticular essentiality on a phased gradient—in other words, *shut up* in there—everything had to work. The six P's: Prior Planning Prevents Piss-Poor Performance.

He paced until almost dawn, battling with himself, battling with his better judgment. And when at last he collapsed in despair onto his fiberglass bed, sleep dangled out of reach for a long, long time.

CHAPTER

10

There Goes
the Neighborhood

It was three in the morning when Danny finally got to the address Sting had stuffed in his pocket, and what an address it was—way out in the ritzy suburbs. Danny suspected that a black kid was probably as welcome here as a stray dog this time of night, but he was stunned almost into happiness as he trudged the last few steps and took it all in. The lawn under the moonlight was a motionless sea of immaculately clipped grass; the house was almost as big as most of the stores he'd been in. There were two driveways and two garages, a gleaming white Cadillac parked near one, the silver limo parked near the other. This was a house like the ones on television—the Brady Bunch's multibedroom house, that mansion where J. R. Ewing cooked up so much trouble. And to think that he, Daniel Zack Frakes, was about to become a part of this fine business enterprise. A gang, most people would call it? No way. This was class.

With the last of the rain tickling his face, he ambled down the winding sidewalk, admiring the flower beds, the small concrete statues of horses in various postures, the water fountain off to his right that sprayed mist across beams of colored light. At the door he punched the doorbell and was immediately aghast. Instead of buzzing or ringing once, it went haywire, causing a chorus of loud chimes to clang. They eventually came together in his mind as a song of some sort. It was still clanging away as the door was pulled open, and Danny stood apprehensively looking up at Sting. He had a bottle of whiskey in one hand and was rocking slightly on his feet.

"Yo-ho," he grunted. "Ding, dong, the mouse ran up the clock."

"I did it," Danny said. He held out the dollar. "Just like you said."

Sting took the dollar and eyed it drunkenly. "Come on in, my man," he slurred, and walked away. Danny eased in and pushed the door shut. The house was a potpourri of unusual smells: new furniture, new rugs, fresh plaster, new paint, lumber, cigar smoke. It looked like the place was only about two weeks old. At the end of the hallway he had a choice of three directions: left, right, or up some carpeted stairs.

"In here," someone brayed, and Danny heard laughter. He followed the noise into a huge sunken living room where the gleam of brass and glass was bright enough to make him blink. He stopped and looked uncertainly at what he was up against here.

The wino Danny had rolled was across the room, sitting on a white leather couch, dressed in rags, waving the dollar. He grinned at Danny, exposing a silver tooth.

"Bugga-bugga," he said, and roared his delight to the accompaniment of other voices. There sat Big Mac, busting a gut. One of the white kids from the huddle a few rainy hours ago was laughing so hard he was crying. Sting was sprawled in a velvet recliner slugging down Jack Daniel's between laughs, two ribbons of it trickling out of the corners of his mouth. Danny felt his face get hot. This was about as bad as when the kids made fun of him at school.

"You did it!" Big Mac howled. "I knew the Mouse had it in him! Yeah!"

Danny debated whether to laugh or to cry. This was horrible.

"Park your ass," the wino said, waving to indicate the furniture, of which there was plenty. "Sting, get the boy a drink." He stood up. The familiar aroma of cologne drifted off him, something no real wino would bother with. Danny felt like giving himself a swift kick. Talk about being duped.

"Whaddya want?" Sting asked. "We got whiskey and gin and vodka and four cases of Schlitz M.L. Translated into kiddie talk, that's malt liquor. Got some wine somewhere, but I bet you're sick of the stuff. Get it? Wine? Wino?"

They all got it. Danny wished for a hole in the floor to conveniently open and swallow him up as they roared at his expense. Instead he pasted on the fakest smile of his life, and went to a couch. It was new and he was wet, but what the heck. Whoever owned this house could surely afford to buy another sofa. When he turned and sat, Sting was already gone.

"The dollar was marked," Big Mac said when the ruckus had abated some. He crossed the room and, with a mutter of subservience, took it from the wino. "Red mustache on George Washington. That's how we knew you didn't crap out and get one someplace else. Brilliant, huh?"

Danny nodded. "Yes."

"Want to keep it?"

He flapped a hand. "I'd rather not."

More laughter. Now he knew the name of the gang: the Laughing Idiots. He ached to get up and leave, but he had no place to go.

"They did the same thing to me," the Latino said with a heavy accent. "They did it to all of us, right there in that dead-end alley where the real winos are too scared to go. That way Ice won't get his own ass mugged by a real one."

Danny saw the boy's gaze suddenly dart across the room to the fake wino. "S'okay to use your name now, isn't it? I didn't blow nothing?"

"Not at all." The wino—Ice—looked at Danny. "Mouse is in. I've seen kids run fast, but this was the first time I ever saw one vanish—fucking *vanish*—into thin air. How'd you do it, little Mouse? Got Spiderman feet?"

They all chuckled. Danny felt his discomfort taking a hike; they were admiring him now, and God, did he need it. "Only the Shadow knows," he mumbled, and had the satisfaction of watching the others howl with laughter. It was strange and probably a little too early, but he felt that here, with these guys, he could fit in quite well. Maybe he'd found a new home.

Sting came back with an oversized blue and black beer can. "Don't let the bull getcha," he said, and popped it open, losing only a small squirt of foam. Danny took it. Cold as ice. He had tasted beer before but never finished a whole can, especially a sixteen-ounce one. He plugged the can into his mouth and took three long swallows. That done, he wiped his lips with a hand, and grinned. He thought the stuff tasted awful, but he couldn't admit that.

Ice stood up and walked out, grinning with satisfaction, dropping his ratty clothes as he went. Sting took his place on the couch. "Lookee here," he said. "We'll start you in the morning." He looked drunkenly at his watch. "We'll start you tomorrow afternoon. You'll run with me until you're ready to solo."

Danny nodded. "What are we going to do?"

Sting took a long drink of his whiskey, burped, and looked around blearily. "Don't worry about it now, Mousie-mouse. You'll just do what I say."

Big Mac stuck his fists in the air over his head, yawning. "I'm out of it for tonight," he said, and stood up. "Mouse, this greasy Puerto Rican here is Lightning, because he's slower than cold shit. The dude picking his nose is Hooter, for reasons no one understands. You'll meet the rest of the crew as time goes on."

"Fuck you!" the boy named Lightning roared. Danny's insides shrank a little. Not a fight, not here, not now, please, but Lightning stood up and drew back a fist.

"Grease this," he growled, and lashed out. Danny flinched, involuntarily blinking. Lightning's fist struck the top of Big Mac's head.

83

"Noogies!" he cried, and scrubbed Big Mac's scalp with his knuckles. They began to wrestle, panting and grinning.

"Idiot greaser," Big Mac howled. "Mouse, he's after me! Hep me! Hep me!"

Danny relaxed. This was kid stuff, all of it a joke between good friends. The white kid called Hooter gave Danny a lopsided grin. "Shocking, ain't it? Messing with each other right here in broad daylight."

"Watch it!" Big Mac screeched, and dived for him. They all wound up in a tangle on the floor. Good friends, a super house, money soon to be in his pockets—maybe this was what Danny had been looking for all along.

A place to belong. He swore he'd be the best businessman they ever had, no matter what he had to do, if that would enable him to start a new life free of pain. Grinning, sometimes sucking up some beer out of the bottomless can, his heart thudding hard in his chest, he watched them wrestle, and he knew these clowns would soon be his friends.

When Ice strolled back in wearing a shimmering blue suit, the kids knocked off the horseplay. He eased himself onto a chair and snapped his fingers. "Party's over," he said, and they all wandered out of the room except Sting. Danny waited for a hint; should he leave too?

"You can choose any bedroom you want upstairs, and there's a lot of them," Ice said. "But don't be poking around in my room, which is downstairs, or Sting's either, for that matter. Got me?"

Danny nodded.

"There's food in the kitchen, and if you need a ride home in the morning, I'll arrange it. You passed the test and everything's set."

Alarm flared in Danny's mind. Homeless again. He stood up. "Thank you," he said dispiritedly.

"You don't look so good," Ice said, frowning at him. "Is that beer going down sideways?"

Danny shook his head. "No, it's fine. Really."

"What, then?"

Sting eyed him. Just past his drunkenness Danny could

see in his eyes a flicker of mistrust. "Something here you don't like, kid?"

"No, it's great. Really. But see, I don't . . ."

Ice, darkly: "Don't what?"

"I don't have a home to go back to." All of a sudden the tears were trying to resurface, and he willed them away before he humiliated himself utterly. "Couldn't I stay here for a while? A few days, maybe?"

"Ah." Ice relaxed, and Sting went back to work on his bottle. "Mouse, as long as you work for me, you've got a home. Dig?"

Danny grinned. "Dig."

"So go on and find a room."

"You bet," Danny said. He walked out practically on air. He was here. He was accepted. He had a home.

Ice and Sting watched him go. Ice reached out and pushed the bottle away from Sting's lips. "What do you think?" he asked.

Sting considered it. "Looks good."

"Yeah." Ice tapped a finger on his chin. "He's perfect, Sting my man. The perfect replacement for Jonny."

They looked at each other. They grinned. Ice leaned back, crossed his legs, and laced his fingers behind his head.

"Perfect."

Sting drank to it.

CHAPTER

11

Put It on My Tab

Her heart was beating too fast. It was getting harder and harder to scoop enough air into her lungs to keep her walking. People were hurrying back and forth, shoving her at times, colliding with her at times. She kept her head erect but behind her sunglasses her eyes were darting, looking, waiting.

Was she playing detective? she asked herself for the tenth time. Was Assistant District Attorney Jane Kozinski, who only yesterday had been ordered to hand the Ice file over to that bumbling sexist John McCoy, actually here, cruising the busy lunchtime sidewalks, waiting to be robbed?

The idea had seemed logical enough last night. Sleep had been hard to come by. She'd spent most of the night staring at her blank television screen with a cup of tea cooling in her hands. The echoes of her boss's words had pounded in her head; "You've become obsessed. You've put your heart and soul into this case, and you should know as well as I do that hearts and emotions and all that other sentimental crap don't belong in the judiciary. . . . Give it to John McCoy." Frank was her boss and he had ordered her to drop the Ice case. Fine and dandy. Here you go, John-Boy, a new file just for you, and its name is Ice.

A fat man in a burgundy suit thudded into her, nearly knocking her briefcase out of her hand. She recovered and walked on, impassive, hoping only that the camcorder in that briefcase was still rolling. She had cut a hole in it with a knife and murmured an apology to the expensive leather. The camcorder was a little bulky and she'd had trouble closing the briefcase over it this morning; she'd practically had to sit on it. Now she worried about focusing the thing. Would the automatic focus work with just the lens sticking out?

It was just past twelve-thirty on this fine Tuesday. Downtown businesses were disgorging employees for the noontime food fest as skyscrapers made of steel and glass watched over it all. She had been walking for six blocks, worrying that the tape might run out, worrying about the focus, worrying about everything but the condition of her kitchen sink, which might warrant looking into if she survived all this without going beserk.

She searched faces, looking for anything familiar, seeing a meaningless blend of bobbing heads in this ocean of people. She wanted to find the one they called Sting, the only one of the nameless gang's leaders she had a photo of. Not much of a photo, though, grainy and fuzzy, bad lighting, too many shadows behind his dark face. He favored mirrored sunglasses and almost always wore wing-tip shoes. Big help. Half of the men on the sidewalk had on wing tips. There were a lot of dark faces, a lot of sunglasses.

This crowd was ripe for the picking of pockets, fairly begging to be taken advantage of. Working this case for so many months had given her, she hoped, a criminal's sense of business. She could almost guarantee that every wallet and purse here held at least fifty dollars in executive lunch and three martini money.

She knew how Sting operated. Sometimes one of his underage cohorts would bump into the target to give Sting time to do the pickpocket number that he was so good at. Other times the younger kid would panhandle while Sting fleeced the target from behind. That was the daytime M.O. At night the nameless gang appropriated more expensive items: silverware, electronics, jewelry—all of it stolen very professionally, usually from family homes while the people were away or sleeping. No one had yet been killed by the gang—except Jonny Bates and quite possibly other traitors, she mused unhappily—but the time was coming. They were getting more brazen, so it was only a matter of time before someone, either an underage crook or a surprised homeowner, got killed. It was the law of averages in the business of crime. The clock was ticking toward the gang's first bona fide murder of an innocent.

A pedestrian who was concentrating on a submarine sandwich crashed into her, apologized with shreds of lettuce dangling out of his mouth, and moved on. Jane adjusted her corporate power suit, realigned the tie.

Last night's rain had pretty much evaporated into small puddles, leaving the air cloying and moist. The day would come, Jane Kozinski hoped, when she could abandon the Midwest's foul weather and head for beach country. But first she needed to accumulate a few successful cases to put on her résumé.

That thought blew a cold draft of apprehension through her mind. She was disobeying a direct order here, so what kind of résumé would she wind up with? Fired from her very first position? That would make her look worse than John McCoy and his repeated bar exam fiascos. But if her boss could see for himself how young these crooks were, he might change his mind, give her the case back. That was a pretty thin straw, but she was grasping at it.

She was bumped slightly from behind, no big deal. The crowds were beginning to thin out a little as she reached the edge of the downtown area. Jane turned and headed back the other way, wondering if she'd made a bad decision, wondering if she should at least buy a hot dog from a street vender and wolf it down before lunchtime was gone, wondering how Hobson was doing in his cell while his newly appointed prosecutor walked the streets and worked another case.

She checked her watch: pushing one o'clock. The camcorder had probably run out of tape by now; that, or the battery was dead or dying. What the hell, she could try again after work. The recharger was in her office.

She hurried across Jacoby Street against the light, got honked at, didn't care. With the idea of quitting in mind, her stomach was able to relax, and instead of churning with anxiety it began clamoring for food. She'd been feeling too blah for supper last night, too nervous for breakfast this morning. My dear, she thought crazily, it appears the woman is anorexic.

Something grabbed at her sleeve. She looked and saw a little black kid with an angel face, shabbily dressed, a little dirty, trotting beside her. "Can you give me a quarter for a bus?" he asked plaintively. "I'm lost and I'm afraid."

She stopped. Poor kid. How come he wasn't in school?

Something nudged her slightly from behind, a whisper of a touch near her left hip. Certainty blossomed in her mind. She raised her briefcase and aimed it at the boy, hoping to catch a shot of his face while his partner— maybe Sting himself—skillfully fleeced the pockets of her suit coat. He would get a bulging wallet, the promise of a nice haul.

She smiled at the kid and reached inside her pocket for the wallet. Gone. She could have laughed. Check this out, Frank. I'm *doing* it!

"My goodness," she gasped. "I've lost my wallet!"

She turned. The partner was already walking away without a care in the world. He was wearing wing-tip shoes. She swung her briefcase around in his direction, hoping to tape even a moment of his face if he should turn.

He didn't. She turned back, but the scruffy little boy was gone. Absolutely vanished.

Wow. Talk about teamwork. She walked again, her heart thudding in her chest, praying that the camera had done its job. It would be nice, she decided, to see the look on the thieves' faces when they opened the wallet and saw that it contained wads of tissues and one lousy dollar bill, payment for their pickpocketing services. She had

89

thought of cutting up paper into dollar-shaped rectangles, but that would have looked like an obvious trick, and the last thing she wanted to do was scare them off. This way, with the tissues, they'd probably think she had a terrible summer cold.

She hurried back to work, full of gleeful satisfaction. Detective Jane Kozinski, master of deception. Oh, yeah.

"Got a minute, Frank?"

Her supervisor looked up from his uncluttered desk where he was doing a crossword puzzle. Scarcely twenty minutes had passed since she returned to the courthouse, and here she was leaning through his doorway, her ammo loaded and ready, the moment of truth at hand.

"Sure," he said. "Come on in."

She shook her head. "I've got something I need you to see in courtroom four."

He stood up, frowning. "Who's the judge?"

"No judge," she said. "That room's unoccupied right now. Coming?"

"Ah, why not," he said, and stood up. He was a large man with black hair that was rapidly turning silver, a slightly inflated belly, the aroma of Brut cologne floating perpetually in the atmosphere around him. He skirted his desk, and they walked down a marble corridor that had been built before they were born, their footfalls echoing. Jane was in a state of high hopes. The tape had turned out fairly well, not much in the swaying picture of Sting but his back and his swaggering walk, but a hell of a good shot of the little boy's face. She only hoped her plan would work on the human cement block known as Frank.

Courtroom four was big and empty right now. She guided her boss past the bench to a rolling table with a government-issue VCR and a TV on it. "You got tapes of Hobson?" he asked with a puzzled frown. "What the hell for?"

"Hold on." Everything was ready. She pressed the Play button and mentally crossed her fingers. Please, God, please.

The sound was distorted, but the picture was fine. It showed a black kid so young it wrenched her heart.

"That is just one of a league of little kids who make a living by committing crimes," she said. "This kid appears to be eight, maybe seven years old. They do all the footwork and get a small cut while Ice and God knows who else rake in thousands of dollars every day. If one of the kids gets popped, he's dumped. And judging from what happened to Jonny Bates, he gets killed as well."

Frank crossed his arms. "I see."

"Now here's his partner walking away with my wallet. I turn around again, and *poof,* the younger kid's gone, too."

"A class act," Frank murmured.

"This happens all over the city during the day. At night the crimes get more serious—break-ins, burglaries, even an occasional stickup of a convenience store. Surely you can't trust McCoy with something this hot."

Frank tapped his chin. "Mmmm." He looked as if he still had crossword puzzles on his mind.

"Here's the capper," she said, suddenly uncomfortable. "When I identified Jonny's body at the morgue, I didn't have to be the coroner to see how he died. He was hanged, Frank, a little kid was *hanged.* They told me his neck had not been broken. He died of asphyxiation, a slow and horrible death. If you'd seen his face you'd—"

"When did you tape this?" Frank asked.

She put both hands behind her back and crossed every available finger, praying for a good reaction. "About a half hour ago," she said. "I rigged up a camera in my briefcase. Pretty slick, huh?"

He stared at the television, which was now airing snow, his features drawing together in a dark and unfathomable expression. Behind her back Jane crossed her fingers so hard they burned.

"You wasted your lunch hour," he grumbled.

"Huh?"

He rounded on her. "Jane, you are not a cop. This tape can't be used in court."

"I know that," she said, reddening. "I just wanted to show *you* how twisted Ice's business is, his business of recruiting kids. Next he'll be using toddlers."

"Fine," Frank said darkly. "I am moved beyond measure. What do you have worked up on Hobson?"

"Hobson? Well, actually, not much, but . . ."

He pointed a finger directly at her face. "McCoy keeps the Ice case," he rumbled. "You get Hobson done or you'll be looking for a new job. Is that clear enough for you? No more Ice. Only Hobson. If I have to spell that out, I will: H-o-b-s-o-n."

"Frank, you're not even trying to—"

"I'm trying to think of a reason not to toss you out of criminal court and downstairs to the file room, where the work is not much fun and you could go blind in the dark."

Jane clenched her teeth and heard them grind together. She was furious and ashamed at the same time.

He jabbed his finger at her. "That's my final word. Do you understand me now?"

She could have hit him. She could have curled her fingers into fists and popped him one on his big fat nose.

"Do you get me?"

"You're got," she said through her teeth, and watched him turn stiffly and stalk out of the room.

As if moving against a tide of icy water, she made herself eject the tape and turn the machines off. That done, she proceeded directly past her office without even glancing inside, caught the creaking old elevator to the ground floor, went outside and walked two blocks, turned at a sign that proclaimed the establishment was called the Schooner Anchor, Home of Fine Spirits and Libations, and went inside.

She was drunk in the space of twenty minutes, and stayed that way until the place closed for the night.

CHAPTER

12

Officer, Arrest That Man

By the time Jane made it home, miraculously without killing herself or anyone else during the drive, the city was falling asleep and Darkman was just getting in gear. The moon in the night sky was fatter tonight, the rain gone off to drench other cities in the East, the temperature a little chilly. Not that the weather bothered him. He would have hiked through snow to get what he needed, because his computers were his only true link with the outside, his only real means of effectively completing the new task he had set for himself.

Under a bloated white moon, Darkman prowls the streets in his endless quest for truth, justice, and the American way.

"Crap," he muttered as he left the factory and lowered the bay door behind him. He felt there was a real possibility that the Rangeveritz technique was cleaving his brain in half so that he could hold conversations with himself like a schizophrenic. It was a scary thought. Clad in his black raincoat and his black hat, wearing the battered and blistered black shoes he'd worn the night of the fire, he trudged through the alley without an artificial face, without smooth hands, without bandages. If some-

93

one saw him this way, sorry about that. No one should be up this late anyway.

There was a computer wholesale warehouse not far away, barely a half hour's walk, where he had . . . shopped before. In truth his "shopping" was outright thievery, but he always left some money scattered about, for whatever good it did. As far as he knew, the owners of the warehouse hadn't yet called the cops, hired a night watchman, or put dogs on patrol. They stocked everything from Atari to Zenith—complete systems, two-dollar parts, what have you. Of course Darkman could have put on a face and an act, gone there during business hours, claimed to be an average Joe, and bought the stuff like a normal customer, but the warehouse sold wholesale only, and he was not a corporation yet.

Darkman, Inc. Check it out. Specializing in Mad Scientist hardware.

"Funny."

He walked with a gentle northeast breeze wafting against him that smelled slightly of Lake Michigan: fishy. He pulled his coat tighter and his hat farther down, then shoved his hands in his pockets, not really wanting to deal with any terrified people tonight. He counted it as his good fortune that the winos of the area avoided his alley as if it were full of crocodiles, or worse. Too many of them had seen him—caught a glimpse of him, at least— and the rumor had spread fast. The fact that the one wino who had tried to molest that Mouse kid had the courage to go there showed only the power of alcohol, or that he was a total stranger. Darkman was, after all, a notorious and frightening creature of the night. Right?

I'll ask the questions here.

Touché. He grinned without lips. Two could play this game, even if there was only one player and no way to win. As the moon cruised slowly across the black night sky, he walked on nerveless feet while the stars glimmered overhead in points of cold white light. As a scientist he had never spent much time dwelling on the beauty of nature, or on its cruelty, preferring to watch his own world through the lens of a microscope. Now, as Darkman, assigned forever to the night, he was developing new senses. Catlike senses, he liked to think, better eyesight, the ability to catch nuances of motion others would have missed, a keener awareness of danger. Or perhaps that was merely a fantasy, born of his desperation to find meaning in all he had suffered, but if the fantasy helped him cope with his despair, then so be it.

He was drawing nearer to the warehouse now, crossing Thirty-second Street over to Jackson, able to see it as a squat block of darkness not far ahead. There were dull lights in the windows, the usual nighttime security. Beyond it rose the jagged outline of the new city, the one formed after the Great Depression closed down all the factories in the old sector, including the Reyton Soap Company, and the people had to leave. Voilà, instant slum, instant repository for winos and rats and Darkman.

Standing finally in the shadows of the warehouse, he surveyed it once again. Brownstone, arches, and pillars —welcome to the world of modern architecture. The sign proclaimed it to be DigiTek Electronics Wholesale. He had spent most of the day trying to repair his IBM with parts taken out of the old NEC, but his efforts were wasted; the computer still didn't work. It had been like trying to put a vacuum tube into a solid-state television fresh out of Japan—meaning, of course, forget it. Hence this middle-of-the-night walk, this burglary. He had thought about stealing a whole new computer—to hell with repairs—but he'd grown attached to his old big-blue. Like him, it was beat up and abused, but it got the job done.

He knew the front entrance was locked, of course, but around back, protected by barbed wire, was a small loading area with two big doors much like the ones at Reyton Soap. There was a trick to getting through one of them—a trick that had worked in the past.

He checked the area. Dead. He crouched a bit and darted through the pool of light cast by a streetlamp, then ran to the back area and the fence. One more cautious look, and he wrapped his hands around the top strand of wire.

Electrical charges suddenly popped and buzzed. Spitting blue sparks danced around his hands like Fourth of July sparklers. Startled, he let go.

Sneaky bastards.

A trace of smoke was wafting in the air. More of his skin had disintegrated. He found that his heart was beating fast, that his mouth had gone dry. This was too similar to the horror that had transformed him, the electricity that had baked his hands to cinders in the first place. Anger began to twist inside him. His whole life revolved around electricity somehow, from his toaster to his computers to the immense electrical charge that made the artificial skin, the same charge that had almost killed him.

He wrapped his hands around the wire again. Sparks jumped. With a growl he snapped it in two. Let's see an ordinary man do *that,* he thought, and touched the broken ends to the second wire. A brief display of sparks. Near the building something exploded with a satisfying *whump.* Smoke billowed out in a cloud from whatever had just gotten fried. He smiled inside. You don't mess with Darkman.

He scaled the fence and scurried to the closest door. This was the hard part. The door was locked from the inside, of course, by a central handle that pushed two thin aluminum bars into slots on the door's tracks, preventing movement. There was no way to get to those bars, no way to get inside at all, unless he simply snapped the bars off from the outside. Which was difficult.

He bent and wrapped both hands around the outer handle, knowing how unpleasant this would be. He took a breath, two breaths, dreading what was going to happen. He tightened his grip.

And he made himself think of Julie. And the mole on her thigh. And Strack's taunting voice:

"Once you are in the coffin you deserve, I will make Julie my bride."

Strack had moved a hand up, stroked her breasts. "These are my treasures now, you ugly son of a bitch. Remember that mole on her thigh? I will be seeing it again and again while you rot in the hell you came from."

Darkman clenched his eyes shut at the memory. While

he had been recovering, while he had been searching for her, she had been sleeping with Strack.

He began to quiver. His vision was blurred by a sheen of red. An anger too intense to understand was gripping him and thanks to the Rangeveritz process that anger would become strength.

Strack had been sleeping with Julie. And she probably loved it. Sleeping with her while Darkman roamed the streets in a daze and a misery so profound that it should have been fatal. He'd been legally dead for only a few days.

And Strack was making love to her.

He clenched his teeth, trying to hold the strength in his jaw back, not wanting to lose any more teeth. He could see Julie now, actually see her sharp and clear in his head. She was naked. He saw her lie down on a bed with a red velvet cover. He saw her open her arms invitingly, and then there was Strack, there was Strack, there was Strack. . . .

"Rrraaafffff!" he heard himself roar, a mindless belch of rage. The door strained and groaned, as if straining to stay shut. Then came two distinct sounds—*ping! ping!*—as the aluminum bars snapped, and the door flew up on its tracks with a noise like a passing train. One of the rails overhead broke free and the whole structure sagged to the left. Darkman covered his face with his hands, screaming into them, and lurched into the building like a troll, ready to rip and tear anything he saw. For this reason he kept his eyes shut, kept his fingers tight against them. He dropped to his knees and bowed like a Muslim before Allah, willing the rage away, ordering it away. And in time it did go away, leaving him stunned and exhausted. He rocked backward and rose shakily to his feet, breathing fast, his jaw hanging slack now. Next time, he thought dully as he probed his teeth for new damage and found a split molar, he would bring a bullet to bite.

Before him, rising dimly in the light, were racks of boxes and crates that almost reached the ceiling, bearing the logos of IBM, Apple, Panasonic, Brother, Commodore, and NEC. The smell was wonderful—brand-new plastic and miles of fresh electrical wire. If they'd had personal computers when he was a kid, he mused as he wandered the aisles looking at the equipment, he could have invented a perpetual motion machine by now, and he'd be rich. As it was, he had about four hundred dollars left in the bank, and of the six local branches of the Erie National Bank, only one still accepted his automatic teller machine card and spit out money as requested. Apparently no one had bothered to tell that branch about the premature death of Peyton Westlake. The fact that he still had fifty thousand dollars in a briefcase back at the factory was not important. That was dirty money from one of Strack's drug-running operations; it might even be counterfeit. When his bank account ran dry, the former Peyton Westlake might dip into it.

Because all superheroes are moral to the bone. Remember?

He snorted. That alone was grounds for opening the briefcase and throwing one hell of a party. He wandered past rows of delightful machines, making his way to the parts section. Here he found the usual gold mine, half a million items in small plastic drawers, each labeled by manufacturer and model number. In the IBM section he located eight drawers that contained parts for his model, each drawer divided into sixteen sections, the microchips mounted on plastic slides. He took one each of everything, damn the expense, and stuffed eighty dollars into the last drawer. It occurred to him that he would make one hell of a cat burglar. To hell with fighting crime. He could be a criminal instead. But what use did he have for stolen loot? Well . . . he could put some new lamps to good use.

He was wending his way out when a motion caught his eye. A flash of red, a flash of blue, a flash of white. Colorful things were going on outside. He peered around a corner and saw that a police car now partially blocked the open loading door. Even worse, two cops were getting out of it, their leather gear squeaking as they jerked their revolvers out.

He shrank back. This was not good. Those cops did not

realize that he was a fledgling champion of justice. They would see him only as a burglar. Apparently the good folks at DigiTek Electronics had installed not just an electric fence but a silent alarm as well. Thank goodness for modern technology, eh?

He quickly reviewed his alternatives. He could work himself up into a frenzy of superhuman strength, but his hide would not deflect bullets. He could swoop toward them with his raincoat flapping like the wings of a bat, but he sure as hell couldn't fly. He could jump higher than any man, but the speed of a kangaroo he did not have. That left just one method of getting out of here in one piece.

He dropped down to the floor and closed his eyes. The rest would take care of itself.

It took the police a full minute to find him. As their footfalls grew closer he concentrated on breathing without motion, short puffs through the nasal openings in his naked skull. Suddenly one of them was trotting fast, his shoes clipping out a good beat. He knelt beside Darkman and drew in a breath.

"Jesus!" he barked. "Toby, over here! Jesus!"

Officer Toby came running. His breath left him in a whoofing grunt. "My God," he breathed. "Jesus."

Here we have, Darkman's alter ego informed him, *two deeply religious men.*

He could have laughed. He *wanted* to laugh, though the only thing funny here was his own predicament.

"Is he alive?" one of them asked.

A snort. "Nobody looks like this and stays alive. Radio for a meat wagon. I'll keep looking, see if I can find out who did this to him, see just what's going on here."

"Right." Rapid footsteps, receding. The remaining cop grunted as he pushed himself to his feet. "Fucking psychos," he whispered, and trotted away.

Darkman snapped his eyes open. All clear, both ways. He sat up, checked the floor for anything that might have slid out of his pockets, got up. He heard the hiss and crackle of the police radio, heard the cop named Toby talking into it. What to do now? Wait for the meat wagon—ambulance or hearse or whatever it might be—play dead, wake up, and scare the driver into premature old age? Or get the hell away?

He waited briefly for his alter ego to say something useless and sarcastic, but it was strangely quite now. Good-bye and good riddance. Darkman crept on through the maze of steel racks and cardboard boxes, peeking, moving, looking, darting. Toby the cop was standing beside the open door of his police car with his back to Darkman, his black gun belt shiny enough to throw off reflections. The cherry lights on top of the cruiser winked their multicolored message. Darkman shrugged to himself and stepped out into the open, ready to simply run at the car, scramble over the hood, and make tracks.

"You there!" someone shouted behind him, and he could almost smell his own goose being cooked. "Hands up and don't move!"

He raised his weird hands. Take that, copper.

"On the floor! Spread out on the floor. Now!"

The other cop looked over. Darkman spun around and gave the nameless one a good frontal view of his missing face. Sure he'd seen it before, but had he seen it walk and talk?

"Boo," Darkman said, and snapped his mouth open and shut. *Click-click.*

The cop's jaw sagged. His eyes got big.

Darkman turned and charged toward the car, tramped over the hood with his bulky shoes squeaking and sliding on the paint, dropped back to the ground, and hauled ass with his hands in the pockets of his raincoat to keep the hard-earned repair parts from bouncing out. He expected a shot, heard a shout, made it to the neutered fence, and hurdled it, heard the cruiser roar, heard tires squeal. There was darkness and safety in the dead center of the city to which he ran, and he used it as any clever crime fighter would.

He hid in a trash can.

CHAPTER

13

Yep, He's Still a Jerk

The following morning started off badly for Penny Larsen, personal secretary and slave to John McCoy, who saw women only as a collective life-support system for his own pleasurable organs. To begin with, her car wouldn't start, which hardly surprised her considering its prehistoric origins. Then she missed her bus by about ten seconds and had to wait twenty minutes for the next one. And finally a jagged tear in the vinyl bus seat snagged her panty hose and rent them spectacularly asunder as she stood up to disembark.

And then, of course, there was McCoy's beaming face when she got to the office late.

"Sleep in, did we?" he jeered, leaning on the doorframe. He had perfect white teeth, which Penny found very annoying. And he really was good-looking, despite being a lecherous toad and a womanizer. How many times had Penny Larsen envisioned smashing his pretty face in with a blunt object? Don't ask.

"Car wouldn't start," she muttered as she unlocked her desk and stripped the cover from her word processor. The cover went into a drawer in the desk. Penny sat in her squeaky old wooden chair. John McCoy watched her every movement, leering, doubtless hoping to catch a glimpse of something he should not be glimpsing. She made sure he didn't.

"Who's on for lunch today?" he asked her. "The mayor?"

You wish, she thought, and got her appointment book out. "Barberini at twelve-thirty, Tokyo Teahouse."

His face fell. "That greasy wop again? Me gagging down Japanese chow? I don't remember that call. Who in the hell made it?"

"You did," she said, and slammed the appointment book shut. "You wanted to swing a deal on his DeLorean and figured he'd be more amenable while sitting on the floor with a cup of rice wine in his paws."

He frowned. "How low did I get his price so far?"

"Sixty-two thousand."

"Damn DeLorean," he grumbled. "If he was still making cars, I could get a brand-new one for about forty-five. The Feds set him up, I swear they did. Barberini agrees on that, too. Heavy competition in the car business, and with a stainless-steel body the DeLorean could never rust. That's why they nailed him, put him out of business."

She put the book into its appointed drawer, and slid it shut. "Did you do that draft of the Thomas closing statement?" she asked. "You said you'd have it by today."

He smacked his forehead with the palm of one hand. "I knew I was forgetting something! I managed to get a few sentences on the Dictaphone, but you'll have to finish it up, okay? You know what I'd say."

She sighed. A speech writer for this imbecile wouldn't work for wages like hers. "No problem," she groaned.

He adjusted his tie, smoothed his suit jacket. "What else have you got lined up for me, besides a midnight roll in the hay?"

She looked at her watch. "You're due in seven-B in twenty minutes."

"Nothing better than that?" He pulled out a pocket comb and rasped it over his teeth, thinking. "Which case is it?"

"Feldmeyer."

"What's the charge? My head isn't working right this morning."

"Assault. He wrapped his putter around his best friend's head when the friend coughed and made him miss his putt."

McCoy nodded and began to run the comb through his hair. "He was going for a birdie, I think, or maybe an eagle, poor bastard. I ought to just drop the whole damn thing, have the judge dismiss it and let the old geezer get back on the greens. He made a hole in one once, if he's not a liar. What's after that, besides you and me and an appointment with some hay?"

"Nothing until lunch with Barberini, and I'm allergic to hay."

He patted his hair with his hands, then pocketed the comb. "Good. If I can get him down into the fifties I'll buy the DeLorean and put it on the market for seventy."

They looked at each other. "You look nice this morning," he said, not at all to her surprise. "Want to take lunch with me and Barberini? Japanese food sound good?"

She shook her head. This was a maddening aspect of his warped personality, this insufferable sexual harassment and then an invitation that sounded sincere. She could not let herself believe one word he had to say. "I have to work on the Thomas closing statement."

He nodded. After a moment he began to saunter off to his own office, then stopped. "Hey, Penny?"

"Yes?"

"Ever had sex in the back seat of a DeLorean?"

She shut her eyes. "DeLoreans don't have back seats, Mr. McCoy."

"Really? I never noticed. Ever have sex in a car at all?"

"I prefer bicycles." She watched him walk away laughing. Thinking evil thoughts, she rolled her eyes. The indignities she had to put up with.

"Penny?"

She swiveled in her chair at the sound of this new voice. Jane Kozinski stood in the doorway, the only nice A.D.A. in this nest of attorneys, standing there slump-shouldered and looking bedraggled. Her hair was tousled, and her eyes looked like big dark bruises. Penny's curiosity went on alert. "Hi, Jane," she said.

Jane shambled in. Her clothes were nice, but she looked small and thin inside them. "Coffee," she croaked. "I smell coffee. I didn't plug my coffee maker in last night."

"I'll get you a cup." Penny got up and moved to the small corner table where her programmable Mr. Coffee was already done brewing, thanks to modern technology and her diligence yesterday at closing. She poured Jane a cup and guided it into her shaking hands. "Bad night?" Penny asked her.

"Oog." She took a sip while steam curled around her nose, then a swallow. She grimaced and fanned her mouth. "Has McCoy done anything on the Ice file yet? I need to know."

Penny went mute for a second. This Ice business had dragged her all the way to a lounge called the Blue Flame a few days ago, where McCoy had insulted her with his gracious offer of sexual pleasures. Just the thought of it made her mad again. She pulled Jane by the elbow out into the hallway.

"McCoy is sitting on it," she whispered. People were drifting past, none of them familiar. "He knows it's a setup."

Jane's eyebrows arched. "A setup? What in the hell . . ."

"He knows you pawned that case off on him to make a fool out of him, make him work on a kiddie case while all the other A.D.A.'s do important stuff."

Jane deflated visibly. "Oh, God. You don't believe that, do you?"

Penny shrugged. "It kinda makes sense. I think McCoy knows he's not very popular."

"With good reason." She took another gulp, fanned her tongue. "Where is the Ice file right now? At home hidden under his bed?"

Penny shrugged her shoulders. "He told me to hide it in my desk, but there were too many folders in those drawers already. So I hid all of it at my place, under *my* bed."

Jane shook her head, seeming very weary. "Great. I swear this place is a loony bin. Frank will probably come by to make sure I turned the file over to McCoy. He's dead set against me working it."

"Why?"

Jane shrugged, then sighed, almost chuckled. "Lawyers in action. Look, if Frank breezes by and asks, tell him you betcher ass McCoy has the Ice file."

"Should I go home and get it?"

"No, I'd rather have it at your place than here." She drank again, stuck out her tongue, and puffed breaths over it. "God, that's hot coffee. Can I have your home address? Have you got a business card or something?"

Penny shook her head. "I don't rate high enough around here to have business cards."

"No problem." Jane rifled through her purse, doing a good juggling act with her coffee, and took out one of her own business cards. "Jot your address and phone number on the back, okay? I'll call first if I need to come over."

"Sure." She scribbled out the information and handed the card to Jane. "Hope I won't be in trouble with Frank."

"No way," Jane said, and touched her arm. "As far as anybody knows, those folders are in McCoy's possession and being scrupulously studied."

Penny almost laughed. "Scrupulously? McCoy? That's stretching things."

Jane grinned. "Okay, he's taking them under advisement."

"I love that lawyer talk," Penny said, and they parted away with a smile.

If he could have, Darkman would have been smiling too.

The image of Bela Lugosi as Dracula flickered against the wall while the film projector ground on. Lugosi held his cape high enough to cover everything but his eyes, which were white and menacing. Darkman, sitting in his battered old office chair in the gloom of the soap factory, had the small microphone pressed to his throat again. The projector's volume switch was turned all the way to off. The IBM was not smoking at all as its screen showed Lugosi's vocal pattern.

Dracula moved his lips.

"Good evening, I am the vampire," Darkman said conversationally. The computer meshed his vocal pattern with the film's and re-formed its wavelength before feeding it back as electrical pulses. The delay could be measured in milliseconds; to Darkman it sounded like no delay at all.

"Goot effnink," he heard himself say. "I am dee vampiyah."

He leaned forward and flipped the projector off, feeling immense satisfaction for the first time in years. Finally, something he had invented worked. He no longer had to try to imitate voices he wanted to copy. All he had to do now was get a tape of someone's voice, run it through the computer, and presto chango, a perfect copy. The only difficult part of this procedure was walking around with his computer strapped to his back, and finding a mile-long extension cord to power it. Oh, well, one thing at a time. Modern science was always coming up with fun new things.

He turned his attention back to the computer, dragging the melted old telephone next to it, ready now to do what he'd wanted to last night. With the computer now working instead of frying itself, he plugged the phone into the modem. Almost instantly he tied a direct link to the police department mainframe on the other side of the city. Ah, the ease of it all. If the cops knew they had a middle-aged hacker peeking into their files, his arrest would be swift and merciless. Not to mention embarrassing for them.

He tapped at the keyboard. "Computer, is there a file on Mouse Frakes, age and address unknown?"

No file. Strange. But maybe not so strange. The kid went around mugging winos. How many winos would bother to report that they'd been robbed for the fiftieth time? Muggings were a fact of life for them.

He bent over the keyboard again and asked for any available Frakes file, then watched the screen fill up. The Frakeses of the city, it seemed, were a pretty sorry lot, but not one of them was called Mouse, and none of the ages matched; the closest one had been thirteen two years ago. Darkman gnawed at a finger bone for a moment, trying to remember what he had heard that gang talking about the other night out there in the alley. Something about a dollar—probably the dollar bill Mouse had in his hand when Darkman saved him. Why that bill was so important he did not know. And what else? Something about food. A hamburger, yeah, a hamburger. A Big Mac.

He cleared the screen and asked for the file on Big Mac. To his surprise the words "Juvenile File" appeared at the top of the screen in squat and sensible IBM letters and, below them, a name: "Loyell 'Big Mac' (Mack?) Donnersley."

Darkman read the file. At age six Big Mac was arrested for taking a loaded pistol to school. At seven he participated in an armed holdup of a pawnshop. At seven another arrest for vandalism. And on and on.

And appended at the bottom of the screen, this: "Cross-ref Ice."

He shrugged to himself and asked for Ice. Probably the code name of the file on the gang or some bigwig involved in it. He stared at the screen, waiting for a flood of data.

He got this and nothing more: "Eyes only active file. Open J. B. Kozinski, 1992."

He leaned back in his chair. Very interesting. Some fellow named J. B. Kozinski was involved in the case. Curious, Darkman asked for personnel, not expecting much interesting information to be available on an unsecured line, and discovered that Jane BeLinda Kozinski, a recent graduate and fledgling prosecutor, had been working in the district attorney's office since 1990.

Darkman turned everything off, nodding, aware of that wonderful smell of brand-new, slightly heated computer guts that floated in the air. The aroma of scientific endeavor, of a job well done. He clicked his bony hands together softly. It was time to take a look at Ms. Kozinski's special eyes-only file, see what this Mouse Frakes kid was really involved in. But would she mind giving him access to what appeared to be a very hush-hush set of files?

Very likely—not that her objections mattered. She would never know he had been there. He considered manufacturing hands and a face, but who should he be? Who *could* he be? His files contained only the faces of men now dead. And what did it matter who he was? Why not be himself, like last night? Oddly, his disfigured face did come in handy once in a while—especially while playing dead.

He picked up the phone to order something to snack on while he waited for the dark of the evening to come, and the reentry of Darkman into the dangerous world of the night.

CHAPTER

14

And You Thought It Was All Fun and Games

Danny Frakes woke up that morning with a bad taste dwelling sourly in his mouth, his eyes hot and bloodshot from lack of sleep, his hair a tuft of knots from the two restless nights here at Ice's expansive headquarters. He got wearily out of bed, sliding across the satin sheets that were driving him crazy, and stood up. He smacked his lips and rubbed his eyes. Another day lay ahead of him, a day full of thievery and crime and innocent people being parted from their belongings. It had been exciting at first, downright terrifying, in fact, this business of distracting strangers while Sting picked their pockets. The first day's haul had seemed staggeringly high to Danny. Nearly nine hundred dollars in cash, a stack of credit cards two inches high, four watches, and some jewelry—fifteen hundred bucks' worth, at least. Out of that, Ice had left Danny with eighty dollars and congratulations on a day well spent. The wad of money had felt hot and bulky in his jeans pocket, so Danny now kept his pay in a drawer in his upstairs bedroom. What he would spend it on he didn't know, since Ice was taking care of all his needs. Yesterday Sting had taught him how to smoke cigarettes —showing him that you don't inhale straight from the cigarette, you suck in a mouthful and breathe it. At least Danny didn't cough much, but the taste of those Kools was ghastly.

He trudged into the bathroom and flicked on the light. An exhaust fan purred to life overhead. The smell of new paint was getting bothersome, and the underlying aroma of fresh lumber was like a faceful of sawdust. He looked at himself in the mirror that still bore the packing label, wondering how he could look so bad after only two days of this. The thought that his mother might be watching him from above tortured him. And now that his dad was gone, too—which direction he had taken was hard to know—he might be spying on Danny as well.

The work was easy; he and Sting had taken frequent breaks for a snack, spent some time in a park while Sting slugged down Wild Turkey whiskey, gone browsing at a mall to check on a CD player for Danny. It was staggering to know that for two measly days of work he would be able to buy one. It would look nice on the dresser here. He hoped his parents would approve of the work he was doing, but knew they wouldn't. Even his dad had left crime behind, eventually.

He stuck out his coated tongue and regarded it in the mirror. He had been having trouble eating. It was easier to just suck down beer, which made a lot of the strange feelings go away for a time. Late last night Ice had gathered a pack of teenage prostitutes, and everyone had gone into a bedroom, except Danny, who managed to slip away from some redheaded girl who was drunk and kept trying to kiss him. The noise of the party seemed to last forever, bangings and bumpings, beds creaking, people laughing and moaning. Danny fell asleep, woke up, fell asleep, woke up. It went that way all night as he tried to keep from sliding off those stupid satin sheets onto the floor. His own bed at home was a cruddy collapsed mattress that had grown shoots of stuffing the way the eyes of a potato will grow sprouts. It was rough and still smelled ever so slightly of his bed-wetting days, but man, was it better than this royal-pain-in-the-butt bed.

He brushed his teeth with a finger, writing an internal memo to himself to purchase a toothbrush. He got dressed in the same old clothes, which were getting decidedly rank. Another errand to do: buy some duds today.

He wandered downstairs wondering what time it was. It seemed quite late. The place was quiet, save for a pair of voices droning away from somewhere in the belly of the house. Beer cans and empty bottles lay about like driftwood on a beach. Some joker had even tossed around some potato chips to be trampled into the carpet. Danny felt it was safe to assume that Ice would not like this much.

He followed the voices down the hallway that opened on the kitchen. He could recognize Ice's gravelly voice well enough; the other was unfamiliar, but not mysterious enough for Danny to care about. He was busy seriously considering a beer for breakfast. He stopped just short of the doorway, not wanting to interrupt anything, and could see shadows moving through the yellow squares of sunlight flooding through the kitchen's many windows onto the floor. He listened, waiting for a break in the conversation, still feeling odd and misplaced despite his two days here, afraid of stepping on somebody's toes.

"You can't tell me Jonny was done right. How did he wind up in the river?"

"It seemed like a good way," Ice said. He sounded mad. "How come *you* couldn't take care of the little shit before he went off and told my name to everybody from here to nowhere?"

A grunt. A pause.

"Just be glad we both got out of it clean. Now for point number two. This damn place looks like a trash pile already," said the unfamiliar voice. "You keep partying all night and see how fast the neighbors call the cops in. This is supposed to be low profile, dammit."

Footsteps. A door opened, then shut; it sounded like one of the refrigerators. A beer hissed open. "Look here," Ice said. "I'll do my job and you do yours. You

111

can't blame us for celebrating, either. Look at that rat hole we lived in downtown for two years."

"Yeah, well, fine. The party's officially over now. And I can't be running over here every two hours to keep you in line."

"Message understood, Bwana."

Danny frowned. The man's name was Bwana, then. And so what?

"Here's the list," the Bwana guy said. Something slapped against something else, a pile of papers on a table, from the sound of it. "From this moment on, we use messengers or the damn mailman. I can't be seen breezing in and out of here every day."

"I'll make sure to buy stamps," Ice said nastily.

"Don't smart-mouth me," the other man growled. "I've got a hell of a lot more to lose than you ever will."

A chair scraped. A shadow moved. Danny bit his lower lip, suddenly afraid. He turned his head and looked back down the hallway. It seemed like a very long stretch now.

"And hey, Marion," Ice said.

"What?"

Marion? Marion Bwana? That was a woman's name. Bwana Marion?

"I already filled Jonny's spot. New kid, only ten, innocent as the angels and no place to call home."

"Sounds good. Just keep him working."

"Got it."

Footsteps again. Danny sidled along the wall, then gave it up in favor of a dead run. There was a door on his right. He dived for it, caught the knob, and bounded inside. It took every bit of nerve he had to ease it gently shut instead of slamming it.

The footsteps became gentle whispers across the carpet. Then they were gone. After a bit the front door opened and shut.

Danny turned and leaned against the door. Sweat was making an appearance on his forehead, and he wiped a hand across it. What a close call this had been, too close. But why should he be afraid of Bwana Marion at all?

Because he sounded like bad news.

It came to Danny then that he was in Ice's bedroom. The red velvet curtains were drawn, keeping everything in gloom. He could see a huge unmade mess of a bed, lots of furniture, a large office desk covered with those instant-developing photographs with the large border on the bottom, a small lamp, turned off, and a telephone. This was no good at all, being here. It was a direct violation of orders. He gently pulled the door open a little, then peeked out.

Ice was headed down the hall, a can of Schlitz in one hand and a sheaf of papers in the other. He looked haggard this morning as he read them, wearing only baggy brown slacks and a white sleeveless T-shirt. Danny pushed the door shut again while a strange feeling tried to paralyze him, a feeling usually called utter panic. He jumped toward the bed, intending to hide under it, dropped to his hands and knees, and promptly bonked his head against solid wood: water bed, no hiding space available.

He got up, a small groan of misery slipping through his teeth. He spun in a circle, at a loss, saw a dark square of emptiness under the chair parked at the desk, and tried to crawl into it. Too small. As he groped his way out, almost in tears, his hand brushed the edge of the desk top and one of the photos slid off to the floor. Danny scrabbled through the fat nubs of the carpet, snatched it up, and stuck it back.

But not before his eyes caught and held the image in the photograph.

The closet. He tore the sliding doors aside and dived in, closed the doors, and tucked himself into a deep, dark corner. Ice entered the room muttering to himself. Danny waited in terror while he puttered around changing his clothes. Danny heard the phone clatter, heard it beep and boop. Moments droned by, each one mercilessly slow.

"Sting?"

Brblbrble.

"Fucking Marion was here again, yeah. . . . I'd like to forget I ever got tangled up with that fat ass."

Brblebrblebrble.

"Yeah, maybe someday. How's your little Mouse holding up?"

Brbleberb.

"Why? None of us been getting very damn much sleep lately."

Brble.

"Okay, yeah, he's pretty young. Okay, then . . . Okay, catch you later." He hung up.

Sweat trickled down Danny's face, dripped off his chin. His hands were clenched into hot, slick fists. The smell of new clothes hanging overhead mixed with the smell of his own. The sensation of smothering was about to turn his panic into a mad scream of terror and a dash for safety.

One of the closet doors slid open, letting in a wedge of dusky light. Danny held his breath as hangers clinked a soft tune. The door slid shut.

Ice left the bedroom. Danny heard the door drift shut. He breathed again.

"Hey, Mouse!"

He jerked. Holy Jesus, he was supposed to be in bed.

"Yo, boy!"

Feet thumped on stairs. Ice was going up. Danny worked his way out of the closet, soaked with sweat, and scuttled over to the desk. He had seen one of the photos. Yes, he had. He leaned over the desk and looked at all of them.

They were pictures of a white kid dangling from a hangman's noose; each picture had been shot from a different angle. Blood had spilled out of the boy's mouth and down over his chin, spotting his shirt with brilliant crimson. His eyes were crushed shut in agony. In one shot Ice was looking on as if absurdly proud, wearing his trademark shimmery blue suit.

"Where'd you go, kid?" Ice's voice came from upstairs.

Danny tottered to the door, opened it, stepped out, shut it. The air was nice and cool out here in the hallway, but his skin was numb. He walked toward the foyer, slump-shouldered, his shoes dragging, wanting simply to leave and never come back. Ice had hanged a kid while somebody took pictures. Had he hanged Danny's father, too? Had he been there admiring his work in Danny's own bedroom at home, there where his father hung from the light fixture?

No, there could be no connection. But this was two too many hangings in one week for Danny to endure.

"There you be!"

He turned and saw Ice coming down the stairs toward him. Danny felt like a corpse inside, and how could Ice hurt a corpse?

"What're you doing?" Ice's tone was flat and accusative, his gaze hostile. "How long you been wandering around?"

Danny shrugged.

"Marion don't like any of my boys seeing his face. Did you see his face?"

He shook his head.

Ice took a step toward him, frowning. "Hey, are you walking in your sleep? Mouse?"

"Huh?"

Ice clapped his hands on Danny's shoulders and shook him, peering hard into his eyes. Danny finally understood: Ice thought he was sleepwalking. That he had gotten dressed in his sleep was no mystery. After the party he had slept in his clothes, like probably a few of the other kids had. He blinked, knowing somewhere inside that if he ever wanted to leave this place, it would have to be on Ice's terms, not his own.

"Hmmahmma . . . huh?" he faked. He shook his head, then tacked on a goofy grin. "Mommy?"

Ice laughed and released him. "Fucking Mouse," he chuckled. "Maybe we ought to call you Babycakes or something. Sting's teamed up with Marbles today, so you've got the day off. Want to make yourself some breakfast?"

Danny nodded and rubbed his eyes. "A beer sounds better."

Ice laughed again, giving Danny a good view of his gleaming silver tooth. "There's cold leftover pizza to go with it, you alcoholic. Go ahead and catch a buzz, and then keep cool here until I get back. If somebody rings the doorbell and you don't know them, stay out of sight. Especially if they look like Mormon missionaries."

"Huh?"

He sighed. "A joke, I guess. Catch you later."

He left. Danny went into the kitchen and popped the tab on a beer, doing as ordered, catching a buzz. He realized now that he was in a very, very dangerous line of work, and wondered how long they would let him live if he tried to get out of it.

CHAPTER

15

Quit Griping—The Exercise Will Do You Good

At last: night
And Darkman.

He had often toyed with the idea of getting a car, and every time he had to perform one of these marathon walks, he toyed with the idea a little harder. He could buy one with some of the fifty grand in the briefcase, Strack's old drug-running money, but once again that idea didn't sit well. He could turn himself into Peyton Westlake and try to swing a loan at a bank, but if they found out that Peyton Westlake had been dead for a year and had come back to list his occupation as free-lance crime fighter, they'd probably turn him down.

And so he walked. The night was cool and clear for a change. The breeze from distant Lake Michigan was rather pleasantly fishy, flapping his raincoat and the brim of his hat slightly as he walked. The district attorney's office was in the Frober-Lessing government building, one of those ornate and crumbling old fossils that had been elegantly beautiful a hundred years ago. Now it was dwarfed by the surrounding steel and glass skyscrapers, a squat and embarrassing hunk of marble with collapsing floors and eroded stairways, a wilted state flag perched listlessly on top of the whole sorry affair. And God, was it far away from the Reyton empire.

Time ticked on toward ten, then eleven. With his hands buried in his pockets and his hat pulled down low he got only a few passing stares as he walked through the circles of light cast by the taxpayers' weather-worn streetlamps. Finally he arrived at the building, assuming the place was never locked up. Some kind of special police operation was based here, and cop shops never closed. He trudged up the steps past the stone lions, past the statue of a Civil War soldier, green and white with pigeon guano, past the statue of a World War One soldier frozen in a combat pose, still fighting a war that had killed millions for reasons no one cared about anymore.

That thought made him wonder if declaring war on crime was just as senseless.

At the top of the steps a set of doors barred the way. Bleached almost white by the sun, they were made of ornately carved wood that was cracked and brittle from the decades of heat and cold. Darkman pulled one open—it was a bit of a struggle—and stepped inside.

Gloomy. It looked as if most of its departments were shut down for the night. It smelled like an elementary school, of paint and pencils and crayons and lots of aging paper. There was a bulletin board on the wall and a building directory. Kozinsky, J. B., second floor, 223-F. Darkman nodded. Probably a little rat hole of an office, too hot in the winter, too cold in the summer. Much like the one that Peyton Westlake had occuped at the university before he was tenured and moved up.

The stairwell was to his left. He went up, his shoes squeaking on the steps, ready to duck his head if someone strolled past. Plainclothes cop, they might think. No big deal.

At the top he struck off to the left, watching the doors he passed as the numbers built up toward 223, where he stopped. The door was closed. He tried the knob, not really expecting it to be unlocked, but unlocked it was. He pushed it open and ducked inside.

More gloom. A large area had been crudely partitioned into separate offices—a result of the city's financial woes, probably; there was no money for new buildings. He walked past A, past B, past C and D and E, found F. Light flooded out through the pebbly glass window in the door.

He shrugged inwardly. Jane B. Kozinski, burning the midnight oil. A real go-getter, it seemed. Either that or she'd just forgotten to turn the lights off.

He tried the knob. Unlocked. What a happy evening he was having. He drew the door open, watching, seeing no one. A computer that looked to have been assembled in the early Jurassic era, a real dinosaur, was on one side of a huge and battered desk, still on. On a small table in a corner was a grimy coffee maker with a digital clock set into its front. Chipped and dented metal filing cabinets were parked against the walls, a couple of framed pictures on the desk. A generic office, no different from a thousand others in a thousand other cities. Darkman stepped fully inside, paused long enough to lock the door, and darted behind the desk to study the computer.

Some outfit called Megabyte Dynamics had made it. Darkman nodded as the light of the screen carved his features into lumps and pockets of shadow. Another extinct computer outfit, victim of competition, and the entire city depended on its wares. It was bad news that did not interest him much. Figuring out how to tap confidential files did. Hunched and wary, he tapped at the keyboard, asking for the directory of its files. He got a page full of names, including Big Mac (Mack?), but no Ice. Apparently the Ice file was on paper only. Which meant it had to be here in Kozinski's office somewhere.

Think we ought to try the filing cabinets, big D?

He almost moaned aloud. His alter ego was back to taunt him.

Try the I's, as in Ice.

Darkman turned and stepped over to the short row of filing cabinets, scanning the drawer labels, finding *I*. He slid it open and began to rifle through the folders inside, the aroma of old paper wafting into the slits in his skull that had once been nostrils, bringing back pleasant memories of his university days. He found Ibson, Idleman, Ignowski, Ipplinger, and more.

But no Ice.

Hmmm.

He pressed the drawer shut. Hmmm indeed. If Kozinski didn't have the file here, then where was it? And since all the electrical appliances here were still on and working, where the hell was she?

Gonna ask her for that file, are you?

Point well taken. Until he donned a face and some hands, he could hardly ask anybody anything. But who could he become? No total stranger would ever gain access to her secret files. Only Kozinski's boss or some other supervisor would have access. So Darkman had to become somebody. Somebody with an official interest in this Ice affair.

Mouse Frake's father? His mother, for that matter, now that the voice synthesizer was working and bras could still be stuffed with toilet paper? But no, Mouse's parents wouldn't know anything about Kozinski, even her name, so that scam wouldn't work.

He was weighing his alternatives when the doorknob rattled to signal an entry. He froze for an instant, his eyes darting around the room, then dropped to his knees, pulled the chair aside, and crawled into the dark space beneath the desk, pulling the chair back to where it had stood before.

Keys jangled, she came in. She was muttering to herself, something about losing her freaking mind and locking doors, something about a man named Frank. Darkman held his breath. If she decided to sit down at her desk and do some work, well, she was in for a good scare. Just one cold claw-hand around her ankle ought to do the trick. So he waited.

High heels tapped the floor. The computer clicked off. Papers rustled. The lights clicked off. He heard the door waft open again, then shut. Footsteps receded.

The phone rang.

More footsteps, fast ones, coming back. Darkman clenched his fists. He heard keys, the door, heels on the floor. The light snapped back on. She came close, skirted the desk, giving him an opportunity to see her feet and legs. Nice. She picked up the phone.

"Kozinski," she said in a monotone. "Oh, hi, Penny
. . . No, not tonight. I'm dead on my feet. . . . No, those
files will be safe enough there. . . . I don't know . . ."

She pulled her chair out on its squeaking wheels. She
plopped down in it. Darkman made himself smaller
while sweat began to build up on the back of his neck. If
she rolled the chair forward, it would be Halloween time.

"Tell you what, Penny. Bring all of that material to the
office in the morning. Tell McCoy you won't take the risk
of keeping something as hot as the Ice file under your
own bed. I know, he thinks it's a gag. He'll laugh. Don't
let it bother you."

She paused. She began to swivel back and forth, the
dull reflection of the light overhead winking on her shiny
black high-heeled shoes as she moved. He saw more of
her legs than she would have preferred, doubtless, but
unless she rolled the chair farther, she would never know
that he was there getting an eyeful.

"You're right, that'll make things easier if the big boss
goes snooping like Frank the bloodhound or something. I
suppose I could talk to McCoy about it in the morning."

She stood up. Darkman breathed again. When she
absently pushed the chair back under the desk he had to
shrink again.

"Sure thing, Penny. . . . Yes, isn't it? Okay, then. Bye."

The phone clunked as she hung up. She stayed in place,
tapping a foot for intolerable seconds while he held his
breath again.

She finally moved, turned off the light, and left. He
heard the doorknob rattle as she wrestled with a key to
lock it. Then footsteps, fading, fading, gone.

He let out a huge breath and crawled out from under
the desk. God, there were probably more pleasant ways
to spend an evening than dealing with this crime business, with all its dangers. But then, if he were to become a
true, a true . . .

*A true what? Dashing hero of the downtrodden? Just ten
seconds ago you were hiding under a desk, ready to faint!*

"Screw you," he grunted, feeling suddenly tired, really
tired. He knew this much now, though: someone named
Penny had the Ice file at home for unknown reasons and

would bring it back in the morning. Penny's boss was named McCoy. Most likely he worked in this building as a lawyer. But there were a lot of offices in this old building.

He turned back on the light and sat down in the chair, which was still warm from Ms. Kozinski's admirable form, and looked again at what was on the desk.

Nothing but the same stuff, except for a stapler he had not noticed before. He opened a drawer and found the usual office supplies—paper clips, staples, carbon paper, typing paper. He shut it. The next one down held an old-fashioned plastic Rolodex. He pulled it out and began to leaf through the cards in it, working his way toward the *M* section.

He found it: McCoy, John, office No. 276D & E. And written in pencil beside that information, one acerbic comment: "Asshole."

The remains of his face grinned. Hello, Mr. McCoy in 276D & E, you asshole. I hope you have what I need.

Darkman left Jane Kozinski's office, forgetting that she had locked the door, too intent on his own business to realize that in his excited state he had crunched the locked knob into a position it had never known before, or that ten seconds after he left, the knob simply gave up and fell off, all by itself, to be a source of wonderment the next day.

He entered 276D—another ruined knob.

Darkman left the lights off. This office was bigger. Like the other, it smelled of stale coffee and old paper, tainted with the slightest hint of cologne. Squatting in the dimness before him was an overloaded desk that probably belonged to Penny, the woman who had been on the phone with Jane Kozinski. Beyond it to the left was a door labeled 276E.

He moved to it and found it unlocked. When he swung it open he saw a desk in the gloom, two chairs with chrome legs sitting conveniently out of the way, a golf club leaning against one wall, and a length of screaming green AstroTurf that ended in a putting cup beneath the window. The rising evening moon was showing through the window, big, yellow and fat. He went to the desk and found the usual framed pictures of family—nope, not family. All three pictures showed a smiling man with straight teeth. In one photo he was dressed in a football uniform. It appeared that Mr. McCoy was a very vain man.

Darkman stuck one of the portraits in a pocket of his raincoat. Now came the hard part, though. He had to find a recording of McCoy's voice. And where better to look than the Dictaphone perched on the desk? He opened it and felt for the cassette.

No cassette.

He left the room, frowning, and located another Dictaphone on Penny's desk. When he opened it, he found a cassette inside. He located a button on the side that made a little red light come on. He started the tape, and heard a man's voice say, "If you secretly love me, please get undressed. You see, Penny, I happen to know that . . ."

He turned it off. Apparently McCoy was deep into sexual harassment. No wonder Kozinski had written "asshole" beside his name.

Darkman checked his watch. Eleven-twenty. He would have plenty of time to do what he had to do.

He pocketed the cassette and made his way out of the building, dreading the long walk home, hoping that all of this trouble would prove worthwhile.

It was close to midnight when the last group of boys arrived at Ice's suburban mansion to deliver their booty and get their percentage after a long day at work. The fact that Danny had idled the day away did not worry him; he still had eighty dollars stashed upstairs, a small fortune for a boy his age. After Ice left on his unknown mission, Danny had gone back into Ice's downstairs bedroom, full of wonder and dread, needing to see the photographs of the hanged boy one more time to verify in his own mind that they even existed.

They were gone; the desktop was now a sterile plain, everything neatly arranged. Racked with apprehension, he had searched carefully through the drawers, ready to bolt at the first hint of company arriving. He found no pictures, but he did come across a puzzling item in the top center drawer: a photocopy of a typed list several pages long. It was the sheaf of papers Ice had been reading this morning as he walked down the hallway. It looked tidy and well done, very official. Danny leafed through the pages, frowning. List after list of valuables— jewelry and watches, cash, credit cards. Okay, then, a list of stolen items. Danny had never seen Ice make notes as the gang members unloaded their stolen treasures, so how had he gotten this? From that Bwana Marion guy? Then where the heck had *he* gotten it?

Questions, too many of them. Danny sat stiffly on one of the recliners in the living room as the gang members emptied their pockets and shopping bags into separate piles on the floor, all of them looking to Ice with humble pride, probably hoping for a smile or a wink, something to let them know they'd done a good day's work for their boss. Danny could see that one boy had done something to displease Ice, but it was impossible to know what it was. All that he knew for sure was that his own stomach was twisted up into a knot and his mouth was as dry as ash.

"Okay," Ice said, and held up a hand to quiet the others. "I've got the roster from yesterday, so listen up. One of you is in big trouble."

Silence dropped over them like a black sheet. Eyes got big.

Ice produced the sheaf of papers from an inner pocket of his suit. Danny saw check marks made with blue ink all over the first page. "Our inventory doesn't quite jibe with my list," Ice said, sweeping them with a dark and sinister gaze. "Somebody lifted a platinum American Express card and forgot to hand it in—surely an oversight. Check your pockets."

They did, eyeing each other nervously. Danny wondered how in the world Ice had gotten that list. From Bwana? Had to be. But the only place Bwana could have gotten it was from the police, an official list of stolen items. Ah, to heck with it, he thought morosely. For all he knew, that Bwana dude could be a Martian.

"You," Ice said, and turned to Danny. His face was creased and ugly. "What'd you do with it?"

Danny pressed a hand to his throat, dumbly shaking his head.

"Check your pockets."

He scrabbled furiously at his pants, thinking with a surge of horror that, yes, he might have overlooked a credit card, though he couldn't remember ever having seen a platinum one. Besides, Sting had held on to most of the stuff they had stolen. He spread his hands and shrugged. No, boss, I do not have it.

Ice took a step toward him. "Let me tell you a story, Mouse," he said in a throaty, hollow tone. "A story about a boy named Jonny. He fucked up and he fucked up bad."

Ah, yes, Danny thought numbly. Jonny the corpse.

"I think you just fucked up," Ice hissed, and suddenly spun around. One of his hands blurred through the air and smacked loud and hard against Big Mac's face.

The boy fell backward like a large stone, giving the floor a little shake, and immediately sat up, his face stiff with fear. "Ice, look, man, I didn't mean nothing. I just forgot!"

"Give it to me," Ice said darkly.

Big Mac dug the credit card out of a pocket and handed it up to him.

"Get up."

He got up, cowering, trying to protect his face. "Ice, please! Listen!"

Ice jabbed a finger toward his face. "Mouse is your new boy, and you sure as hell would've opened your mouth to back him up unless you had a reason to keep it shut." He stuck a hand inside his blue suit, and presto, out came a switchblade. He clicked it open and pressed the blade against Big Mac's upper lip, just below his nose. A tiny dot of blood rose there. "Hey, Mouse," Ice called, turning a bit. "This little lowlife was going to let you take the rap for his crime. Where do you want me to cut him?"

The other boys stepped backward, forming a circle, the

125

center ring of a deadly little circus. Danny rose to his feet, cold as death inside, scarcely able to think. What had been a group of boys proudly displaying their wares had become, in the space of a few seconds, an audience to an execution.

"You say the word, Mouse," Ice said softly, "and I'll cut out his heart."

"No," Danny said immediately. "You'll just get . . . you'll just get blood all over the rug."

Ice grinned. His silver tooth winked, reflecting bits of light. "Good point. I believe we need to use a bathtub for this."

He began to drag Big Mac away. The boy couldn't seem to walk upright anymore and was beginning to mutter and groan in his terror. Tears were shining as they tracked down his cheeks.

"Wait," Danny said, unable to watch any more of this. "Let him live. I'll team up with him to make sure he doesn't screw up again. He could . . . he could work for nothing for a week or two, sort of like paying a fine. Maybe a month or two."

Big Mac began to nod his head, blubbering noisily.

"It'd be kinda like probation, like the cops give you, and after a while you'll be able to trust him again. Does that sound okay?"

Ice looked over to Sting, who was leaning against the wall drinking a beer. Sting shrugged, looking absolutely uninterested in all this.

Ice pushed Big Mac away. He staggered a few steps and fell onto the white couch. "Mouse just saved your miserable life," Ice spat. "This is the first time and the last time he'll do it. Two months, no percentage, and you'd better hope to Christ nothing else ever falls into your pockets."

Big Mac nodded. He wiped a forearm across his face, smudging his tears.

Ice cleared his throat. The anger that had twisted his face into an ugly caricature of himself was fading. "Back to business," he said, and the boys dispersed quietly.

CHAPTER

16

He Was Glad
He Didn't Get Slapped

In the late morning Darkman did two things that he had not done in a long time.

He called a taxi.

And he became someone else.

He was surprised at how fascinating the production of artificial skin still was, though he'd performed the process hundreds of times in the old days. The digitization was the hardest part, dividing the photograph of John McCoy's face into mathematical sectors the computer could understand and replicate. When that was complete it had been a simple matter of engaging the servos of the Bio-Press, opening the pipette that fed it pinkish unstructured artificial cells, and watching the machine heat and press a sheet of goop into the shape of McCoy's face. The world's most advanced waffle iron, Julie had once called it.

Then came the wig selection; Darkman hoped the man had not let his hair grow since the photo was taken; if he had, this would be a very poor charade.

McCoy's eyes were green; Darkman's were blue. Contact lenses solved that problem. It was impossible to guess what kind of clothes McCoy would be wearing today, but surely, as an attorney, he would wear a suit. Darkman had accumulated a wide selection of clothing during his Strack-stomping days, so he didn't have to shop at a clothing store.

While he was gluing fingernails on in the near-dark necessary to keep the skin from beginning the process of decay, he phoned Yellow Cab. The dispatcher asked three times if he had the address right; not many winos in that trashy district could afford cabs. By the time the taxi arrived, Darkman was ready. He checked his appearance in the cracked little hand mirror that was a relic of the fire that had ruined his life. Staring back at him was John McCoy, right down to the tiny scar barely visible beside his nose. The only thing missing was the voice. The speech duplicator would not be helpful until he could miniaturize it. Still, though, he had found as he practiced McCoy's voice, that it was helpful to try to match the S-shaped vocal patterns on the computer's screen.

It was eleven-thirty when he pulled the bay door open and stepped out into the daylight. Fortunately the sun was hidden behind a thick fog of gray clouds; muted sunlight would fry his labors slower than usual. He jogged to the cab and climbed in the back, catching a glimpse of the driver. He looked scared.

"Where to?" he grunted, swiveling his head as if looking for interesting things written on the streets and walls.

"Frober-Lessing building," Darkman said in his best McCoy voice, then frowned. It sounded kind of lame.

"The marble monster, eh? No problem."

He ratcheted the meter and pulled swiftly away from the curb to perform a noisy U-turn. "What brings a respectable businessman like you down here?" he asked. "This looks like a good place to get rolled."

"Just business," Darkman replied, trying to hone that voice.

"Lucky you're still in one piece. I got held up just the other day by a kid with a knife. Little kid, almost a baby. I should've strangled the little bastard."

Darkman started. Mouse Frakes? "Little black kid?"

"Nah." He shook his head. Darkman noticed that

dandruff was sifting out of the driver's hair as he moved, and he smelled strongly of sweat. Gak. Darkman rolled his window down. "Little Mexican got me that time," the driver went on.

Darkman saw his Class II chauffeur's license taped onto the sun visor: Morton, Robert J. He did not believe that he ever wanted to meet this man again.

"Hey, watchoo think about that City Council deal?" Robert J. Morton asked suddenly. "Think the guy's a liar? I do. And I think it ain't just him. It goes all the way to the top. They're all a bunch of lying politicians. So what if he bounced a couple checks? Everybody does, but no, they gotta howl bloody murder."

Please shut up, Darkman thought as the city scenery blurred past.

"And then there's the City Council caught sitting on their thumbs. So who takes the fall? The big guy? Do you think the big guy does? Well, guess again. It's the little guy who takes the fall."

Please . . .

"And who winds up losing sleep over it? The big guy? The mayor? The state senators who've been parked on their fat asses since kingdom come? Well, guess again. It's the little guy, sure as shit, every time."

Darkman fished a five-dollar bill out of a pocket and tapped the driver on the shoulder.

"Hey, whoa!" Morton said happily when he turned and saw it. "What's the occasion? National cab drivers' day?"

Darkman took a breath. "Is it worth five bucks to you to keep your mouth shut so I can think?"

"We aim to please," he crowed and snatched the bill away.

Darkman settled back, relieved, and checked his watch, a nervous habit that was not entirely foolish. Few things were more annoying to him than having his face erupt with blisters and start to melt in the middle of an important conversation. And the smell of the smoke was as awful as the stench of burning hair, maybe worse. So yes, it made sense for Darkman to worry about the time.

He checked his watch again. Nine seconds had passed.

He switched his train of thought to another track. He had learned, while hiding under Jane Kozinski's desk when she was on the phone, that McCoy's secretary, Penny, was supposed to bring the Ice file to work today. He hoped that something in that file would lead him to Mouse Frakes.

And then what?

His McCoy face pulled down into a frown. And then what? Go to his house and ask him to give up gangs and crime?

What if he says no?

Well, if he says no, then, then . . .

Will you adopt him? Make him your partner? The fantastic adventures of Darkman and his youthful pal, Darkboy?

"Shut up," he muttered dismally.

Robert J. Morton turned his head. "I ain't saying nothing."

"Not you. Sorry."

Robert J. Morton frowned. His expression clearly indicated that he thought the red-haired guy in the back seat was a nut.

"I'm rehearsing for a play," Darkman muttered.

"Do tell."

He turned his attention back to the road while Darkman turned his attention back to himself. Okay, the Ice file would lead him to Mouse Frakes, or at least to that Big Mac kid, and then he could break up the gang. Get the leader thrown in jail, tear the organization apart from the top. Or something like that. Sound good?

No comment.

In time the cab wended its way to the Frober-Lessing marble monster. Darkman paid the eight-dollar fare and got another sneer from the driver. The cab pulled away to merge with the traffic and the noise, and Darkman turned to go up the shallow tiers of steps. His heart was beating a bit too fast, and the stink of exhaust fumes was making his stomach squirm, but he made it to the top without keeling over and nearly bumped heads with the real John McCoy, who was hurrying out.

Oops.

Darkman whirled, raising a hand to shield his face, and nearly stumbled as McCoy thudded against him. "Watch it, Mac," McCoy snapped, and Darkman replied with a noncommittal grunt. Then McCoy was gone on his way, his loafers slapping on the steps, blending into the lunchtime crowd.

Darkman stepped inside the building. The real McCoy had been wearing a light-colored suit—camel or beige, maybe tan, but the fake McCoy was wearing dark blue. The real McCoy's hair was a shade lighter than the wig reposing on Darkman's skeletal head. And a lot of his fingers were adorned with expensive, shiny rings. The fake McCoy had none.

He considered getting a cab, going back, spending another day working on getting this right. It had not hindered him before, but should he go breaking into government offices again?

"Aw, screw it," he muttered, and went in. Enough time had been wasted. He took the stairs to the second floor, glad that most of the workers here seemed to be out to lunch. At 276D he paused, hoping Penny was out, and put his hand on the knob.

"Yo, John!"

He froze.

"Are we still on for tomorrow, eleven o'clock, handball court?"

When he turned his head he could hear his neckbones creak. He saw a young man, a generic junior executive in suit and tie, the standard uniform for yuppies. "Yes," Darkman said.

"Prepare to have your ass waxed. Just a warning."

He walked on, laughing, obviously pleased with himself and the world. He doubtless had a Beamer, three girlfriends, and an apartment full of plastic furniture. Phony bum.

Darkman steeled himself, cranked the knob, and went in. No Penny, just a desk covered with folders and papers, her computer, a slender glass vase with a wilting rose sticking out of it. He checked the drawers, working fast, trembling slightly, breathing fast. Being no one for a year had taken its toll on his nerves. In the old days he had impersonated crooks with the possibility of getting shot if he goofed up. Now the worst that could happen would be a lot of confused people and one highly embarrassed Darkman. But still he trembled, still he breathed too fast, still he considered simply giving up and going home.

No Ice file. He straightened, frowning hugely, the remains of his skin under the wig hot and sweaty. He crossed to the filing cabinets and gave them a quick going-through, mentally chanting *Ice-Ice-Ice,* finding nothing but the fact that he had gotten pretty rusty in the alphabetization department. He slid the last drawer shut, thinking that Penny must have forgotten to bring the damn file. Great, just great. What now?

The door swung open and she came in, ending the search. There was a submarine sandwich in her hand with crinkly strips of lettuce hanging out of it like green streamers. She stopped and stared at him while he stared back. "That was a fast trip," she said. "I thought you were going to take your DeLorean to the shop and eat across the street."

"I was," Darkman said. His mind was a tangle of nerves and doubt. "I decided to work on the Ice file first."

She pushed the door shut, eyeing him strangely. "I thought you were going to ignore that case."

"I changed my mind."

She squinted at him. "Are you feeling okay? You look pale."

Well, it's like this, Penny. I didn't realize that the picture of McCoy had been taken in the winter, so I didn't add enough toner to the goop before I made it into the waffle that is currently serving as my face.

"Mr. McCoy?"

He smiled at her while his excuses were fizzling out inside. "Where is that file? Still at your place?"

She would not stop squinting at him. Her sandwich was drooping open while lettuce pattered down on the floor and a slice of tomato was slowly trying to slide out from between the various meats. "How come you changed clothes?" she asked.

"Spilled coffee on my tie," he croaked. The inside of

his mouth was as dry as the Gobi; his stomach felt like a hollow bowl. "Silly me."

"So you changed your whole suit?"

"Hey," he said, grasping at his last chance. "I'll take my clothes off if you will too."

"Hmmph." She turned and sat at the desk. Darkman could breathe again. Saved by a sleazy remark. Penny put her sandwich on the blotter and shoved her chair away from the desk, then bent and began loading her arms with file folders. "You want Ice, you've got Ice. I'm just the hired hand in this loony bin."

She swiveled and dumped them into his arms. "Ice. Nothing but Ice. Take a week off and read it all."

"Jesus," he grunted, trying to keep them from sliding apart. "Don't we have a condensed version?"

She barked out a shrill laugh. "I don't have to condense. It's in my contract: 'At no time will the secretary be forced to condense, fix plumbing, or have sexual relations with the boss.'"

He smiled as if enjoying her wit, thinking furiously. Should he leave and read this back at the soap ranch, or try to sift through it here? Did he have time before McCoy got back or the false face went belly up?

Penny went back to her sandwich while he stood debating. What did he really want out of this gigantic file? Just Mouse's address? Or some kind of insight into the whole sorry affair? Both?

He went through the doorway into McCoy's sparsely furnished office with its putting green on the floor and dumped the folders across the desk. Still standing, he picked one up and leafed through it. Most of it was handwritten comments, probably Kozinski's workup for her boss. He tried another. Typed reports, complaints from citizens about gangs in general. Then another. It looked like Kozinski was preparing a doctoral thesis, focusing on gangs in general and the Ice gang in particular. There were some fuzzy photos of little value, some police reports, interdepartmental memos, depositions, clippings from newspapers. One interesting report was a transcript of the questioning of someone named Jonny Bates. The interview looked encouraging to begin with, but it soon became obvious that Bates was hedging, willing only to name Ice as his boss, which of course Kozinski had known for quite some time.

And after that, a photocopy of a coroner's report listing asphyxiation by hanging as the cause of death, stapled to a photograph. Darkman lifted the coroner's report and was looking at a photograph of a young kid lying dead on a slab in the morgue. His eyes were open slightly, dim and lifeless. His purple tongue stuck up from his mouth like a grotesque Popsicle. The rope had dug hideously through the flesh of his neck.

Darkman shut the folder while a chill rippled up his spine and back down again. To hell with insight into the whole affair. The next body they found might well be Mouse's, but Darkman was doing this not just for Mouse's sake but also for the sake of a dozen, a hundred other kids.

He realized belatedly that he was growing angry again, furious. He was just this side of an attack of rage that might end with the destruction of this entire room. Little kids were dying, and to help them he was forced to be both detective and undercover cop. Someone very big, very powerful, had to be the secret top dog of the gang, yet it was the kids doing the work, doing the dying.

With shaking hands, he picked up another folder. The top page was a police report on Loyell "Big Mac (Mack?)" Donnersley. Darkman nearly passed it by, having seen the name on his computer already. Then he realized that this report was different, more recent. This was a pickpocketing charge. It listed the boy's address as 3319 Pike. Darkman seared it into his memory, knowing that Kozinski had probably used it and gotten nowhere, then flipped through the rest of the folder looking for a police report on a Mouse Frakes.

Nothing. Darkman scowled, breathing hard. That was pretty skimpy info for all this trouble, but it was a start. He checked his watch as he picked up another file, a bulky one. He had plenty of time. In the folder he found only a videotape with no label on it. Might be worth looking at, might be absolutely blank. He put it in his jacket's inner pocket, checked the bulge and found it negligible, and went back into Penny's office, where she was done eating and was blowing on a cup of coffee, looking lost in thought. She glanced up at him, awareness coming back into her eyes, and new doubt. She had probably been wondering anew about this suit business, and decided something was still not kosher.

"Oh, keep on blowing like that," Darkman crooned, putting a hand on the crotch of his slacks. "Don't stop, baby."

"Pervert," she growled, and while she sat there darkly stewing about this newest harassment, he went out—and never came back.

CHAPTER

17

When in Doubt, Panic

Danny couldn't sleep. Again. This was his fourth night in Ice's house, but he still felt cold and lonely here. The bed with its slippery satin sheets and the bedroom it was parked in were as strange and ugly to him as the inside of a jail might be. And that was another thing keeping him awake: he knew he would go to jail someday if he stayed in this line of work. It might not happen for a month, a year, ten years, but it *would* happen, and he would be behind bars for a long, long time. He wasn't sure if this feeling that was trying to eat him alive could be called guilt or fear. He knew that if his mother was indeed watching from above, she would be sick that her son had gone so far astray so fast, a sick angel up in heaven crying for him and his sins.

He sat up in bed, holding handfuls of the sheet to keep from sliding, a knot forming in his throat while hot tears filled his eyes. He did not belong here. The kids acted as if stealing was all just for fun, but they had to know it wasn't. When Ice wanted to kill Big Mac the others hadn't said a word; they were stunned into silence. But Danny had not noticed any real surprise on their faces.

They all knew the facts of life in this business—and the facts of death, for that matter.

He slumped back down. The satin pillowcase made an unpleasant rasping sound whenever his hair brushed across it, which was another annoyance. He closed his eyes and immediately saw a bright and clear picture of a kid hanging from a rope around his neck. He opened them and saw a dull and clouded image of his father hanging dead from a light fixture. A small moan squeaked out of him. Was it possible to die from shame and lack of sleep?

He crawled out of bed, weak and aching from today's endless walking, and put his clothes on. Somehow that felt better, because he could almost believe he was just a visitor here who would soon be going. A little clock on the dresser told him it was almost two in the morning, but downstairs heavy-duty rap music was still playing, probably Hammer pounding out a message. He had come to learn that Ice went to bed last, like a chicken guarding the roost, but Danny doubted that he stayed up out of concern for anyone. More likely, he wanted to fleece the kids who happened to straggle in late.

Today Danny and Big Mac had worked Greenwood Center, a mini-mall to the north, but their haul was skimpy. Big Mac was lethargic and gloomy, unable to do much except stare at his feet and mumble incoherently to the prospective hit while Danny did his best to pick some pockets without getting caught. He'd found that the best defense when he did get caught was to meekly offer the item back with the lie that the person had just then dropped it. Not all of them bought the act, but the worst he'd gotten so far was a finger wagged in his face and a scolding from an old lady who demanded to know why he wasn't in school. At dusk they had trudged back here to the Ice Palace, as Big Mac had begun to call it sullenly. Here Danny lived in luxury he had never known before, but he was miserable and frightened.

He went into the bathroom to face himself again. When the light was on he took a look at what he had become, a scruffy kid with big bags under his eyes and a set of teeth that hadn't seen a brush in a week now and were turning a melancholy shade of yellow. Not to mention the state of his clothes. Somehow, it seemed that if he bought a toothbrush and some new clothes, his stay here would be permanent.

The music died downstairs. One annoyance gone, at least. But now he could hear voices drifting up through the stairwell and the floors, Ice's raspy one and somebody else's. Well, maybe they wouldn't mind some company, and if they did, he'd just grab a beer and bring it up here.

He went out and ambled down the steps in his bare feet, thinking idly that if he drank a lot of beer, two or three cans, it would probably make him sleepy enough to check out of this nightmare for a few blessed hours. When the music kicked back on suddenly, he groaned inside. More torture. In the downstairs hallway he strolled unhappily to the kitchen with the beginnings of a headache starting to throb between his eyes and promising to get worse if he did not medicate it with beer. The kitchen doorway was a bright rectangle of light. It was apparently Ice's favorite room in the whole house, and that was where the voices were coming from. And now he could recognize the other voice, too. It belonged to Bwana Marion.

If he had known the meaning of the phrase "déjà vu," he would have thought it. Instead he seemed to slip sideways a little without moving, as he felt a quick jolt of alarm. Was this a strange repeat of two mornings ago? Was he dreaming? Had all of the past few days been a nightmare?

"Don't even think it," Bwana was growling. "My neck's on the chopping block, and if I go down, you go down. Get me?"

Ice snorted. "Frank, all I have to do is talk to one of your little chickens down there. I'll plea-bargain and walk away free while your stupid ass goes down the tubes. Get *me?*"

A chair scraped across the floor. The two men grunted and strained. Danny shrank back into the hallway, his eyes big, all of his own troubles forgotten as he listened to a wrestling match between the two. Glass shattered like a noisy bomb. Objects thumped and fell. And then the sound of a fist hitting flesh, once, twice, three times, registered louder even than the blasting of the music.

"You big fat puke!" Ice bellowed. *Boom!* Another fist struck flesh. "You think your old white ass is any match for me?"

Moving slowly, as a dream, his mind a solid block of fear and wonder, Danny stepped closer and through the open doorway. Broken glass sparkled on the clean white linoleum floor. A chair was lying on its side. Bwana Marion was stretched across the table on his back while Ice held him down. Nose to nose they were shouting at each other:

"I'll fuck you up so bad you won't—"

"Fucking try to take me on when—"

"Swear to Christ I'll—"

Danny pulled back. What a fancy-dressed rich dude would have to fight with Ice about he could not imagine, unless it had to do with those lists of stolen things. Somehow Bwana knew what had been stolen, and he gave—or sold—the lists to Ice. Heck, he might even be the secret leader of the gang, a crooked lawyer or politician, like in the TV cop shows sometimes. That possibility was, of course, absolutely none of Danny's business.

He remembered with a rush of apprehension that the last time he had snooped like this, he'd wound up hiding in Ice's closet scared half to death. With this in mind he turned and hurried down the hallway on tiptoe. Forget the beer, forget the music, it was time for a quick retreat and another stab at some sleep.

Feet were thumping down the stairs, keeping time to the blast of the music, a rapid-fire beat. Danny wilted inside. Was he in trouble? Ice hadn't been very happy to see him up and about yesterday morning, the morning he had found those hideous pictures. And hadn't he heard Ice say that none of the kids should ever see Bwana Marion's face?

He did the only thing his tired and frightened brain

139

could decide in that fraction of a second. He ducked into Ice's bedroom and hid himself in the closet again to await whatever the future might bring.

The sound of glass breaking had pulled Sting out of a drunken sleep in which his dreams had been meaningless tatters and his snores had rattled the windows. He tromped down the stairs in his boxer shorts, puffy-eyed and grouchy, and barely caught a glimpse of a small foot disappearing through the doorway of Ice's bedroom. Then the door clicked shut.

Something huge thunked to the floor in the kitchen. The crash was loud enough, Sting assumed as he broke into a trot, to have been a refrigerator falling over. He burst into the kitchen and was immediately walking on broken glass. He let out a shriek of pain and surprise and hobbled backward leaving thin trails of blood from two or three puncture wounds. He plopped down on his butt and squeezed his ankles, rocking slightly, groaning, not wanting to look at the damage.

The noise hadn't been made by a refrigerator at all. There on the floor beside the table lay Frank Marion with Ice wrestling on top of him. Marion was the greedy fat bastard who thought he ran this show. Ice was strangling him.

"Knock that shit off!" Sting shouted. All this commotion would wake up some of the other kids, and the last thing they needed to see was Frank Marion lying dead on the floor. Whoever had ducked into Ice's bedroom had already seen too much.

Ice snapped his head around, his face shiny with sweat, his lips curled in a sneer. "I'm gonna kill his ass," he panted. "He ain't worth our time anymore."

Sting gaped at him. "Use your head, man. You can't kill the fucking D.A. He's the only thing standing between us and the cops!"

Ice deliberated this while Marion's face went from beefy red to ugly purple. Finally Ice jerked his hands away and rose up to stalk off to the sink, where he got himself a glass of water.

Marion sat up clutching his neck, his tic hanging over

one shoulder, his silvery hair a sweaty tangle. He coughed and looked over to Sting with hate bright in his eyes. "Good counsel, Mr. Thomas." He coughed again.

"Sting."

"Yeah, Sting." Marion got laboriously to his feet and began to rearrange himself. "If you can't talk sense into that idiot, I know some people who can. I got a little lady named Jane who wants a piece of his hide real, real bad."

"Who you calling an idiot?" Ice roared.

Sting flapped his hands. "For God's sake, Ice, shut the fuck up!"

Marion jerked stiffly at his jacket, then dusted off the lapels with angry little sweeps of his hands. "I paid over three hundred grand for this place, and you've managed to turn it into a fun house. It's supposed to be a place of business, a cover, nothing more or less. If Ice can't handle the responsibility of managing this outfit, I'll find somebody who can. Maybe even you, Sting."

He stormed out, crunching over glass, the aroma of his cologne competing with his own body odor as he passed. Sting guessed that he was not a man who worked up a sweat very often.

"Fat little whitey," Ice growled. "I'd give my left arm to see him lose everything."

Sting examined the soles of his feet. "Cut to ribbons, that's what I am."

"Fat-ass honky. One of these days, man, one of these days . . ."

Sting looked up. "None of these days, man. Without Marion we'd still be stealing the wheels off of cars. We got to do what he says, or he'll blow the whistle on us and it'll be our word against his. We'll get royally screwed."

Ice snorted. "I say we kill him. Then we'll be on our own."

"And the reports? The inventory?"

Ice filled his glass again. "Even if we lose ten percent off the side to the kids, we'll still clear a profit. Fuck Marion, and fuck his reports. He's a dead man." He drank, then dumped the rest of the water in the sink.

Sting got done plucking glass out of his feet and cleared an area on the floor with his hands, then stood up, wincing. "Fine. But how are you going to do it? Send him a letter bomb? Run him off the road? Put poison in his coffee?"

"All very good ideas, but I got to think of something better, smartass." Ice moved to the refrigerator and pulled out a jug of orange juice, which he set on the table. Then to the liquor cabinet, where he got a bottle of vodka. He righted the fallen chair and plopped down on it. "I can't think too good without some oil. Pull up a chair."

Sting shrugged. The clock on the wall above the sink read 2:06 A.M. A little early, but no one had ever had to twist his arm to get him going. He picked his way to the table, sat down, and poured himself a glass of vodka, then added a dash of orange juice. "Power screwdriver," he muttered, and began slugging it down.

"I could hide in the back seat of his car," Ice said, "then pop up and cut his ugly throat."

Sting coughed and began pounding a fist against his chest, gasping. "He'd crash and you'd both burn," he sputtered. "Plus you might be seen."

"Maybe. How about I burn down his house?"

"His house has more alarms than all the banks in town put together."

"Mmm." He sipped at his drink, frowning, then slammed it down, a grin spreading across his face. "Sting! You remember old Poppy from back in the neighborhood? The guy we used to call Hoppy Poppy?"

"Yeah. So?"

"You remember what he used to do in his garage? Remember what got him arrested so many times?"

Sting thought about it. "Well, I ain't seen Poppy for five or six years, so I was pretty young, but I think he made some kind of explosives. He knew the formula."

"Yeah! It was his own recipe, and damn if he wasn't proud of it! He made a cannon out of some sewer pipe and used basketballs for shells. He could shoot them so high they'd go right out of sight."

"That's right," Sting said, smiling. "And when they came down, people thought the sky was raining basketballs. Hah!"

"Then check this out," Ice said. He leaned forward, making head motions to get Sting closer. "I'm gonna visit old Poppy, make sure he ain't in jail. And if he ain't, he's gonna make me up a batch."

Sting nodded. "So how do you get Marion with the explosives? Shoot it through a window like Poppy's old cannon?"

"Nah." Ice leaned back, took a reflective drink. "Briefcase," he said suddenly.

"Say what?"

"In a briefcase. He always carries one. Well, we make him a special one, give it to him, tell him it's full of money. He opens it, and boom. Good-bye, Mr. Big."

"Only one problem," Sting said. "He won't ever let us be seen with him. How are you going to get the bomb to him?"

"Don't know yet. Somehow, though. Somehow I will."

They both settled back, when suddenly Sting popped upright. "Damn!" he roared. "I almost forgot!"

"What? What?"

"I seen one of our boys ducking into your room when I came down. If you got something in there he shouldn't see, the shit might start hitting the fan."

Ice jumped up, his thighs shoving the table across the floor a few inches. Fresh screwdrivers slopped across it. "Big Mac is one dead boy," he said darkly. "He's looking to get me, looking for a way to do it."

Sting stood up. "Did you leave those pictures of Jonny in your room?"

"They're in my desk, along with the others."

"Jesus H. Christ, Ice, I don't see why you have to take . . ."

But Ice was already hurrying out of the kitchen. Sting turned and jogged after him, shaking his head. If Big Mac found the pictures, it was Ice's own damn fault for taking them in the first place. Some kind of dark perversion made him do it, and that was too sick for Sting.

Ice stopped at his door and pressed an ear to it, frowning. "Nothing," he whispered. He turned the knob slowly and eased the door open. After a moment he stepped fully inside. Sting followed him into the darkness, grimacing at the smell. Ice flipped the light on.

The room was a mess. Sting had of course been in here before, but that was shortly after the gang moved into the house. It appeared that Ice was a slob.

Ice turned. "You sure somebody's in here?"

Sting shrugged. "I don't know if he's still here, but he was. My eyes never lie."

Ice raised a hand. "Hold on. There's only one place to hide in here, and that's right over there."

He pointed to the sliding closet doors. "That's the only hiding place."

He stalked over and whisked the doors apart. Sting waited, knowing that if somebody was in there, he was in for a world of hurt, probably Jonny-style hurt. Ice didn't just have a fondness for photography; he especially enjoyed executions. Sting didn't mind them, either. As second-in-command to Ice, he felt it his duty to keep the troops in line, whether that meant a good beating, or death. He smiled to himself now, imagining Big Mac dangling below him on a rope. He liked the kid well enough, but not enough to care whether he lived or died.

"Empty," Ice said. He began to kick at the shadowed floor inside the closet, seemingly more out of irritation than anything else.

Sting tried to measure his own feelings about this development. Was he happy or unhappy that no one was hiding here? In truth, he recognized without much joy, he was unhappy. Somehow executions made all this kiddie-crook business seem bigger than it was. If you take candy from a baby, you're just playing a game. But if you get *killed* taking candy from a baby, you're doing something significant. Killing was important. It gave meaning to the whole operation.

A muffled yelp issued from the closet. No mystery there. Ice's face contorted into an artwork of delight. Good-bye, Big Mac, Sting thought. Maybe you'll find a place in hamburger heaven.

Only it wasn't Big Mac that Ice dragged out, kicking and squirming. Sting stared in astonishment.

It was Mouse. Man, what a crazy world this was.

CHAPTER

18

Send In the Clowns

This, Darkman decided, was definitely strange. He had spent thirty-five years being a white man, one year being Darkman, and on this fine morning he was a black man. And quite a dapper one at that.

The suit was a hideous pink polyester, the tie a screaming red, the flower in his lapel blue and green. He had considered getting ahold of a walking cane and maybe a top hat, but in the end, he'd realized that he would look dangerously like an actor in an old-time minstrel show. That would be no good. The impression he was trying to achieve, for the sake of Loyell "Big Mac (Mack?)" Donnersley's mother, was that of a professional man who knew how to spend his money. He only hoped that he did not look, instead, like a clown.

It turned out that the kid lived fairly close, according to his police file, only about a twenty-minute walk from the fossilized downtown area Darkman inhabited. Her neighborhood still had a few die-hards left hanging on. Pike Street was not hard to find, once he began finding corners still marked with street signs.

With the sun shining merrily on his new face, threatening to end its existence, he located 3319. It was a run-down apartment building—no big surprise there—a squat and ugly brick structure that bristled with graffiti and old TV antennas. Shards of glass winked dirtily in the cracks of the sidewalks. Rusty fire escapes, partially dismantled, still clung to the walls, of no use to anyone. One building not far down on Pike was a shattered, burned-out hull with a tree growing out of its center. Quaint.

Darkman ascended a few crumbling steps and entered a foyer of sorts. Some of the mailboxes still sported names, and he quickly located Donnersley, 2C. He almost laughed. He had thought it would be tough to find this place.

He went up the eroded old steps to the accompaniment of their squeaks and groans as his footfalls echoed loudly in the dusty stairwell. At the landing he squinted through the gloom of a hallway, his nose picking up the smell of rotted carpets, many people, many babies. He found 2C and rapped on the chipped and crumbling door. He could hear a lot of noise inside, kids squalling and a television roaring. He knocked again, harder.

The door popped open a bit, and a small brown face peered out from under the chain. "Who is it?" the boy demanded. "Whatchoo want?"

"Hello," Darkman said with a smile. "I would like to speak with your mother, if I may."

The kid turned his head. "Maaaaaaaaaaa!"

From inside: "Who is it?"

He turned and said, "She wants to know who you are."

"The name is Frederick Jones, my little friend. I am a friend of the family."

The boy shut the door. He hollered something, and then Darkman waited.

And waited.

Scowling, he was about to knock again when the door was jerked open a few inches, stopped by the chain. A young woman stared at him. "I don't know any Frederick Jones," she growled. Her eyes were full of mistrust. "What do you want?"

"Just a few minutes of your time," he replied.

"We don't need nothing, so don't try to sell me anything."

"I'm not a salesman," he said. "I have a business transaction to complete with Loyell. You see, the boy and I have known each other off and on for years, and in the early days of our friendship we made a promise that if one of us got rich, the other would get fifty percent. That way, two people can be happy instead of one."

"Uh-huh. Well, Loyell ain't close to being rich, and no boy would make a deal like that with someone your age. That story is just plain stupid. What are you selling?"

He had expected some skepticism from Big Mac's mother, but not this open hostility. "Madam, I am not selling anything. I am here to make good on my promise. Is Loyell at home?"

"No, but my old man's sleeping on the couch, so I ain't helpless."

Darkman nodded, not believing her. "Where might Loyell be, then?" he asked. "I have quite a sum of money to give him."

"Yeah, and donkeys can fly," she said sourly and shut the door.

"But . . ."

He tapped his artificial chin with a finger. It seemed he had come across like a clown after all. He looked down at himself. He had assumed that a recently rich black man might dress like this, but that had to be the result of his own cultural bias. And why would *anyone* dress this way in a ghetto? A sure-fire way to get mugged, or worse.

He shook his head. Talk about stupid. Now not only had he been white and dark and black, he was also red. Racially ambiguous. A regular laugh riot.

He shoved his hands in the pockets of his absurd pink slacks, chagrined, wondering what to do. Was time of the essence here? Any reason for haste? Yes. For a kid named Jonny Bates, he was already too late. For Mouse, time might be running out. It was running out for all the others in the gang as well. He tapped on the door again. Lady, I'm on a mission from God.

"Wake up, Tyrone!" he heard her shout. He waited,

tense, uncomfortable, but a minute dragged by and Tyrone was still asleep, because, of course, he wasn't even there, probably didn't exist at all.

He remembered his money then, the wad of bills he had peeled out of the briefcase full of Strack's money before leaving the factory. It was just for show, and he hadn't yet shown it.

He pulled the wad out and counted out five one-hundred-dollar bills. He squatted and shoved them under the door as far as they would go, then waited, very much worried now that some Schwarzenegger type might amble down the hallway and beat him up just for the pleasure of ruining his clothes. It was mildly hot up here on the second floor, definitely stuffy. When too much time had passed he got down on his knees and peered through the crack under the door.

No money. The door was jerked suddenly all the way open. He looked and was staring at the lady's house slippers, then her knees, her torso, her face. He put on an apologetic grin and got to his feet.

"How much more of this?" she asked, smiling this time, waving the money. "How much more for Loyell?"

"A lot," he said. "Thousands and thousands."

"You can give it to me. I'll see that he gets it."

"Well, thank you very much," he said, "but I wouldn't miss the opportunity of seeing his face when I hand him the bags."

"Bags?"

"Bank bags."

She stuck her head out into the hallway. "I don't see no bags."

"They're in a safe," he said promptly. "It would be far too dangerous to carry that kind of cash around the city."

She crossed her arms and eyed him. "Is this drug money? Is that where all this cash came from?"

"Hardly." He coughed into his hand. "I am, in fact, the owner of my own business now. A very large business."

"Making what?"

"A lot of money," he said, and almost cracked up, so witty did he feel. "I'm in the soap manufacturing business," he went on. "Soap, cleaning agents, laundry detergents, any product that gets things clean. I could bring some samples by later."

"Free?"

"A gift for the fair maiden." Uh-oh, he thought. Would a real black guy talk this way?

Apparently so. She lowered her head, grinning coyly, obviously embarrassed.

Good Lord, Darkman, are you a lady killer or what?

"Now may I speak to Loyell?"

She lifted her head. "He ain't here."

"Is he in school?"

"Nope." She sighed resignedly. "He's running with a gang. I don't hardly see him at all anymore."

"I see. Maybe if I talked to him, offered him a job?"

"Good luck on that one."

"It's worth a try," he said. "Where would he be right now?"

She fingered through the money again. "Used to hang out on the streets, run with a bad gang. Now he's in some kind of business—he calls it a business, anyway—that keeps him on the streets just like the other gang did."

"Do you know anything about this new gang?"

She looked at him, frowning. "You sure you ain't a cop?"

He gave her more money, two hundred dollars. "Cops can't afford to throw this kind of money around, can they? Here, go ahead and have another one."

She took it. The whole wad went into the front of her blouse, tucked under her bra. "The gang used to operate real close to here, but they moved. Loyell told me that if I ever need him bad—and he meant real, *real* bad—to find a street called Courtney Circle and look for a silver limousine. Sometimes he stays there, sometimes he stays here. Where it is, I can't say. I know I never heard of it in this city before."

"Courtney Circle." He nodded agreement. "Sounds pretty ritzy, pretty new."

"Could be." Something crashed in the room behind her. She turned and barked at someone she called Tyrone. A child began to cry. "If you go there," she said, giving Darkman her attention again, "they'll know somebody told on them. From the way Loyell talks, you don't *ever* want to cross those people, or you can wind up dead. Some business he's in, huh?"

"I prefer my own," he said. "I'll find a way to get ahold of him, and it won't involve you, so not to worry."

"If you can do it, do it. Elsewise give me your number and I'll have him call next time he shows up."

"Thank you," Darkman said, feeling pleased with himself after all. "I don't believe I have a pen on me. Could I bother you for one?"

She was staring at him strangely, not into his eyes but at something else, his nose or cheek. "What in the world?" she said softly.

Darkman touched his nose. A blister was growing there. It popped under his finger, and a wisp of yellow smoke drifted up. Ah, that destructive sunlight. At least it had given him enough time to do what he wanted to do here.

"Gotta run," he said, whipped around, and sprinted down the hallway trailing smoke while his face snapped and crackled and popped just like the cereal, turning itself into mush, exposing the charred skull beneath it.

CHAPTER

19

You Saw What?

Danny Frakes did not know why he was still alive. He thought, murkily, that it must be his angelic face, his tender age, his small size, or simply the grace of God under the influence of his mother. It was nearly six P.M., and he had not yet been hanged.

Outside his bedroom window the evening was beginning to steal the day. The sun hung low and bloated on the horizon, the shadows it made long and fuzzy. Early this morning, when Ice's probing foot had kicked him and made him yelp, he thought for sure he was as good as dead. Ice, shaking with rage, had hauled him out of the closet, cuffed him twice with the back of his hand, making his upper lip bleed freely, and dragged him into the kitchen for an interrogation, with Sting hobbling behind. Danny had discovered what happened when two bare feet were made to run over broken glass: blood and pain. Ice did not care. He slammed Danny down into a chair and backhanded him one more time.

Sting located a broom and swept up the shards, limping on the outer edges of his feet, obviously not concerned about a little kid who had dared to enter a

151

forbidden room. Ice, on the other hand, was positively rabid.

"What were you looking for?" was the gist of his questioning. Danny knew, of course, that somewhere in that big desk of his Ice had hidden a pack of photos. He also had some police reports or the like on the stolen property that he shouldn't have—gifts from that Bwana Marion guy. While Danny was hiding in the closet he thought he had heard the name Frank mentioned. Frank Marion, then? Or Bwana Frank Marion? It was all just too confusing.

"I was scared, and I was hiding, that's all," he told Ice. Tears were leaking out of his eyes at a good clip, dripping on his lap. "I heard a fight when I came downstairs, and I got scared."

"Why *my* room?" Ice roared. "You *know* it's off limits!"

"I forgot!" Danny yelled, and wiped his eyes with his knuckles. The chunks of glass in his feet felt like hot shrapnel.

Ice turned. "Sting!" he barked. "Make a note. Every kid gets reminded every damn day that my room is dead-man's-land!"

Sting looked up from his sweeping and nodded. "Dead-man's-land."

"There'll be a curfew every night at midnight. Once your ass is upstairs, it stays upstairs!"

"Upstairs," Sting repeated.

Ice turned back to Danny. "Where'd you come from anyway, kid? What have you and Big Mac got going here?"

"Huh?"

"Were you gonna blackmail me? Set me up?"

"I was just scared," Danny wailed. "Please don't kill me."

Ice's frown twisted into a suspicious grimace. "What gives you the idea I kill my kids, boy? Did you see something you shouldn't have?"

Oops. Danny's thoughts went wild for a moment. How did he know? Because of the pictures, of course. Then an idea struck him. "You said you were going to kill Big Mac the other night. You were going to stab him for keeping that credit card."

He expected Ice to see the logic of that and let the matter go. Instead Ice's hand blurred through the air and smacked Danny's face hard enough to bowl him and his chair over. "I didn't say I was going to kill him!" he bellowed. "I said I was going to *cut* him!"

Danny could only stare, lying absurdly on his back on the floor. The man standing over him hardly seemed human anymore, a huge stick figure swelling and growing, about to burst with rage. Danny crossed his arms over his eyes, dimly aware that he now had a goose egg on the back of his head from the fall.

Ice kicked the chair out from under him. "Get out," he panted. A line of drool was actually slipping from a corner of his mouth. "Get out before I do kill you, you nosy little shit."

Danny was up and heading for the front door when Ice screeched again. "Not outside, dammit, *upstairs* where you belong!"

Danny ran in a curve and barreled up the stairs three at a time, burst into his room, slammed the door. His first instinct was to hide under the bed. Bad idea. It was hiding that had gotten him into this mess in the first place. So instead he climbed onto the bed and covered himself from head to toe with blankets. It was hard to breathe and his feet were electric with pain, but after a while sleep crept over him, pulling him away from reality, unplugging him from the world for a merciful little while.

And now: evening.

Danny was standing at the bedroom window on the edges of his bare feet, the only position that made walking possible, his elbows on the sill and his chin on his palms. The day had dragged on endlessly; the house had been quiet with everyone out on duty, and there had been no further word from Ice or Sting. Hunger gnawed at his stomach, which occasionally growled its displeasure. Drinking water helped, but the boredom was the worst. One moment his mind was whirling with replays

153

of the night's terrors; the next moment it was drowsy and calm. He fully expected to have been hanged by now, but with a guy like Ice in charge of his fate there was no telling how long he would make his littlest criminal, his little Mouse, wait and suffer.

Danny caught a glimpse of movement among the greenery outside. Two boys with whom he had not had much contact were strolling toward the house carrying innocuous-looking brown grocery bags—the day's haul. Now it was time for the gang to kick back and party down. Through the window he saw another duo, maybe Big Mac and someone else less familiar, also on the way home. He hoped that Big Mac would at least come up and say hi, maybe tell him how much longer he had to wait either to be killed or to be fed. The hamburger man owed him that much and more.

Time drifted past as Danny stood there watching the day unwind into night while the noise and clamor grew downstairs in Bwana Marion's hated fun house. How the neighbors in their stately houses put up with this racket he did not know, but the rich types around here were probably too hoity-toity to demean themselves by stopping by to complain. More likely they just cranked the Beethoven up a little higher to mask the noise. It surprised him to realize how much he hated those rich people who had never done him any harm. His mother in heaven would definitely not approve of his attitude. But look: so far he had not uttered a swearword, had been obedient, had tried to do good in this business, and here he stood awaiting execution for the crime of hiding in a closet. For the first time it occurred to him that death would not be so terrible; he would be with his family again.

And he could almost hear his mother whisper, "You tried to do *good* in this business? This *bad* business? Off to bed with you, Daniel. No supper tonight."

He emitted a short, miserable chuckle. Heaven and earth were conspiring against him.

More motion outside. Sting was approaching, much taller than his partner—a partner whom Danny had not seen before. New kid? Newer than him?

His replacement?

He shuddered. Despair was sinking bone-deep into him. He saw Sting's head jerk around suddenly. He seemed to be looking into a small copse of trees that bordered Ice's huge back yard by the privacy fence. He said something to the new kid, and they separated. Sting headed toward the trees in his usual drunken strut. He paused long enough to fish inside his clothing. Voilà! He produced a small bottle, drank from it, made it vanish again, walked on.

And then something strange happened. It happened in a second, maybe less than a second. As Sting entered the stand of trees an arm flashed out, grabbed him, jerked him out of sight. Danny waited, full of surprise and a crazy kind of glee—Sting wasn't as bad as Ice, but he was nobody's idea of Wally Cleaver, either—but saw no more except a tree or two shaking hard enough to make a few leaves dislodge themselves and drift down.

He frowned. That arm that had flashed, something was strange about the hand attached to it. Danny's first thought was that the man was wearing a white glove, Michael Jackson style. But no, it was large and bulky, too big to be a glove. More like . . . more like . . .

Gauze. A hand wrapped in gauze.

The mummy-man.

He hobbled to the bed and sat down to do some serious thinking, but wound up aimlessly wondering who, what, when, why.

CHAPTER

20

Where Did You Say
You Bought It?

Darkman worked with furious speed, not really knowing why, knowing only that something big was about to happen. Something big, something deadly.

Darkman suspected, without really believing it, that he was developing some kind of sixth sense in this business of fighting crime. He had found Courtney Circle without much trouble and dropped by for a visit. He'd brought along a camera and a small tape recorder, wondering if he was doing something utterly useless, even silly, but unable to shake the feeling that bad things were about to happen here. The file photograph of Sting had been grainy and blurred, but at least it had enabled Darkman to recognize him on sight. It hadn't been hard to find the right house; it was the only one that kids of many colors were streaming to, looking much like trick-or-treaters with their bags of loot.

Sting had strolled past the little copse of trees where Darkman was hiding near the house. Darkman had shouted, "Come here," to attract his attention. Then *boom! pow! smack!* Sting was out like a defective light bulb. Darkman took a few pictures from various angles, then used a length of old twine to keep him hog-tied for a while. Next, Darkman had slapped him awake, turned on the recorder, and captured Sting's voice as he cursed, threatened, and demanded to be untied. Finally he had stuffed a rag in his mouth and dashed back to the soap factory.

Within an hour he was Sting, and in another hour he was ready to walk into the house for a purpose he did not fully understand. He was scared stiff, of course, as he stood at the door listening to music thundering inside.

He stepped inside and was immediately hit with the smell of spilled whiskey and recently smoked marijuana. For some reason his brown contact lenses felt too big and he wished he could pop them out, but that would have to wait. He heard voices above the music, some laughter, ice clinking in glasses between songs. An after-work gala, apparently. He sauntered through the house mentally practicing Sting's voice, not very eager to try it out and fail. Then again, there was always that best of old excuses: "Sorry, I've got laryngitis."

He passed kids who seemed to defer to him, making way for him, saying hi. Well, he was the second-in-command here, so why not? He affected Sting's banty-rooster strut as he walked, beginning to loosen up a little, able to grin and feel cocky.

"Where in hell have *you* been?" someone shouted behind him, and he whirled.

A big guy in his early twenties. Darkman had found the man named Ice.

"Yo," Darkman said. "Just checking out some babes."

"Yeah, well, let's get down to business," Ice said, and turned. Darkman followed him. "I found Poppy right where he used to be, puttering around in his back room inventing Flubber or some goddamn thing. The old coot almost talked me to death. But guess what he sold me?"

Darkman shrugged inside. Drugs? Magazine subscriptions?

"Enough to put Marion on the moon. I'll show you."

Who in the hell was this Marion guy who was going to wind up on the moon? That named sounded vaguely familiar, irritatingly familiar. For no reason that he could fathom Darkman thought of Jane Kozinski.

Ice led Darkman into a dim bedroom that smelled stuffy and needed maid service in a very bad way. He clicked the light on and went to a desk. A new briefcase was perched on the blotter.

"Check it out," Ice said, grinning, and opened it.

Darkman checked it out, as offered. He saw road flares bundled together, some wires, nine-volt batteries taped together. The whole affair smelled slightly like gunpowder.

Dynamite. Probably homemade. The flares had been hollowed out and filled with an explosive. It looked as if the den of thieves was opening a new era.

"All I have to do is set the switch on this hinge," Ice said. "Marion opens it up, he's out of luck forever."

"When's he coming for it?" Darkman asked.

Ice drew away, frowning at him. "He ain't coming for it, you know that. This is gonna be a special delivery."

"Oh. Right."

"You want to get him?"

Darkman's thoughts raced, going nowhere. Get whom? Marion? "Where's he at?"

"I kept him in his room all day, the little bastard. He's probably half starved to death. And check this out: if he opens the briefcase to get his hands on some cash for a hamburger, it's good-bye to Mouse. If he hangs around at Marion's too long, it's good-bye to both of them. Man, sometimes I amaze myself."

Darkman nodded. His sixth sense had been right: something big *was* about to happen. Mouse and Marion were about to be erased. Now, then, who in the hell *was* Marion?

"Get the kid down here," Ice said. "I'm going to set the ignition on our very special gift."

He bent over the briefcase. Darkman moved away, wishing he knew where the stairway was, thinking stupidly that in a house this magnificent there was probably an elevator. He went out and down a hallway, found a huge kitchen with some spots of dried blood on the floor, another hallway, rooms, a stairway. He went up, expecting to get even more lost, but all the doors were open except one slightly to his left. He tapped at it.

It swung slowly open, and there was Mouse with a gaunt face and a dreadful gallows look in his eyes. His upper lip was puffed out and crusted with old blood. Darkman considered scooping the boy up and charging out of the house with him, but he knew that Ice would simply pick another kid to carry the bomb. "Come on downstairs," he said instead, trying to sound gruff, hating it. He escorted Mouse back down to the room where Ice was waiting. Mouse balked at the door, obviously terrified.

"It's cool now," Ice said, motioning him in. "I'm sorry I lost my temper like that." He hefted the briefcase. "Think you can carry this?"

Mouse stepped in and took it. "It's not too heavy," he said.

"Good. Do you remember that fat guy who was here? The white dude?"

He nodded. "Bwana Marion."

"Huh?" Ice touched his forehead. "I don't know where you got that bwana shit. The dude's name is Frank Marion. He lives in a big fancy house not far away, and I want you to take this to him. He's expecting you, so don't worry if a bunch of alarms start going off. Anybody tries to stop you, you say Frank Marion's waiting for this. You got all that?"

Mouse nodded.

"I'm going to tell you one more thing. The briefcase is full of money, so I want you to stay there while Marion counts it. Can I trust you not to screw this job up?"

Mouse nodded again. "I'll do it just like you want."

"Fine." Ice patted his shoulder affectionately. "You'll walk to Marion's, but Sting will be driving just ahead of you in the limo, show you the way, make sure nobody messes with you. Marion don't want any of us within ten miles of his place, but you're new so he won't mind if you show up there. Better get going now."

"Right." Mouse turned. Darkman could see his expression now: relief. He thought his head had been pulled off the chopping block.

"Wait a second," Darkman said. This question was

going to be a little risky. "What's Marion's address? I forget."

Ice frowned at him. "You must have chicks on the brain, man. It's down there on Wilshire, in that fancy neighborhood where all the doctors and lawyers and plumbers live."

Darkman tapped a finger on his chin. "What's the number?"

"Jesus. It's that big gray house that's lit up all the time. Shit, you've seen it a dozen times!"

Darkman backed away. "I just don't want to mess up."

"Let me know how it goes. And Mouse?"

Mouse looked up at him.

"This job is important, so don't screw up."

"I won't."

They left. Questions were gnawing at Darkman's mind, the uppermost one concerning Frank Marion. The name was more than just familiar; he'd seen it on paper a very short time ago. Frank Marion. Frank Marion.

Frank Marion—the district attorney! Darkman almost grinned. The old brain takes a licking and keeps on ticking, by God. And Frank Marion was one crooked son of a bitch.

The keys were in the limousine. Mouse was already cutting across the huge front lawn, stepping high and maybe a little proudly, though it was hard to be sure. The poor kid thought he had been saved by the grace of Ice.

He glanced at the digital dashboard clock in the limo. The Sting face had been in existence now for the better part of an hour, give or take. No matter. The artificial Sting had served his purpose for now. When the real Sting wriggled out of his web of twine and showed up at the house, well, some people were going to be very confused. And when Mouse Frakes and this exquisite limousine never returned, all kinds of trouble would erupt.

So then, Darkman wondered as he started the limo, was it all over with? Could he simply shanghai Mouse and keep the limo as a reward? He did need a car, that was for sure, and this was nicer than he would ever buy for himself. But the whole situation felt anticlimactic.

Dangerous or not, it was *fun* to be other people, to thwart bad guys and save good ones. That was what being a superhero was all about, wasn't it?

He dropped the car into gear, thinking hard, but something moved off to the left and he glanced over.

It was Ice, jogging toward him, waving a hand. Darkman thought of just peeling out and to hell with him and his gang, but it seemed that the mission wasn't over after all. There were still a lot of little Jonnys in that house.

Ice ran around the car and hopped in on the passenger side. "To hell with you," he said by way of greeting.

Darkman's heart jumped. Had he blown it? "What'd I do?"

Ice grinned at him. "Screw you if you think you're going to have all the fun. Why should I be stuck in there baby-sitting while you watch the fireworks? I can't wait to see Marion blown all to damnation, him and his fortress."

"Oh. Okay."

Darkman drove. Now he was furiously trying to find Wilshire on his mental map before getting to the street where Mouse was waiting. He would have to turn either right or left, and Ice didn't seem to have much patience with bunglers. He felt like banging his fist on his head. Wilshire! Wilshire!

It was no good. The city was just too big.

He cleared his throat. "Don't you know some kind of shortcut to Marion's?"

"The usual way is okay."

Rats. "Aren't they working on the streets nearby? I think some of them are closed."

"Man, you worry a lot lately. Go ahead on downhill toward Latham and we'll see what it looks like."

At last, a direction. The only way downhill was along the slope, and when he found Latham he could fake it from there. "Why don't we just drive the kid?" he asked.

Ice let out a snort. "If that K mart briefcase pops open by itself I don't want to be too close."

That made sense. Darkman slid his window down and pointed the way for Mouse. He nodded and started off, taking small slow steps. Ice settled back and crossed his legs, clicked the air conditioner on, and lit a cigarette. "Where's your baby bottle today? Going on the wagon?"

Darkman frowned. "Um, my gut's acting up."

"After all that goat piss you drank, I ain't surprised. What have we got to drink in this car?"

"Don't know," Darkman said. What was he, the regular driver, the chauffeur? "Probably some gin or vodka."

"Lower the divider. I'll scout around."

Darkman nodded. The privacy window was right behind his head, and he knew he would be in deep trouble if he couldn't find the switch that lowered it. And, man, did this limo have switches.

"Roll it down," Ice said again, irritated. "What's wrong with you today? First you don't remember where Marion lives, and now you can't operate the limo. And how come your voice is so weird?"

Uh-oh. Darkman's thoughts began to tangle while sweat broke out under his wig. "I, uh . . . I got ahold of some bad dope," he said at last. It didn't sound too bad, for an amateur.

"No wonder you're scrambled in the head. Forget about the booze, let's just get there and watch the show before your brain starts leaking out of your ears."

He could stand the abuse. He tooled along at a good eight miles an hour, according to the bright digital speedometer, keeping an eye on Mouse in the rearview mirror. He hoped Marion's house was not too far away, because in about twenty minutes his hands and face were going to turn into soup and smoke. No bad dope in the world could be blamed for that.

It took sixteen minutes to get there, another two for Mouse to catch up and then reach the house. Darkman had never before suffered a nervous breakdown, but now seemed as good a time as any. Sitting in the limo with the engine idling, he analyzed his options. There weren't many. He had to get out of the car and into the house before Marion opened the briefcase. There was only one way to do that.

He cracked his door open and looked over at Ice. "I'm gonna puke," he said, and though his face was not real he knew he looked sick. He felt a sudden tickle on his left cheek and touched it. A blister, primed and ready to pop.

"Don't get any on the limo," Ice barked at him, and he got out just as the blister ruptured with a sharp snap and a puff of yellow smoke. The evening breeze captured the stench of burned hair and smoldering rubber and blew it back into his face. He let the door swing shut, walked behind the car, and took off at a dead run, streaming smoke in earnest now, his melting face oozing down on his chest like hot taffy, dissolving into strings of goo that dripped from his hands.

He heard Ice shout something at his back, heard Ice's shoes smacking the sidewalk, but the only thing he could do was fire up the afterburners and hope like hell that Ice was not a fast runner.

Danny Frakes had to agree with Ice in one respect: Frank Marion was not a fun guy to have around. He was large and solid and if a smile ever crossed his face it would probably break it in two.

Danny had been ushered in by an honest-to-God butler, a black man wearing white gloves, a penguin suit, and a permanent expression of disdain; he was not exactly a comedian. Danny tailed him through the maze of the house and was taken to an ornate door, where the butler knocked gently and Marion called out a reply. When the door was opened, two things struck Danny's eyes: the guy behind the desk owned tropical fish by the dozen and had two black eyes.

"That'll do, James," he said, and the butler shambled out. "Okay, kid, let's see the money," Marion growled. "Ice wants to buy out my interest in the project, consider it sold. You tell that slap-happy coon the next time I see him it better be in hell."

Danny nodded. Better be in hell.

"And as far as the house goes, he keeps it as long as he wants, but if he sells me out or starts bandying my name around, that house is gone." He snapped his fingers while colorful little fish swam aimlessly about in the aquarium behind his desk.

Danny nodded.

"Hand me the briefcase."

Danny stepped closer to the desk and passed the briefcase over to Marion.

"Okay, kid," Marion said as he took it from Danny's hands, "take a hike. Forget you ever saw me."

Danny turned, then remembered his instructions and turned back again. "Ice says I have to watch you count it."

"Why? To see if I know how? Get out of here."

"If I don't do it right, he'll kill me."

Marion eyed him hatefully. "One less porch monkey on the planet—who cares? James!"

Danny felt like weeping. Didn't anything ever go right anymore? "Please, Mr. Marion," he said. "You don't know—"

Marion had jumped to his feet. "Who told you my name?" he roared. "That son of a bitch!"

James opened the door and stood there looking constipated. "Sir?"

Marion waved a hand at him. "Get this creature out of my sight!"

Two strange things happened then. First, one of Marion's flailing arms connected with a globular fishbowl on a wooden pedestal beside his desk and sent it crashing over. Fish and water sluiced across the floor. Second, a dark shape suddenly appeared in the window, crashed *through* the window, and snatched Danny up as if he were made of lightweight plastic. Danny saw the briefcase teetering at the edge of the desk while Marion stood there shielding his face from the explosion of glass. Danny saw it overbalance, saw it fall. And then he was hauled through the window and slammed rudely to the ground.

The world went nuts. There was a titanic explosion and a burst of yellow light. Glass belched through the window to tinkle down all around him. The concussion felt big enough to push his eyeballs all the way back into his head.

A bomb. He was no dope. The grass that his face was mashed into smelled sweet, but the guy lying on top of him was too heavy to bear, and God did he stink. Danny twisted and squirmed, turning around far enough to see the man's face.

Or what was left of it.

The mummy-man unmasked.

Danny didn't even realize he was screaming until he finally stopped.

CHAPTER

21

And They Hadn't Even Been Introduced

Penny Larsen was reading a paperback romance novel when someone knocked at her door. As a teenager she had absolutely been in love with romances, envisioning herself as the beautiful, flawless heroine, but a few years in the big city, and her job with the less than romantic John McCoy, had stripped her of those fantasies. She was not exactly beautiful, more like pleasant-looking and cute. She had a tendency to drool in her sleep. If her dream lover ever did show up, he would not be on a white horse. Most likely, she had to admit, she would bump into him in an elevator or on a bus.

Another knock. She looked up at the clock above the dark and silent television that was decked with flowers in vases: too late for visitors. This was probably her lonely neighbor across the hall coming by to ask for a cup of sugar and an ear to hang on to for about five hours. She closed her book and set it on the stand beside the couch, got up, stretched, and went to the door. She opened it.

Nobody there.

Penny frowned, then realized that she was looking over someone's head. It was a little black kid who looked decidedly shell-shocked. His clothes were dirty, and a few sparkling shards of glass were tangled in his hair. He had a fat lip and eyes that were shot through with bright scarlet veins. She looked down the hallway in both directions. No one with him.

"The mummy said you'd let me in," the boy said. "He said I'd be safe here."

She stared down at him, her mind utterly blank.

"He said that where he lives is no place for a kid. It's a soap factory."

She blinked. What strange quirk of fate had suddenly transported her into the Twilight Zone?

"My name's Danny Frakes. It's not Mouse anymore. Can I come in?"

She backed away robotically and let him in. She shut the door and stood there mentally unbalancing while he looked around. "He said you wouldn't mind."

She came to herself. "Who said?"

"The mummy-man," the boy said with a degree of irritation, as if Penny and everybody else in town should be acquainted with the local mummy.

"And your name is Danny?"

"Yeah." He plopped down on the couch and sighed wearily. "If you don't have an extra bed I could probably sleep on this."

"Hold on a second," she said. "I don't even know you, and I certainly don't know anything about a mummy." She squinted at him. "Are you on drugs?"

He shook his head. "No, but I'm really hungry."

"Well." Penny put her hands on her hips, reminded of John McCoy and his arrogance. She was not about to be pushed around by a kid. "Unless I get some straight answers," she said, "I'm going to call the police."

"Oh, I remember," Danny said. "I'm supposed to mention Ice."

"Ice? Why?"

"I was in his gang up until about an hour ago."

It hit her then: the notorious Ice and his gang of babies. She moved to the couch and sat down beside him. "Am I supposed to call somebody? Does Jane Kozinski know about you?"

He shrugged. "I dunno. Have you got any doughnuts?"

"Wha—doughnuts? No. Who's this mummy-man? Another kid in the gang?"

"Nah. He's the man with no face."

"Like Ice?"

"Ice has a face."

She made a chopping motion in the air. "Everybody has a face. What I mean is that nobody has ever seen Ice's face."

"I have. He has a silver tooth."

"Oh." She looked down at the carpet between her feet, frowning. Here was a kid who had seen Ice. Here was a kid who could probably lead her to him. No, wait. This was Kozinski's pet project, not hers. She should have the chance to rally the police and lead the charge. But how had this kid wound up in *her* apartment?

Maybe this mummy-man was an informant, she thought. He was too scared of Ice and his crew to do the snitching himself, so he'd recruited Danny Frakes and sent him here.

But how did the mummy-man know where she lived?

She felt a rush of fear. The Ice case was McCoy's now, and so, in effect, it was her case too, in a tenuous way. She was being drawn into a dangerous situation, with no way to control it. Unless . . .

She turned her attention to the kid named Danny. "The fridge is full of food," she said. "Help yourself. I have to make a call."

He toddled off to the kitchen while she looked up Kozinski's number. As she dialed, she tried to picture a man with no face. Sunglasses, probably, and a stocking over his head to blur and flatten his features. A trench coat buttoned high. A hat pulled down low. Only the Shadow knows.

When there was no answer after ten rings Penny gave up and reluctantly put the phone down. Danny came out with a can of Coke and a handful of Oreo cookies that were disappearing fast. "Nothing like good nutrition," Penny joked, but he was too busy eating. Well, one bad meal wouldn't kill him.

He sat down and spoke with his mouth full. "Yougogganybeer?"

"Goggany? Have I got any beer?"

He nodded.

"Not for you, kiddo."

He shrugged good-naturedly.

"Where do you live?" Penny asked him.

He shook his head.

"Where are your parents?"

He slashed his throat with his finger.

"Murdered? They were murdered?"

He shook his head, then swallowed. "My mom died, and my dad hung himself."

"Oh. I'm very sorry, Danny, but I have to know more about you. Who's raising you now? Grandparents?"

"Uh-uh. Ice."

She grimaced. "And a fine childhood I'll bet you're having. Does he make you rob people? Stuff like that?"

Danny seemed to mull that over, frowning. "I don't think I ought to say. I don't want to go to jail for the rest of my life."

"I can sure understand that. Have you been in jail before? Or in reform school?"

He gobbled down the last cookie. "No, but I probably will be as soon as the cops find me."

"Are they looking for you?"

"Probably." He licked his fingers. "Can I get more cookies?"

She waved him on to the kitchen, then sat back to organize her thoughts, which were as hard to arrange as Rubik's Cube. Again she tried to call Jane Kozinski; again nobody answered. She considered calling John McCoy, but she figured that he would probably laugh the whole thing off, the creep. That left Frank Marion, but she doubted anybody that high up in government would have a listed phone number.

Danny wandered over and watched her leaf through the phone book.

"What are you looking for?" he asked, sounding alarmed. "You gonna call the police?"

She was running her finger down the *M*'s, and shook her head. "Don't worry. I'm looking for a guy named Frank Marion. I work at the same place he does. He'll know what to do with you."

Danny dropped the whole handful of cookies. Then he dropped the Coke, which gushed brown foam onto the rug in a sudden spray. When Penny looked up from the phone book, startled, he was backing away, his eyes large and full of fear. "You work with Marion? Bwana *Marion?*"

He spun around and bolted for the door.

"Wait!" she cried, and jumped onto her feet. "You don't have to be scared of Mr. Marion. He's a lawyer!" It struck her with comical absurdity that many people would disagree with that. Amazed at her own crazy thinking, she lunged forward and caught a handful of Danny's shirt, hauling him backward. "What are you afraid of?" she shouted. "I'm your friend!"

He struggled to tear free. "Not if you work with Marion you're not!"

She felt a fingernail break. Oh, great. With one tremendous heave she swung him around like a kid playing crack-the-whip. He slammed into the couch, his shirt tearing out of her hands to the tune of another fingernail snapping, and landed on the floor. The neighbors would start complaining soon.

"Listen to me!" she whispered harshly. "Nobody is going to hurt you. I won't go near the phone. I won't even touch it."

He pushed himself up on his hands. "You promise?"

"I promise."

He stood up, his shoes crunching on Oreos, grinding them into the carpet. Penny groaned. The landlord would get her for this. "Why in the world are you so afraid of Frank Marion?" she asked him.

"I'm not afraid of him. I'm just of people like him."

"What people are like him?"

He sat on the couch and began scraping the white Oreo frosting off the soles of his shoes. "Crooked people. People who do bad things in secret."

"I see," she said, not seeing anything except Danny

Frakes sucking the Oreo gunk off his finger. "Don't do that, it's dirty," she said. "Do you mean to say Frank Marion is a crook?"

"He ain't nothing now," he replied. "Ice had me take a—I mean, Ice set off a bomb in Marion's den. Killed him and his butler, or at least tore them up so bad they'll die."

"You're kidding."

He twitched his eyebrows.

"Good God." She dived for the phone. "Don't panic, I'm just trying to get ahold of a lady named Jane. How long ago did this happen?"

"'Bout an hour."

"You saw it?"

He made a noise. "I was *in* it."

She saw the glass in his hair twinkle again. Your Honor, exhibit A.

Eight rings, nine. Ten. Eleven. What the hell, a few more won't hurt. Twelve.

The phone clicked on the other end. Jane said, "Hello?"

"Jane?" said Penny.

Something heavy thudded against the apartment door. It thudded again, and the door broke open with a wooden crunch, the latch bursting into shards. As Penny watched in horror the doorknob fell off and thunked to the floor.

"Hang up the phone!" shouted a tall black man wearing a shimmering blue suit as he thundered into the room.

She tried to set the phone in its cradle, but missed. The handset dropped to the floor.

"Mouse, we're going to have a nice long talk," the man said. It was more of an animal snarl than a statement of fact. Penny's breath locked in her throat, and her eyes grew huge. The man had a silver tooth.

She was face-to-face with the man Jane Kozinski had been looking for all these months. She was face-to-face with Ice.

CHAPTER

22

Didn't You Used to Be a Jerk?

"Hello?" Jane Kozinski shouted into her telephone. She had just come home from a short trip to a convenience store and heard the phone ringing. She lowered her grocery bag onto the sofa and sprinted across the room for the telephone, knowing that as usual the other party would hang up the moment she said hello.

"Hello?"

"Jane?"

"Yes." She did not know who the caller was, and began running the voice through her memory channels. It sounded a little like her sister in Vermont. "Carla? Carla?"

No response. Then she heard a crash, things breaking, the phone hitting the floor. Distantly she heard a man growl, "Mouse, we're going to have a nice long talk."

Footsteps. A door banging shut with a crunch.

Silence.

"Hello? Hello?"

She pulled the receiver away from her ear and stared at it. Prank call? No way. Her sister? Not likely. Carla's line of work in Vermont was cosmetics. Not many of her customers were men, nobody would ever give her the nickname Mouse, and even if she'd accidentally over-charged someone, who in the world would batter her door down and haul her away?

Who, then? That voice had been fairly high, probably not a very old person. But who was Mouse?

The line was still open, but no one was speaking. Maybe she could go next door and use her neighbor's phone to get a trace on the call.

Suddenly she realized that the woman on the phone sounded familiar. She knew that voice, had talked with the caller many times before. Marge Hinkley at the beauty salon? No. Stephanie Rabern, the waitress at her favorite lounge? Nope. Someone from work? Marie Christensen in the copy room? Penny Larsen in John McCoy's office?

Yes.

She hung up the phone. In one of the grocery bags a quart of ice cream was steadily melting. Frozen vegetables were going soft. Botulism might be secretly fermenting in the can of tomato soup. But Penny Larsen was in enormous danger so who gave a damn about groceries?

It occurred to Jane that the man speaking in the background might have been Ice himself. That thought sent a shudder of fear and excitement through her. Fear for Penny, excitement because Ice was finally making a move without three dozen kids fronting for him. She'd known his armor would crack someday; too bad that Penny was the one who might suffer because of it.

She hurried out of the house. Penny lived fairly close, and traffic was usually thin at this hour. With luck she could make it there in ten minutes.

She was pulling out of her driveway, her Toyota grumbling at being called on to do extra work, when it occurred to her to call Lieutenant Tremont at the police station, and maybe her boss, Frank Marion. But telephoning them would only delay her, as they subjected her to a barrage of endless questions, and she couldn't afford the delay just now.

Her heart beating fast, she peeled out onto the road, knowing in the part of her mind that was not impressed by heroics that she was off on a dangerous adventure that could only mean trouble in the end.

She got to Penny's place in eight minutes, setting a new world record for the number of stoplights ignored at high speed. Penny lived in one of those elderly brownstones that seemed charming if you could ignore the rusty plumbing and the fact that each apartment had only one electrical socket to power little frills like the refrigerator and the stove. Jane charged up the shallow steps to the door and located Penny's flat almost immediately; it was the only apartment whose door was split wide open. Jane slowed down, breathing hard, wondering if she would come face-to-face with Ice inside. But no, the place seemed to be deserted. Maybe whoever had been there had said his piece and left, kidnapping Penny and Mouse, whoever he was.

She was about to push the door open when it struck her that Penny might be inside, dead on the floor, a blood-drenched corpse. Could she handle that? Of course she could. After seeing Jonny Bates dead and blue on his morgue slab, she could stand anything.

She shoved the door open and looked inside. Wood chips and sawdust. The aroma of flowers. A paperback romance novel on the floor. "Penny?" She cleared her throat. "Penny?"

No answer. But no corpses, either.

Something touched her from behind. She jerked away with a startled little squeak, then spun around.

McCoy. Of all people.

"Christ, John," she snapped, "don't ever do that again."

He was looking past her. "What the hell happened? Where's Penny? Where's Mouse?"

She frowned. "You know about Mouse?"

"Yeah." He looked sick, almost trembling inside his casual clothes. "He's a—"

Across the hallway a door was jerked open a crack and a watery blue eyeball peered out. "How long are you going to keep banging and bumping things?" an old lady grumbled at them. "Some people like to sleep once in a while!"

"No problem," McCoy said, and they ducked inside. He pushed the door as closed as it would get.

"Okay," Jane said, almost a whisper, "what's this Mouse business?"

"First I need to know about Penny," he said. "What happened here?"

"Penny called me. Before she had time to say a word somebody kicked the door down. I heard a man—he sounded like a jive street-talker—say something to Mouse. And that was it. They all left, but I don't think by choice."

McCoy looked down at his shoes. "I guess I get the award for all-time stupidest man."

"Meaning?"

"I brought Mouse here to stay with Penny a while. Ice followed me."

Her mouth dropped open. "You've seen Ice? I didn't think you were even *trying* to work the case. And who the hell is Mouse?"

He looked up, his expression grim. He was oddly pale, as if his tanning-parlor brownness had been suddenly washed away. Nerves, maybe. But somehow the angles of his face seemed off-kilter. Jane shrugged it off.

"He's a little boy, one of Ice's kids," McCoy said. "I've been playing cops and robbers, I guess. I dropped Mouse off here and figured he'd be safe until this whole thing was over with."

"Over with? You're about to wrap up the Ice case?"

He looked at her glumly. "Thought I was. But now he's got Penny and Mouse, so there's not much we can do. He'll kill them if we try to move on him, even if ten SWAT teams are breaking down his doors."

Jane sat down on the little couch. "Do you know where he lives? Where he operates?"

He nodded. "Yeah."

She could only stare. Months of work, and she didn't even have a picture of Ice. McCoy gets the case and three days later he's got the man's address. Maybe, she thought dismally, she had underestimated him.

"Well," he said with a shrug, "I guess I'll go home. There's not much I can do now."

"Home?" She frowned at him. "What about Penny? Ice will probably kill her. I say we should hand this over to Mark Tremont."

"Who?"

"Lieutenant Tremont."

"Ah. The police department."

She snatched up the phone, hung it up, put the receiver to her ear, and heard the dial tone. She was about to punch in a number when McCoy pulled the phone out of her hand. "No cops yet," he said. "Give me a day or two on my own."

She made a noise that was close to contempt. "You? What could you possibly do?"

He put the phone back together, then hesitated. "I have another angle."

"Then the police ought to know about it. As Frank Marion says over and over, we're lawyers, not cops."

"Oh." Now he was looking at her strangely.

"What's wrong?" she asked.

He jerked his head. "I guess you haven't heard. Marion's dead."

"Dead?"

"A bomb went off in his house."

She stood up. "Who would want to kill Frank? Wait, I take that back. There's probably a hundred people he put behind bars who would want to see him dead. Revenge. But, Jesus, when did this happen? I didn't hear it on the news."

He rubbed his hands together, then examined his fingernails. She began to get irritated. He was obviously keeping things from her because he wanted the limelight for himself, the bum. Frank Marion just got murdered, and still McCoy wanted to play politics. "Well?" she snapped.

He sighed. "Frank Marion was Ice's business partner. The relationship went sour. Ice eliminated him."

"Oh, for God's sake, McCoy, that's just plain silly. Frank wouldn't—"

"Wouldn't pull you off the case just when you'd started making progress?"

"Well, he did that, yeah, but—"

"And assign it to the most incompetent bumbler on the staff?"

"Okay, yeah, but—"

"In effect, bury it and all the work you did?"

She eyed him, the strength draining out of her. She slumped back down onto the couch, staring at the blank television screen without seeing it. Of course. Frank Marion's insistence that she abandon the file should have made her suspicious, but who would have believed that he was in league with Ice? And how had McCoy, the most incompetent bumbler on the staff, found out all these things?

"We won't phone the police," he said. "They might be corrupt, too. All we know right now is that I'm clean, you're clean, and Penny is missing. Once I get her and Mouse out of danger, I'll move on Ice myself."

"Yeah. Sure," she said wanly. The picture tube of the TV was as dark as her heart felt. She'd been betrayed and humiliated by her own friend and boss, Frank Marion.

"I'm serious, Jane."

"And if you wind up dead?"

He put on a small grin. "Superheroes never die. They just change identities."

He sketched a salute and went out while she contemplated that statement. Then she remembered that she wanted to ask him where Ice's headquarters was in case something went terribly wrong. She ran out into the hallway to stop him, but he was gone. And so she left, too.

The night was long and miserable.

CHAPTER

23

Fright Night
at the Ice Palace

Penny had never known terror like this. The closest she had come was many years ago on a camping trip with her father. Darkness had fallen, and he was still out in the forest doing whatever fathers do, when the moon rose high and cold and bears and ghouls and goblins cackled at her from high in the trees. The tent's walls were flimsy, the fire had gone out, she was only eleven, but she knew that someday a hunter would stumble across her bones in the rotting remains of her tent, dead of fright. That had been pretty scary.

But nothing like this.

Some Latino kid was up front driving the limousine while slugging down beer. In the belly of the limo she was perched on a luxurious leather seat with Danny Frakes beside her. Ice was sitting across from her, his silver tooth seeming to glow in the dark. She had never seen a man grin so big and so long. What a cheerful character this Ice was turning out to be.

He had escorted Danny and her at knifepoint to the limo that was waiting outside her brownstone. None of her usually nosy neighbors had bothered to be nosy. Her heart was thundering in her chest, her breathing tight

178

and hot in her lungs. She could now understand why some people fainted from shock.

The limo smelled like cigarettes and booze. Ice held a martini in one hand, the knife in the other. He kept on grinning as they drove through the city. He grinned as the limo swerved and skidded, but he did not spill his drink. And he grinned when the driver stopped at a convenience store and came out with a package of white clothesline.

Danny was a shape beside her in the dark. Penny was glad for the darkness because Ice had one fist on her left knee, the fist holding the knife, and was slowly pushing it between her legs, under her skirt. She did not squirm, did not move at all as he invaded her, the knife a mere shape that was lifting her dress like the fin of a killer shark. Terror had frozen her muscles and deadened her nerves. He toyed with her for a moment, then leaned back, chuckling under his breath, which smelled strongly of gin.

"You'll do fine," he informed her, and all she could do was close her eyes and hope to fall into a dead faint and wake up in bed at home.

The limo slid smoothly into the driveway of an enormous house ablaze with light, and stopped. The beer-drinking chauffeur opened the door for them and belched loudly into her ear as she climbed down. He laughed and slammed it.

They marched toward the house. Penny nearly stumbled, walking in shock, reminding even herself of old war footage of the survivors of bombing raids, her face slack and dead as she stumbled forward like a zombie, dazed beyond words. But she knew that the real terror lay beyond these ornate yard statues and the colorful fountain in the middle of the lawn. The blackness that settled over her mind was nearly a physical pain.

The cement walkway became carpet as they entered the house; the chill of night became heat; distant insect chatter became human voices. She saw faces, black and white and brown, saw curious eyes, frowns, sneers, grins. The floors were littered with beer bottles and cans, McDonald's bags, cigarette butts. She walked behind

Danny with no thought of trying to escape, wanting only to meekly oblige these people and end this misunderstanding. Being kidnapped by a gang leader was not on the grand chart of her life; somebody would pay for this.

They tromped into a dark and smelly bedroom, Penny squinting when the light went on after the door was shut. Ice straightened up. He had a photograph in one hand. "This is what happens to people who don't follow my orders," he said, and held it in front of her face. Her eyes were still closed. He tapped her nose with the picture, and she opened them.

What a mess. Perhaps if she offered to make the bed? The only way for a nice person like herself to handle mean persons was to be so God-blessed nice that they would have mercy, begin to like her, and in the end become her buddies. It had worked before, but that had been in high school, and the mean person was a fat girl named Desdemona who liked to pull Penny's hair in gym class. After the guaranteed super-nice treatment they had indeed become friends, and still exchanged Christmas cards. So then, it was time to start charming this Ice fellow.

He was bent over a desk, rummaging through a drawer. Penny touched her throat. Perched and tense. "Should I make the bed for you or anything?" she was able to say.

He stopped and slowly turned his head to look at her. "Say what?"

"Anything I can do? I can clean house."

"You can stand there and keep your mouth shut, that's what you can do," he snarled. "And as far as the bed goes, if you make it, you and me are just going to mess it all up again."

He grinned. The tooth gleamed. Penny let her eyes slide shut, rocking on her feet.

Jonny Bates. She recognized the boy from Jane's files. She made one last desperate attempt to faint, the image of the ghastly picture imprinted inside her eyes forever, and was aware that her knees were coming unlocked and that she was falling.

* * *

180

Danny had to duck out of Penny's way as she crumpled to the floor. She hit her head cruelly hard on a corner of the oaken water bed, causing the water in the mattress to slosh audibly. Her skirt was rumpled in a decidedly unladylike way as she lay, and he saw that she was wearing blue panties. He was glad that he was not her, because it was possible that what Ice had in mind for her was worse than what he had in mind for him.

"Look at this, Mouse," Ice demanded, wagging the picture. "Look what happens to my enemies."

Danny looked. It was nothing that he hadn't seen before, even in his own bedroom in his own house, where his father probably still hung from the light fixture with flies going at his dead eyes.

Ice put the picture away and shoved the drawer shut with his knee. The Latino kid was standing with the package of clothesline in one hand, casually staring down at Penny.

"Put her on the bed," Ice told him, motioning toward it. "Use some of that rope to tie her down."

"You got it," the kid said, and dropped the clothesline on her stomach. He bent and picked her up in his arms. Her head lolled like the head of a corpse. Danny saw a small river of blood running from a cut on her scalp above her right ear.

"Any sign of Sting yet?" Ice asked.

The kid dropped Penny on the bed. The mattress heaved. "Nope." He went to work opening the package with his teeth.

"We might be having double fun tonight if I get my hands on the bastard," Ice muttered. He shoved a hand inside his suit coat and hauled out a cigarette. The other hand produced a lighter. He puffed and blew the smoke in Danny's face. "Mouse my boy," he said, "I want to know why you didn't follow my orders tonight."

Danny had no idea what he meant.

"I ordered you to stay at Marion's and watch him count the money."

"Oh." Danny shrugged. "I tried, but he told his butler to throw me out."

"Aha. And that guy with the hat who dived out of there with you was the butler."

"Well, no."

"Who was he, then?"

"I don't know."

Ice wagged his head slowly. "A perfect stranger crashed through a window just as your ass was about to get blown away. He pulled you out, saved your life, then walked you to this bitch's apartment, and you didn't even know him, never seen him before." He took a puff, still shaking his head. "I saw it all, Mouse. There's a lot of it I don't understand, but that's between me and Sting. All I want to know from you is the dude's name and where I can find him."

Danny swallowed. His throat creaked. Should he say anything about the soap factory and the mummy who inhabited it? He owed his life to that strange man whose face was a skull, whose hands were ravaged and ruined. He was like a guardian angel. But life was hell; there was no room for angels in it.

"I don't know his name," he said. "Honest. And I've only seen him two or three times. But I think he lives, he lives . . ."

No. He couldn't do it. He already had one foot in the grave and was slated to die very soon. At least he should check out of life with his dignity intact. "I don't know," he said flatly.

Ice grinned. "Oh, I *like* this," he crowed. "A hero among us rowdy boys!"

He stepped over to Danny with all the grace of a lumbering Frankenstein creature and snared Danny's right hand. "Be a hero now," he said sweetly, and bent Danny's thumb backward until it touched his forearm. His metacarpal bone broke with a small, wet snap that was inaudible over his wild shrieks of pain.

"I don't joke around!" Ice shouted in his face. "I can break every finger you got and then start on your arms! Where does the mystery man live?"

Danny opened his mouth but could not speak. Tears dripped down his face and were salty against his tongue.

His thumb was bent comically, hideously backward, an impossible position that was impossible to believe.

"Where?" Ice bellowed.

"Duh-duh-duh," he was able to stammer, "duh-downtown."

"Downtown's a big place, Mouse! Where downtown?"

"At a . . . a . . ."

The bedroom door crashed open, and Sting stood there looking wild and disheveled. "Why didn't anybody come looking for me?" he shouted. "What's wrong with you?"

Ice whirled. "Where the hell have you been? Why'd you run off like that?"

"Run off like what? I've been at the edge of the back yard tied up for half the night!"

Ice advanced on him. "If you can't handle the drugs you eat, then *stop eating them!*"

Danny thought they were going to fight. Instead Ice spun around and shouted at the Latino kid. "Is that gonna take all night? Tie her up!"

"All done, Ice. Be cool, man."

"Give me the rest of that rope."

The bag of clothesline flipped through the air. Ice snagged it. "Nobody touches the bitch while I'm gone," he said darkly. "Sting, get the camera. If I have to kill all of you in this house to straighten you out, I will. Mouse!"

Danny was staring raptly at his ruined thumb. He looked up. "What?"

"To the limo. Sting, you drive, and I don't want to hear anymore bullshit about your hallucinations."

They all stood staring at Ice. "Well?" he roared.

Everyone started to move fast.

CHAPTER

24

We Thought Walking Was Good for You

Darkman had considered buying a car many times, but he had never done it. Now, parked in the alley where the wino and Mouse Frakes had shaken him out of his weariness of spirit sat a 1991 Chevrolet Corvette, doubtless worth upwards of thirty thousand dollars. He had, of course, gotten the special Darkman rate, stealing it from one rich neighborhood where Marion used to live. It didn't sit well with him to heist some poor fool's pride and joy, but time was short here, almost gone. Perhaps it was a sort of poetic justice that the car was beige. He did not like beige very much.

He was working feverishly at his computer, his McCoy face and hands a boiling puddle in a far corner, sending up smoke, stinking up the place, self-destructing in the usual way. On the computer he was performing a task that he had known he would have to do at some point in his career, a task that he had dreaded. For this mad project he should have allowed himself four or five hours of work. Now he was trying to do it in mere minutes. It was not much fun at all, this business of trying to create a mask from memory alone. He had no photograph for the computer to digest, just thousands of pixels on the screen that had to be individually arranged into a face.

He was discovering that he was not much of an artist.

He paused long enough to check his watch. Penny and Mouse had been shanghaied about twenty, maybe thirty minutes ago. Darkman had become John McCoy in order to present himself at Penny's apartment and help keep watch in the night when few lights would be on to ruin his artificial skin. Now, because of his monumental stupidity, the whole affair had collapsed. He should have known that Ice would follow him to Penny's place. Some hero, this new Darkman. But that was a mistake he would not make again.

The face forming on the screen looked a little like Tim Conway. Darkman adjusted the tint, trimmed some of the curves off the cheeks, made the ears smaller and flatter, the nose wider. Ice was not an average-looking man. If memory served him right, Ice's eyes were unusually close together, his chin a little longer than normal, the bridge of his nose a little too large, probably as a result of a broken nose or two. And his cheekbones were more prominent.

Darkman hunched over the keyboard again in the dim light, forming, shaping, reshaping, his bony fingers clacking eerily as he worked, the staccato bursts of sound disappearing into the bowels of the huge factory. Thoughts of that damned silver tooth kept distracting him, nipping at his internal worry center, telling him in small whispers that there was not a silver tooth in the house, and just how did he plan to make one? He tried to brush the thought away. He would pull this off, somehow. Or die trying.

He sat back and examined his work. The image looked like Ice now. A tab on the keyboard caused the face to shift slightly to the right, a head turning on its neck as he tapped and tapped.

The side view was not satisfactory. The profile could have belonged to almost any black man or white man who'd had his nose rearranged in a fight. Darkman frowned at it without lips. Something was missing.

Artistic talent, maybe.

He mentally said to hell with it, and activated the Bio-Press. The big Honda generator in its distant room chugged harder, fighting to produce the necessary voltage buildup for the bullet charge that would zap the pink fluid into temporary life before it was shaped.

The procedure was done inside of twelve seconds. Darkman rolled his chair across the floor and peeled the steaming face off the Bio-Press. He held it up. It looked like a wet brown rag. If he'd had skin on his fingers he would have been howling with pain now; the bullet charge heated the pink fluid to slightly more than eight hundred degrees during those twelve seconds. Another famous benefit of the Rangeveritz technique: no need to buy forceps to handle the stuff.

He emitted a humorless chuckle while he waited for the skin to cool. The remaining fringes of his own facial skin were still quite sensitive, and after his experience in the world of the terminally burned, nothing was quite as disturbing as another burn, no matter how minor. He turned around to look at his supply of wigs. No problem. He still had lots of Revlon artificial fingernails in various lengths, and the uncomfortable brown contact lenses were swimming in the jar with the others. There was eye makeup and there was lipstick in a dozen shades. Best of all, he still had a large supply of the smelly mastic he used to glue the phony faces onto his ruined skull. He looked at his watch again. It was getting late. Time to make the hands—generic ones tinted the right color would do fine—and then a few easier faces. Soon he could be on his way.

The generator groaned again as Darkman prepared more skin on his jumbled, burn-blackened lab equipment, his energy-hog machinery demanding more voltage, always more voltage, and getting it.

Not much later he found that he was beginning to like his Corvette a lot. The big engine didn't make much noise, which made it easier on the ears and safer from a ticket, but when he floored that accelerator and the carburetor got into the act with all four barrels, look out.

He whizzed through town at a respectable speed, despite the temptation to wring the thing out like a rag, drove on toward suburbia, found Courtney Circle, and cruised past the house once without stopping.

There were two cars sitting dark and silent in the driveway, but no limousine. Darkman assumed that a man like Ice wouldn't deign to be seen in anything else, but that assumption wasn't necessarily valid. Ice might be inside the house watching television, playing checkers, knitting booties. There was only one way to know for sure.

He parked a safe distance from the house and watched figures move inside the lighted downstairs windows—the kids, enjoying the evening. He got out and let the door swing shut, then hesitated, breathing the crisp night air, noticing that the moon was veiled by a curtain of scudding clouds. Rain seemed likely.

He shrugged to himself and went up the sidewalk to the front door. He was reaching for the knob when it struck him anew: he didn't have a silver tooth.

Hmm.

A minor brainstorm sparked inside his head. The Corvette smelled heavily of cigarette smoke, a smell that would probably dissipate if he aired the car out for a few days . . . if he decided to keep it, of course. He jogged back to it and leaned inside. On the dash was an open pack of Marlboros. He fetched it up.

The surgeon general says these things are bad for you, he thought crazily, and tore the package apart. Voilà! Aluminum foil.

He wrapped some of it around one of his canine teeth, snugged it in place with his tongue, moved his ersatz lips up and down to see if it would peel off. Seemed likely not to.

Back to the door. The usual music was blasting inside. He shoved it open and strode down the main hallway that led to the heart of the house, moving in the hyperkinetic fashion he had seen Ice use, trying to assemble the remains of his facial muscles into something resembling Ice's permanent sneer. A small kid trundled toward him, gave him a brief smile, almost passed by without comment. Darkman nipped at his sleeve with his fingers, trying to get his attention.

He stopped. "Man, Ice, you got back fast."

"Yeah." Darkman's fire-damaged vocal cords were coming in handy for a change: Ice's voice had been cooked by too many cigarettes and probably a lot of grass, crack, and whatever else he could inhale. "I thought maybe somebody would like to tag along."

The kid looked at him quizzically. "You got Sting and Mouse. Where you going, anyway?"

Great. He had no idea where he was going. "Hey, look," he said in Ice's jive-and-boogie voice, "go get Big Mac for me, willya? I need to, uh, discuss something with him."

"Sure I will, Ice. Hold on."

He scampered away. Darkman heaved a sigh of satisfaction. So far so good. After a few seconds Big Mac was headed down the hallway toward him, looking a little bit like his name. Beefy, maybe fourteen years old. He had a round and pleasant face. This kid a crook? No way.

"Yeah, Ice?"

"Yo, Big Mac," Darkman said, bobbing his shoulders like an old-time gangster. "I thought maybe you'd like to tag along."

The boy's eyebrows drew down into a frown; his eyes grew large beneath them. "Where to, Ice?" He looked very scared all of a sudden. "Not to the river, Ice. I don't like it at the river." His voice was quavering.

Yes! Darkman rejoiced inwardly. *Jonny Bates's body had been found in the river!* "Not to worry, my man. With the little lady along, we'll have a good time."

"Lady? You got her tied up in the bedroom. And we haven't touched her, just like you said."

Darkman tapped his head. "Guess I got hooked up with a bad batch of grass. Hey, I heisted me a car. Want to test-drive it?"

Big Mac looked doubtful. "Isn't that kind of—what do you call it?—high profile, driving around in a stolen car?"

Darkman sighed internally. This banter wasn't getting

him anywhere. "Just come on," he snapped, irritated and sounding like it. "You drive."

Big Mac backed up a step, raising his hands. "Just tell me we ain't going swimming, Ice. You know I'm sorry I messed up with that credit card."

"Consider it forgotten. Let's roll."

They went out. The sky was a dark gray, and the smell of rain was heavy on the air. "Ever driven a Corvette?" Darkman asked him as they approached the car.

"A 'Vette? Hell, no. But I always wanted to."

"Keys are in the ignition."

Big Mac opened the door and looked inside. In the glow of the dome light Darkman could see the ecstasy on his face. "I'm not very good with a stick," he said as he dropped into the seat.

Darkman skirted the car and got in. "Just don't ride the clutch. The bearings burn out fast that way."

"Does that mean you're going to *keep* this thing?"

"Get it repainted, file off the serial numbers, stamp new ones in—why not? I might even give it to you."

"Wow. Can you get me a fake driver's license?"

"Consider it done—if you'll do one or two small things for me."

He hesitated. Then, meekly: "What kind of small things, Ice?"

Darkman chuckled. "Number one: start the car. Number two: chase down the limo."

Big Mac let out a breath. "Those things I can do."

After one false start, and with a lot of tire screeching, Big Mac cranked the Corvette through a jerky U-turn and headed toward the outskirts of the city, out to the riverside where the water was foul and the blackened hulks of abandoned factories huddled in the mud and the stink.

CHAPTER

25

Not All Endings Have to Be Happy, Do They?

The rain started to fall at about eleven o'clock, pattering lightly on the limousine's roof, speckling the windshield, and misting through the beams of the headlights. Sting was behind the wheel looking none too happy even from behind, muttering under his breath, constantly glancing into the rearview mirror to eyeball Ice with raw hostility.

Danny did not understand why they were mad at each other, but it was of no concern to him. At ten years old he was preparing himself for the upcoming trip to heaven or maybe hell. He could not stop the tears and the sobs that racked him like convulsions, could not stop the agony of his broken, throbbing thumb that was attached to his hand at such a weird angle. Ice was a dark and silent figure in the seat across from him toying with his camera, seeming to reek with rage.

Danny did not feel that death was warranted here. He had delivered the briefcase to Bwana Marion, and it had exploded. The only problem was that Danny had survived, had been saved by the mummy-man. All Danny wanted now was to get away from Ice and his gang and stay away from them forever.

"Still being a hero?" Ice asked sullenly.

Danny held his tongue. In the silence the noise of the rain was growing louder as the storm kicked up in earnest.

"Where downtown?" Ice demanded. "Where, exactly, does this character live?"

Danny considered his options as he cried. Would it save his own neck if he blabbed? The mummy-man was a grown-up who could take care of himself. Perhaps he would not mind this tiny little betrayal.

"In an old factory," he mumbled, and hung his head. There, it was out. The deed was done, high treason that made no sense at all.

"Which old factory?"

"Reyton."

Ice snorted. "The old soap place? There ain't nobody there but the rats, and they're starving to death. Give me the truth."

"It is the truth. I don't know his name but I know he lives there. He's the reason most of the winos are too scared to hang around."

"Why did he bother saving your young ass, if you don't know him?"

Danny frowned at that. Why had the man with no face bothered with him at all? His was a lost cause. "He never told me," he said.

"It doesn't make any difference," Ice replied casually. "If he lives there, I'll find him and I'll kill him."

Danny accepted the news with weary calm. "Are you still going to hang me? I did what you wanted. You could just let me out and I'll vanish forever."

He saw the silver tooth flash. "I'll feel much better if I vanish you myself," he said, and laughed. "Vanish you myself. I like that."

The limousine slowed down and turned into a bumpy street. Through the dark windows Danny could see only destruction, a moonscape of shattered machinery and leaning warehouses bordering the river. This was the place, he realized, feeling a dead and careless ambivalence about the whole matter. He would not live to see another sunrise or another sunset. Only this dismal rain, and then heaven or hell or the blackness of eternal nowhere.

Sting turned the headlights off as the limo crawled along the bumpy street. Ice was casually twirling his camera on its carrying strap, humming an unidentifiable tune under his breath. The package of clothesline was up front somewhere. Danny watched him, wondering how Ice could do this terrible thing to him and not be concerned about it at all.

Suddenly Danny imagined his own small hands jerking outward to encircle Ice's scrawny neck, imagined his fingers clamping down so hard on Ice's throat that his eyes bulged comically as he was strangled. And then he imagined himself crashing through the privacy window, getting a good hold on Sting, smashing his head against the steering wheel until it shattered and he was dead. And then he saw himself calmly driving the limo to the nearest police station, and turning himself in. The End.

The limo slowed, its tires crunching to a stop on the gravel. Danny pulled himself out of his hopeless fantasies and got out after Ice swung a door open for him. Hunched against the rain, they walked up a decaying wooden ramp toward the huge black maw of an abandoned warehouse. Sting tagged along behind, perhaps feeling regretful that it had come to this, perhaps feeling nothing at all.

Danny shivered as he crossed the doorless threshold. "Only a few steps more," Ice said. Was he concerned that his little Mouse might stumble and fall, maybe scrape his knee? It came to Danny quite suddenly that Ice was not a very smart man, perhaps even stupid. The thought was not all that comforting.

"Hold it," Ice said. Danny sensed him groping around. His cigarette lighter flared alive, and in its glow Danny could see that two or three candles had been attached with melted wax to a bar of rusty steel that sprouted out of an odd construction made of steel and tin. How nifty. Ice was prepared for unexpected night executions too. A regular boy scout.

Danny looked around as the candles began to glow.

Odd things in here—crooked pipes and strange scaffolds, discarded crates, mounds of debris. It looked vaguely familiar, though he was sure he had never been in here before. Another instance of déjà vu?

His breath left him in a sudden wheeze. Indeed he *had* seen the inside of this warehouse. He had seen it the pictures that Ice kept in his desk.

Sting tromped up some stairs and started working with the clothesline, fashioning a sloppy noose at one end. He draped it over a pipe and let it descend almost to the floor. Danny felt his eyes slide mercifully shut at the sight of it. He wobbled on his feet, very close to falling over. Dear Mom and God: please let it be swift and painless. Ice took him by the elbow, almost gently, and guided him to the rope. He was breathing hard, most likely because he really enjoyed these executions. Why else would he take pictures?

They stopped. Ice lifted the noose and settled it around Danny's neck, then snugged it tight. His breath reeked of gin. Maybe, Danny thought without emotion, that would be the last thing the kid code-named Mouse would ever smell.

Ice stepped back, his shadow bobbing along like a dark ghost, and checked his handiwork. He raised the camera and looked through the viewfinder. "Fucking flash better work," Danny heard him grumble. The camera clicked as he adjusted it. This was crazy. Danny knew it had to be a nightmare or some form of insanity. Ice had not even bound his hands.

Ice looked up at Sting, nodded slightly, and turned his attention to Danny. "The punishment for disobeying me is death. I find you guilty of disobedience and am forced to do this."

He snapped his fingers, then pressed the camera to his eye.

The rope twitched. It became taut, then tight, then too tight, then unbearable. Danny tried to scream, but the only thing that came out was a wet and hideous gobble, the voice of a turkey on the chopping block.

Sting kept pulling. Danny was pulled up onto his toes, off his toes. He swayed slightly, his eyes screwed shut, his

193

DARKMAN

face contorted with agony as his feet completely left the floor. He began to twirl in slow motion, desperately clawing at the rope around his neck but unable to get his fingers under it. His broken thumb was being pushed in horrible directions, but the pain of it was nothing at all compared to the pain of his dying.

He was aware, as he hung there like a trout on a line, that the camera's flash did indeed work, because though his eyes were shut he was seeing brilliant flashes, flashes the color of blood as Ice circled him like a shark, gathering photos for his ghastly collection.

CHAPTER

26

The Color of Roses and Blood

"Faster," Darkman said. Big Mac obliged him, made the engine howl like an Indy racer at full throttle, wandering all over the road like the novice driver he was. The rain on the windshield was an endless barrage, the black scenery outside blurring past too fast to make sense of. The reflections of the 'Vette's headlights on the road were two shiny ribbons splashed with raindrops the size of nickels.

"How's this?" Big Mac asked.

Darkman was holding on to the dashboard. The car sat so low he could almost hear his ass dragging. He looked at the speedometer. Eighty-five. Not bad, considering that this little back road was posted at thirty. "How much farther?"

"Farther?" Big Mac took his eyes off the road to glance at him. "You've been this way a dozen times, Ice."

"It's the damned dark," he answered immediately. "I'm losing my night vision. Suppose I need glasses?"

"Might be." Big Mac was watching the road again. "We'll be there in about thirty seconds, but I hate to drive this car through the muck."

"We can always wash it later."

"Yeah." He grinned. "Or just drive it through the river. It's close and it's handy."

Darkman laughed for him. Of course the execution site was close to the river, probably in an old boxcar or warehouse. Why waste time dragging Jonny's corpse all over the place, when the river was located so conveniently nearby? What a horrible business this business was.

Big Mac slowed down, pushing a little too hard on the brakes, making the wheels skid on the slick pavement. He turned right onto a muddy lane that wound down to a clot of abandoned warehouses near the river.

"There's the limo," Big Mac said. "Can you make it out with your defective eyeballs?"

"Very funny. Go ahead and stop here."

"Here? You're gonna get soaked, man."

"Just stop. I want to go on foot, make sure nobody's snooping around."

Big Mac coasted the car to a stop, then killed the headlights. "Ice," he said nervously, turning to face him, "you're not, like, setting me up? I mean, you walk away, the car explodes or something? Boom, no more Big Mac and the trouble he caused?"

Darkman smiled for his benefit. "No exploding cars, kid. Go on back home."

He hesitated. "Ice?"

Darkman had his hand on the door lever. "Yeah?"

"Mouse is gonna get it tonight, ain't he? Is there any way I can change your mind about offing him? Mouse is just a little kid."

"I know," Darkman said heavily. "But rules are rules."

"Please? I mean, he's only ten."

"That's old enough to know better than to cross me." He bent and fished under the seat, found his lightproof bag of tricks, then swung the door open and got out. Big Mac frowned as he watched him.

"What's in that bag?"

He pushed the door shut. "Nothing that concerns you, Mac. Get out of here."

"But, Ice—"

"Drive, dammit!"

He did as ordered, making the rear tires throw clots of mud as he turned in a wide, uneven circle. Then he was at the road; then he was gone.

Darkman heaved a sigh of relief and jammed the bag inside his pants. Part A of the plan was complete: Big Mac had brought him here. The rest of it was up to Darkman himself. He turned and saw that traces of yellowish light were leaking through the cracks in the walls of the nearest warehouse. He slopped and skidded through the mud, holding his arms out for balance, not very worried about the noise because the rain was loud enough to cover it. He found a wooden ramp that led into the building. Stenciled in big black letters on the tin wall, nothing more now than a few flakes of paint, was the warehouse number: A-22. At some point in the distant past the number might have had significance for the barges that used to ply the river, signaling the skippers to unload their cargo here. Now it was just a leaning eyesore. Through the wide doorway he could see candles burning inside the warehouse, casting long, trembling shadows across the floor.

And then he heard a sound he would never forget, a sound imported from hell itself: *Agggggggghhahssss.*

They were hanging Mouse. Darkman's heart jumped. He wasn't too late yet. He raced up the ramp, which cracked and threatened to snap under his muddy feet, and stopped long enough to peer deeper into the dark maw of the entrance. Rain hammered the tin roof; there was a smell of rotten vegetables in the dead air. And a man in a suit that shimmered like molten blue diamonds was walking in a circle taking snapshots of Mouse, at times squatting to shoot from a new angle. Mouse was kicking and squirming, his head cocked at a grotesque angle from the noose, gagging on his own blood, by the sound of it.

"Let him down!" Darkman bellowed in a voice that was not Ice's, not even his own: the voice of raw disbelief. "Sting! This is Big Mac! You've got to let him down!"

Hidden up in the shadows, Sting was invisible. His voice floated down. "Why?"

"Because . . . because . . ." *Because why?* "Because he's just a kid!"

Sting let out a snort. "That never stopped us before."

Ice was prowling around, trying to see who had spoken. There was a mighty frown on his face. "Mac," he shouted angrily, "get out of here!"

Darkman could scarcely believe they were buying his act. His Big Mac imitation sucked as bad as the Donald Duck impression he had been trying to master since grade school. "I've got a gun!" he bellowed at them. "God damn you, *let the kid down!*"

Sting did better than let him down. He dropped the rope. Mouse hit the cement floor and keeled over sideways. His head smacked the floor with a fleshy thud and he took a long, sobbing breath.

"Who is that?" Ice barked. "You ain't no Big Mac."

"Why don't you come over here and see?"

Ice strutted a few steps, but he looked more scared than angry now. "Don't be shooting at nobody," he said. "Are you the cops? Did Mac turn me in? Well, he's nothing but a liar, I can tell you that."

"No cops," Darkman said. "Something better."

Ice was close, walking out of the feeble light. He held his cigarette lighter over his head and flicked it on. "Okay, hotshot," he said, his eyes still searching, his face dappled with shadows and light. "What's better?"

Darkman felt his anger trying to rise as he stood here so close to Ice. The raw desire to rip the man's throat out surged thickly through his veins, but he forcibly squelched it. He stepped away from that light, keeping his distance, drawing Ice away from the warehouse. The rain extinguished the lighter. Darkman heard him flick it a few times, heard him mutter to himself.

"Damn it, where are you?" he howled into the night. "Who are you?"

Flame burst from the lighter again. Darkman bared his teeth in a grin. "Me," he said, and lunged at him, already feeling the surge of strength, the adrenaline that turned him into a powerhouse of rage. Before he smashed into Ice he saw a look of disbelief in his eyes, disbelief and sudden terror at the sight of his identical twin on the attack. And then Darkman was on him, bowling him over, hearing his head slap into the mud, going for his throat. His vision was misting over with red, the color of roses and blood.

Ice tried to scream. Darkman hoisted him up by the throat and hurled him into the mud a good distance away. Ice splashed down like a large rock and immediately jumped to his feet. A bolt of lightning cracked the sky, and Darkman saw Ice turn, saw him raise a foot to run in that brief light, saw the camera still dangling from its strap. Again Darkman jumped at Ice, who resembled an oversized bat wearing a blue suit that shimmered and changed when lightning again arced across the sky. He crashed down behind Ice and captured him in a huge backward bear hug.

He squeezed. His anger was an earthquake; his rage was slipping out of control again. Ice grunted, his feet pedaling uselessly as Darkman lifted him off the ground. Darkman squeezed harder. Small things inside Ice's body popped and snapped; anyone watching would have seen one broken rib sprouting out of his midsection, punching through his shirt. Ice tried to scream but it came out as a wheezing gurgle. Darkman continued to squeeze, his own eyes crushed shut, overwhelmed by the rage and the inner pictures of Jonny Bates lying on a slab, Mouse twirling on a rope. Something plastic in Ice's hand broke with a crunch; Darkman smelled butane, thick and unbreathable. Ice went suddenly limp.

Darkman dropped him in the mud, where he began to snore.

Sting's voice wafted out of the warehouse: "What's going on out there? Ice?"

Darkman took a staggering backward step. His wig was askew, his feet two balls of mud. A line of saliva was running down his fake chin, and he wiped it away with a hand. *Back off!* he ordered himself. *Back off, damn you!*

The red mist began to fade. There might someday come a time when the rage would not go away, and that was a thought so dismal that he nearly choked on his own breath. It was never pleasant to be so utterly out of control.

But anger fills the hole in our soul, does it not?

He groaned. The inner man was back after a blissful hiatus of a day or two.

A junkie needs his fix. You need danger.

Granted. He did. And there was plenty of it here, if the inner voice would simply shut up and let him hunt for it.

"Ice?"

Darkman spun around. Sting had appeared in the doorway, a darker shadow against the shadows. He was peering outside, swiveling his head. Darkman hastily repositioned his wig, slung some of the mud off his feet, checked his face with his hands, having to reposition it as well. A terrible thought struck him: what if the glue that held everything together was dissolving in the rain? At least the faces and hands in the bag weren't getting wet, but from the feel of things the Ice persona was falling apart.

"Come on, Ice, what's happening out there?"

Darkman cleared his throat, searching his mind for the area marked *Ice's Voice.* "Keep your damn pants on!" he shouted out, hopefully in the right tone and with the right degree of annoyance, and slopped his way to the warehouse. Lightning flashed again and he could only pray that Sting had not seen Ice lying in the mud.

"Who was that?" Sting demanded as Darkman crossed the threshold. "Big Mac?"

Darkman brushed past him. "Nobody you need to worry about."

He uttered a noise of disbelief. "Look," he spluttered, "I'm second-in-command, in case you forgot that. Who was it?"

Darkman pretended to ignore him. He stood over Danny's crumpled form, feigning disdain while growing sick inside. He was still alive—was squirming slightly—the most pitiful thing he had ever seen, right up there with the morgue photo of Jonny Bates.

He turned suddenly back to Sting, barely able to control his gorge and his anger. "Phone in the limo still busted?"

Sting frowned, this Sting who was maybe seventeen or

eighteen and liked to hang other kids. "There ain't no phone in the limo," he said. "You know there ain't."

"Shows what you know," Darkman shot back, glad he had turned the question to his advantage. "There's a phone under my seat, been there since before you joined up. It's been broken. I told Big Mac to get it fixed. Just wondered if he had."

"Oh." He shrugged a little. "As far as I know, no working phone."

"Damn. I've got an important message to relay, and I need communication."

"Yeah?" Sting eyed him doubtfully again. "You didn't have a message when we got here."

At last Darkman was able to vent a little more steam. "Just shut up!" he shouted. "Every time I make a decision somebody has to ask me a hundred questions!" He aimed a finger in Sting's face. "You get in the limo, you go back to the house, and you make a call for me! Got it? Can you keep your goddamn mouth from asking questions for a change?"

Sting stepped back, raising his hands. "Okay, man, don't blow a gasket. Tell me what the message is, who it's for, and I'm outta here."

Darkman jerked a pen out of his breast pocket, then slapped at his clothes, searching for paper. And dammit, he should have *brought* paper. Slipups like this could end this masquerade pretty quick.

Sting dug in a pocket. "Here."

Darkman snatched the paper out of his hand. It was a crumpled coupon for a free ice cream cone at Dairy Queen. It struck him again how twisted this gang of lawless children was, so young and so deadly.

He pressed it to his knee, jotted down a number, then scribbled two sentences. He held it closer to the light, nodding. It would have to do. He handed it over and watched while Sting read it.

He looked up. "What the hell?"

"Just do it," Darkman growled. "And go out the back way."

"Back way? What back way? What for?"

"Because," Darkman said through his teeth, "I just told you to. Now do it if you have to cut a hole in the wall."

Sting turned, scowling, and jogged off to where the shadows were thickest. He clomped and clanged around for a full minute, cursing under his breath. A door finally screeched open, and he was gone.

Darkman went to Danny and worked the noose free while his Ice face came steadily apart at the seams and pieces of it slithered to the floor.

CHAPTER

27

A Weird Situation

Sting drove the limo to the house, a frown welded to his face and a sincere desire to kick some ass burning in his guts. Ice was getting very annoying of late. He and Sting had enjoyed a pretty relaxed partnership up to now, Ice in charge of everything, Sting in charge of making sure that everything got done. He had heard the phrase "chain of command" used in some war movie, and understood it pretty well. The officers make the decisions, the soldiers obey. Until now he had considered himself an officer in the gang. Now he wasn't so sure.

He took the last corner to the house with a high-speed squeal of tires even though the road was slick with rain, and roared into the driveway, fuming. A beige Corvette was parked there. So who gave a damn? At the house he stiff-armed the front door open and waded through the trash and beer cans, knocking the slower kids aside. In Ice's top-secret room he slammed the door and dumped himself into the chair at the desk, then grabbed up the phone. When he swiveled he noticed the girl tied up on the bed, a little amazed that he had forgotten all about her. How would Ice feel if he came home and found that she had escaped? It might be worth letting her go, just to get back at him.

He dug the paper out of his pocket and eyed it. Local number, someplace in the south side of town. So Ice was rubbing elbows with establishment types now, eh? God forbid that anything should remind him of his lowly origins. As Sting dialed the number a sour taste formed in his mouth and a desire for some firewater knocked at his thirst control center. The phone clicked and beeped distantly as the connection sought out the mystery person's phone. Then it rang once, twice, and clicked.

"Hello?"

"Got a message for you," he said stonily, then read the note Ice had written: "'Don't be coy, be real. A good grade still counts when you're twenty-two, as long as your ship comes in.'"

"What?"

"I didn't stutter, lady."

"Who is this?"

"I'll give it to you one more time." He had to nip his tongue with his teeth to keep the word "bitch" from sliding out. For all he knew, he might be talking to Ice's mother. "'Don't be coy, be real. A good grade still counts when you're twenty-two, as long as your ship comes in.'"

"But I don't . . ."

He hung up, tired of it, tired of everything. He looked across the room at the cute little lady lying on the bed and found that he didn't care about her, either. The only thing he could keep in mind now was an upcoming date with a bottle. He stood up and stalked to the kitchen, where rows of cabinets held the waters of fast comfort. He cracked open some Russian Star vodka and slugged down a few mouthfuls, wondering if he should even bother going back to the warehouse. But Ice was there without any transportation, and a long walk in the rain would be just the thing to ruin the rest of his day and Sting's as well when Ice finally got home and proceeded to discipline his lieutenant.

Big Mac wandered in and headed to one of the refrigerators. He stopped and looked glumly at Sting. "Did you do it?"

He regarded him wearily. "Did I do what?"

"Kill Mouse."

Sting had to search his memory, which was scary. Getting soft in the head from too much booze? He hoped not. "I got about halfway there, and then somebody showed up and ruined it."

"Yeah?" Big Mac looked as if he might smile. "So Mouse is still alive?"

"Far as I know, yeah."

Big Mac exhaled a large sigh of relief. "I gotta find Ice and thank him."

"Then you'd better put on a raincoat. He's still back at the warehouse."

"That's okay. He gave me his car."

Sting blinked. "Say what?"

"That 'Vette outside. He heisted it, then gave it to me."

"Bullshit," Sting countered immediately. "We don't heist cars."

"Well, Ice sure did. And while I was driving him to the warehouse, he told me I could have it."

Sting wagged his head back and forth and set the bottle on the countertop. "Are you on drugs?"

"No. Should I be?"

"I drove Ice to the warehouse in the limo barely a half hour ago."

"No way, man. I just now got back. See?" He lowered his head and shook it hard. Tiny raindrops sprayed across the floor from his hair. "And see these?" He held out a set of car keys. "How he ever found somebody stupid enough to leave the keys in a car like that, well, it had to be a miracle."

Sting narrowed his eyes. "Ice does not give things away, Mac. Especially not cars."

"But he did! Only about ten minutes ago!"

Sting covered his face with his hands, breathing between his fingers. They smelled like rusty metal, warehouse metal. He pressed hard into his eyes, making colors jump. Now, either Big Mac was crazy or he himself was. Or Ice. Or all three of them. Ice was a man of many talents, but he could not split himself in two. And that brought to mind the small matter of Ice's second-in-command spending half the evening tied up in the weeds while everyone else seemed to think he was doing business as usual.

A cold and terrible thought formed, then fragmented just as rapidly. He almost chuckled. Imagine that, thinking that some kind of human chameleon had infiltrated the gang. It was Ice, had to be Ice, trying to make fools of them all. This was a test of sorts.

"So do you believe me?" Big Mac asked as he opened the fridge and hoisted a beer out. "I may be nuts, but the car is out there and I've got the keys. Maybe Ice is changing, turning nice all of a sudden."

Sting let his hands fall. He snorted tiredly. "Oh, he's changing all right. The question is, what's he becoming?"

He left the kitchen with the vodka in his hand and the question unanswered. Upstairs in his room he eased the door shut, locked it, and moved to his dresser. Unlike Ice, Sting liked to keep a tidy room. In his sock and underwear drawer, nestled in a small leather holster, was his only deadly weapon, a tiny .25-caliber semi-auto with pearly grips. It wasn't exactly a cannon, but it could inflict some damage.

He left the house wondering why he felt it necessary, on this dreary, windblown night, to carry the gun.

CHAPTER

28

Can Somebody Be Confused to Death?

Consciousness surged through him in slow, steady waves, bringing with it questions and pain. Who was he? Ice. Why was he all wet? Rain. Why did he feel as if a hot locomotive had driven over him, slicing him into several large pieces?

Ice. The *other* Ice.

Raindrops were battering his face. He opened his eyes and lifted his head out of the mud. Pain screeched through his chest at the movement while a screech of his own slipped out of his mouth.

He forced himself to sit up. The movement nearly killed him. For some reason he could smell gasoline or kerosene, nauseatingly thick. It seemed to be drifting up from his clothes. He hung his head, panting. The world became harshly white for a moment as lightning walked the sky, and in that brief instant he saw what his problem was.

A broken rib. A *badly* broken rib, sticking out of him like a bloody white knife just above his liver. He opened his mouth and a glop of something salty drooled off his tongue and plopped in the mud between his outstretched legs. It came to him that he had a pierced lung, a punctured liver, a ruptured spleen, whatever. Something fatal, for sure.

He waited. He waited to die while the cold rain drummed on his head. Distantly he heard the foghorn of a river barge, and could imagine that horn being blown by the angel Gabriel himself, just like in the old song, coming for to carry him home.

Time passed while the storm howled through the city. After several minutes Ice decided that he was too young and too crafty to die. Someone who looked a lot like him had appeared out of nowhere and used a sledgehammer on his chest, but the murder attempt had been botched. Though Ice's memory of the struggle was as clouded as the black sky overhead, he felt sure he had put up a good fight.

He worked himself slowly to his knees, holding his side with the rib protruding between his fingers, grunting against the pain, then climbed to his feet, each movement accompanied by a new set of grunts and moans. Taking baby steps, he was able to make it into the warehouse before collapsing to his knees again.

Only one candle was still burning. Ahead and to his left the hangman's noose dangled eerily from the overhead pipes. Mouse was gone, having left only a smear of blood on the concrete below the noose. Sting was gone as well. In the desolation the only sound was that of the rain pounding on the roof.

Ice got to his feet again. This was all very mysterious. Something had gone horribly wrong. He had been deserted, left to die alone. But how? And by whom?

A voice rang out of the darkness, making him slew around with a gasp.

"Hello, Ice. Come for the last hurrah, have you?"

Ice shuffled in a slow circle. He saw only flickering shadows, junk strewn about, dead machinery. He turned clumsily again, frowning, beginning to feel very, very scared. "Who are you?" he whispered.

"You know me quite well, Ice. I'm your partner."

"I don't have any partners."

"Oh, but you do."

Ice frowned, blinking rapidly to clear his vision.

Everything was getting swimmy. "Let me see you," he grunted. "Face-to-face."

He heard a ghostly chuckle and then the slow rasping of shoes over concrete. Something pale began to bob in the darkness, a human head. "Sorry about the frog in my throat," the man said. "I always seem to get laryngitis when a bomb explodes in my face."

Ice made a guttural noise and fell back a step. *"Marion?"*

"In the flesh, Ice. I'm still your partner, Ice. And can you dig this, Ice? I owe you something."

Ice began to stagger as he retreated. That face was blurry and indistinct, but it was Frank Marion, no doubt about that, a balding head without a body. A ghost? Ice was not one to believe in ghosts. "The explosion wasn't my idea," he said. "I didn't even know about the bomb until it was too late to warn you."

Marion laughed. Outside, the wind began to hoot around the corners of the warehouse, and the flame of the single candle inside the building wavered. "The time for excuses is long gone," Marion said. "This time the noose goes around *your* neck."

Ice shook his head, breathing hard now, far more scared of the living than he ever would be of the dead. "We can cut a deal," he said, his voice wavering and desperate. "We'll reorganize the whole operation, put you in charge again. Would you like that, Marion? Will you at least think about it?"

But Marion was gone.

"Hey!" Ice shouted. He groaned from the pain it caused. "Marion! Please!"

Nothing.

Panting, Ice started for the doorway. Lightning stabbed the sky outside, thunder boomed a moment later. In the dark he tripped over some heavy metal object and fell, wresting himself around in time to keep from landing on his exposed rib, knowing that it would be like falling on a knife. As he got to his feet the pain became so huge that he was forced to scream, for all the good it did.

"Hey, Ice?"

He stopped, gasping for air, recognizing that voice. He turned. "Sting? Is that you, my man?"

A black form moved between Ice and the candle. It planted its fists on its hips. Ice peered hard, trying to see a face on that form that was bordered with candlelight. It was impossible. He patted his soggy clothes in search of his lighter but could not find it. "Is that really you?" he called out. "Sting?"

The figure turned. Ice was able to see its profile. If it wasn't Sting it was somebody who had the same facial curves, the same haircut. "Sting, my man," Ice said, nearly blubbering. "I'm hurt bad. Real bad."

"Not bad enough," Sting said coldly. "But then, the hurting always stops when you die, doesn't it?"

Ice gaped at him while new blood seeped out of a corner of his lips and crawled down his chin. The taste of it was like a mouthful of aluminum foil, and he spat on the floor. "So then you, too," he said. "You and Marion are all chummy, and Ice is supposed to die."

The figure nodded.

"We'll just see about that," Ice was able to snarl, and began to totter toward him.

Sting ducked out of sight.

"Sting!"

Footsteps, receding.

"Sting!"

Nothing.

Ice stopped, breathing hard, his entire right side a vise of pain. *"Sting!"*

He grinned suddenly. No, no, he was not going to let them screw him over without putting up a fight. There was a thing called honor involved here. "I can see you!" he shouted.

The walls threw the words back at him as a series of echoes.

"Gonna getcha!"

Echoes, silence.

"Jesus help me," Ice whined under his breath. "Sting!"

Marion's face bobbed into view a far distance away, just beside the hanging noose. He was holding a candle under his chin. He looked like the Phantom of the Opera.

"It's over," he said. Ice saw a pale hand beckon. "The punishment for treason is death."

Ice shook his head. "No. No way. You ain't hanging me."

"Then you'll hang in prison."

Ice went into a fit of laughter that sounded more like crying. "They don't hang murderers anymore!" he crowed. "They use lethal injection now!"

The candle went out. Footsteps crunched across the floor.

"Death to traitors," Sting whispered from a different place.

Ice jerked himself into a turn, weeping openly, his hand still clamped to his side as blood leaked through his fingers and stained his muddy blue pants. He hobbled to the doorway while lightning danced in the sky outside, while thunder walked on giant's feet.

"Where you going, Ice?"

It was Marion again. Ice moaned. Marion still alive, and Ice betrayed by his own lieutenant, his own friend who had known all along that Marion was not dead. The world was going crazy. He staggered out into the rain and saw the limousine parked in the mud. The dome light popped on as the driver's side door swung open, and in that light he saw Sting behind the wheel. Ice drew in a painful breath that was full of cold rainwater.

"You bastard!" he shouted. "Traitor! You ain't leaving me behind!"

Sting stepped out and eyed him.

"So die then!" Ice screamed, and charged at him, weaving drunkenly, skating and sliding in the mud.

A tiny point of orange light winked. Something hard and hot slammed into Ice's right shoulder. He screamed something nonsensical and fell to his knees, then immediately jumped up again. He charged on. Sting shouted a warning that Ice was in no mood to hear. The little gun popped again with a flash of light, and mud spurted at Ice's feet. Far to his left, not registering in his mind at all, flashing blue and white lights became visible.

"Bastard!" he shrieked. *"Nobody beats the Iceman!"*

Another flash. A second bullet crashed into his chest,

feeling like a hot wrecking ball knocking him backward a step. He tried to keep his balance, tried hard, but gravity took over and he slammed on his back to the ground.

He raised his head. He no longer knew what had happened, no longer knew anything but his own made-up name.

And then he knew no more.

CHAPTER

29

It Was a Dark and Stormy Night

Penny Larsen hated waterbeds the way most people hate tarantulas, but it was a new hate and almost enjoyable. For every move she made, the bed reciprocated with a move in the opposite direction. As she struggled in the dark to free her hands and ankles from the ropes that held her, she became seasick after a while, but did not give up. Her hopelessness had lifted a little to be replaced by a desperate sort of courage. So the big bad man named Ice wanted a roll in the hay? How horny would he be after she bit a hole in his cheek and tore his lips off? He'd probably beat her to death, but even death was more attractive than being his love slave.

She had been making some progress on her right wrist, had been able to loosen the length of clothesline a little at the cost of a lot of skin. She took a short breather, gathering her strength, determined to ignore the pain and really go for it. She nodded to herself, blinked sweat out of her eyes, clenched her teeth, and pulled as hard as she could pull.

Something gave as she bit back a scream; something loosened. Suddenly her hand snapped free and smacked her on the chest.

213

Success! She rolled slightly and went to work on the other wrist, glad for the raging music that drowned out the noises she was making.

The light snapped on, and there stood Frank Marion in a wet blue suit with mud up to his knees and the remnants of his hair sparkling with raindrops. She sucked in a breath.

He came wordlessly to the bed and stared down at her. She stared at him with all the wonder of a child meeting Santa for the first time.

He untied her left wrist, then her ankles. He bent over her as if to pick her up. Finally he spoke: "Are you all right, Penny?"

"No thanks to a crook like you," she spat, and slapped his face hard. At which point the entire lower half of his face peeled upward like cheap wallpaper to expose a large part of a naked white skull complete with teeth, one of which was silver.

She screamed while he pressed his face back into place.

"Ouch," he said, and went out.

He assembled the kids the living room and gave them the news: The gang is disbanded. Take a hike, don't let the door hit you in the ass on the way out, don't bother to come back, and for God's sake, go to school on Monday morning. And, Big Mac? I want the keys to the Corvette.

And so they left, all but Penny and the boy known as Mouse who was lying on the couch, still in pain.

Marion who was not Marion gave her the keys and asked her to take Mouse to a hospital and to see that he found a home.

She took him.

Darkman was the last to leave, then, and as he made his way back to his shabby and lonesome home he was passed by a cavalcade of police cars headed into the city. He saw that Jane Kozinski was riding in the first car looking very, very pleased.

CHAPTER

30

Maybe All Stories Do Have Happy Endings

On Monday morning at work John McCoy was surprised to find himself the brilliant hero whose crafty coded message had led Jane and the police to warehouse A-22 on the river. He could not recall having sent any message, but he enjoyed all the attention.